**W9-DFW-278**

## Praise for Kristi Gold:

"Characters who touch your heart and a
story to match. When I finished the last page,
I wanted to start reading it all over again."
—Bestselling author Jennifer Greene on
*Doctor For Keeps*

"Gold shines at creating characters you care about."
—Bestselling author Virginia Kantra

"Kristi Gold is one of those authors whose
books you never want to miss. She touches
your heart in all the right places."
—*Reader to Reader Reviews*

"Kristi Gold's *Renegade Millionaire* will captivate
readers with its undeniably sexy hero and the
combustible attraction between characters.
An exceptionally well-written story
that should never end."
—*Romantic Times* on *Renegade Millionaire,*
2003 *Romantic Times* Reviewers' Choice Award

"Kristi Gold combines her trademark larger-than-life
hero with the Barone Dynasty's sensuous plot and
comes up big in *Expecting The Sheikh's Baby.*"
—*Romantic Times* on *Expecting the Sheikh's Baby,*
2004 National Readers' Choice Winner,
Best Short Contemporary Series

Don't miss Signature Select's exciting series:

# The Fortunes of Texas: Reunion

**Starting in June 2005, get swept up in twelve new stories from your favorite family!**

COWBOY AT MIDNIGHT by Ann Major

A BABY CHANGES EVERYTHING by Marie Ferrarella

IN THE ARMS OF THE LAW by Peggy Moreland

LONE STAR RANCHER by Laurie Paige

THE GOOD DOCTOR by Karen Rose Smith

THE DEBUTANTE by Elizabeth Bevarly

KEEPING HER SAFE by Myrna Mackenzie

THE LAW OF ATTRACTION by Kristi Gold

ONCE A REBEL by Sheri WhiteFeather

MILITARY MAN by Marie Ferrarella

FORTUNE'S LEGACY by Maureen Child

THE RECKONING by Christie Ridgway

# THE F RTUNES OF TEXAS: Reunion

# KRISTI GOLD
## The Law of Attraction

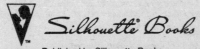

Published by Silhouette Books
**America's Publisher of Contemporary Romance**

Special thanks and acknowledgment are given
to Kristi Gold for her contribution
to THE FORTUNES OF TEXAS: REUNION series.

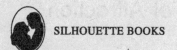 **SILHOUETTE BOOKS**

ISBN 0-373-38933-7

THE LAW OF ATTRACTION

Visit Silhouette Books at www.eHarlequin.com

**Printed in U.S.A.**

Dear Reader,

I was thrilled to be invited to participate in
THE FORTUNES OF TEXAS: REUNION with my
contribution, *The Law of Attraction,* for several reasons:
I'm a born and bred Texan, San Antonio is one of my
favorite cities, I enjoy working with authors to bring
together a satisfying series, and I'm admittedly a
television courtroom drama addict.

This story features Daniel Fortune, a dynamic
San Antonio assistant D.A. who has designs on being
the next District Attorney, and Alicia Hart, who left
corporate law to become a champion of justice for the
common folk. Take these two passionate attorneys, pit
them against each other on a high-profile case, add a
good dose of chemistry, and you're bound to have
fireworks inside and out of the courtroom. As an added
bonus, that high-profile case involves an infamous
exhibitionist known as the "San Antonio Streaker,"
an element that lends itself to more than a little humor,
and a whole lot of fun. And I admit to having had more
than my share of fun writing this book.

Needless to say, quite a bit of research on Texas law
was involved and I've tried to make the legal process
as accurate as possible. However, I'm a writer, not
an attorney, so I did use a little creative license in the
courtroom scenes for the sake of entertainment.

I invite you to get ready for a wild ride, and I do hope
you enjoy *The Law of Attraction* as much as I've enjoyed
writing it!

Happy reading!

*Kristi Gold*

Acknowledgments:

Many thanks to family friend and future attorney,
Wes B., for pointing me in the right direction.
Any errors in legal procedure I might have
made are definitely my own.

Dedication:

To Kathie DeNosky, one of the most talented authors
and best friends I've ever had the pleasure of knowing.

# One

"I can't believe you spent all day with the naked guy."

For once Alisha Hart was thankful for the barroom buzz drowning out the cute and somewhat cocky Joe Alvarado's comment. Unfortunately her current law clerk had a definite lack of decorum at times. But he worked cheap, and with her fledgling law practice, cheap was all she could afford.

Moving her glass of champagne aside, Alisha folded her hands before her on the scuffed wooden table and frowned. "Do you think perhaps we could call him Mr. Massey—his appropriate name—instead of 'the naked guy'?"

Joe loosened his tie, reclined in the high-backed chair and chugged another drink of beer. "I just call 'em like I see 'em. And let's face it, plenty of San Antonio's good citizens have seen him. All of him."

"Not all of him."

He forked a fast hand through his dark hair and gave her his usual impatient scowl. "Okay. Most of him."

Alisha couldn't argue that point, but she would soon have to argue the now infamous case of the "San Antonio Streaker." Without an official public defender's office in the county, she'd qualified to be added to the list of practicing attorneys willing to represent those who couldn't afford private counsel. Just her luck of the draw that she'd been assigned as Les Massey's public defender. True, the man had posed almost in the buff at several notable tourist attractions, but he'd been clever enough to keep certain parts of his anatomy covered. As far as Alisha was concerned, he might be a misguided man on a mission, but he was within his rights to express himself, even if he freely expressed himself practically naked.

"Regardless of what he's done," she told Joe, "he's still a client and deserves my attention."

"More or less a nonpaying client."

Alisha recognized that Les Massey would soon receive the benefit of her services without handing over a dime of his own money—as if he had any—courtesy of the state of Texas. "That's what the system is all about, Joe. Solid legal representation for the indigent. The 'little guy,' so to speak."

He let go a strident laugh. "From what I hear, Les wouldn't be considered a 'little guy.' Rumor has it that was one long coonskin tail he had covering his goods during his little show at the Alamo. Have you seen any evidence of that?"

"Oh, dear God, Joe. I'm not even going to go there." Granted, Alisha had been mildly curious, but she suspected that the legend of Les's "goods" had been blown totally out of proportion. And even though he would be considered a fine specimen, with his buff body and surfer-blond hair, she wasn't interested in his "goods" or any other aspect of his person. Besides, he was seven years her junior, rarely utilized all three of his brain cells at once and was a little too smarmy for her selective taste in men. "Can we change the subject now?"

"Sure. Let's play Twenty Questions. Guess who just walked in?"

"Your wife?"

"Nope. Not yet." He leaned forward. "I'll give you a hint. He's practically a legend in legal circles."

Couldn't be Les, unless he'd escaped from jail. "I give up."

"Would you believe the big man himself?"

"Isn't it a little late for Santa?"

"Try Daniel Fortune."

Great. Just what she needed—the man who delighted in pushing all her hot buttons whenever the opportunity presented itself. The man who ruled the criminal courts like a king. The man she wanted to cling to like cheap plastic wrap every time he came near her—a fact that would remain a secret to everyone, especially the senior assistant district attorney.

"Well, I should've known the iceman cometh," Alisha said, trying to keep her tone nonchalant. "The temperature just dropped a few degrees in here." In reality, her body temperature had risen to rainforest proportions.

"He's brilliant," Joe said. "One of the best prosecutors in the state."

One of the best-looking prosecutors in the country. "Yes, he's got a good record." And a great butt.

"Don't look now, but he's heading this way."

Alisha battled the urge to look and she won out for the time being. Maybe Mr. Fortune would keep walking right on past her. Maybe then she could sneak another peek at his derriere.

Joe slapped his palms on the edge of the table, startling Alisha. "I'm going to go to the boys' room, then give Julie a call. If she doesn't get here quick, she's going to miss the festivities."

Alisha wanted to ask him to please stay, which was totally absurd. Chances were the esteemed A.D.A. wouldn't even bother to say hello. And even if he did, her obligation only required she be polite and toss out a few insults if necessary. "Fine. I'll be here when you get back."

Trying to appear relaxed, she turned her attention to the

wide-screen TV across the room and pretended to watch the Times Square globe beginning its descent, signaling the arrival of the new year on the East Coast. Pretended not to be at all concerned that the preeminent attorney was somewhere on the premises. Pretended she didn't care where he was or what he was doing, even if she did. She'd just sit there and blend into the surroundings—not at all that difficult considering she had blending in down to a fine art in crowded bars.

"Hey, Hart, did you really get the guy with the big schlong?"

Following a spattering of laughter, Alisha's gaze snapped to the man posing the query seated two tables over—the lard-bellied lawyer, Billy Wade Carlisle, not board certified in anything since "bottom feeder" had yet to be designated as a specialty. Right now she would like to take his ratty toupee and stuff it in an orifice where no toupee belonged.

So much for remaining anonymous. Of course, the place was rather loud and a bit rowdy tonight. With any luck, Mr. Fortune hadn't heard Billy Wade's brilliant query.

"Looks like you could use a drink."

The sound of his voice coming from behind her, deep and downright deadly, drew Alisha's complete attention. So did the very masculine hand that slid a glass of champagne before her. She visually tracked his navy coat sleeve up to his wide shoulder and, against better judgment, continued on to his eyes. Tonight those eyes looked dark even though she knew they were green—not crystalline green but a deep green that at times looked almost brown, other times green-gold, depending on the lighting. Intense eyes that shouted power. Considering the definite cast of amusement in his gaze, no doubt he was about to contribute to her status as current courthouse laughingstock.

"Don't even start, Counselor," Alisha muttered.

He had the nerve to look innocent—and stunning, with his brown hair combed back in neat layers and his jaw surrounded by a spattering of evening whiskers. "Start what?"

"Your commentary on my recent appointment to represent Mr. Massey."

He moved beside the table, giving her the full effect of his striking face. "No commentary involved. I just wanted to buy you a drink."

She tried to look pleasant and calm despite her frenzied pulse. "Thank you, but I still have one."

"Save it to toast the new year."

The drink would probably be warm by then, and that definitely complemented her current state at the moment. "I appreciate it."

He surveyed her face from forehead to chin before centering his gaze on her eyes. "I take it you're getting your share of digs about the streaker."

Alisha rimmed her glass with a fingertip, purposefully avoiding his gaze. "He doesn't streak, he poses."

"Poses until he evades the authorities, then he streaks."

"I'm not going to give you any details about my defense, if that's what you're after."

"I'm only wondering how you're handling all the *exposure*."

Cute. Real cute. She risked a quick look at him to find him sporting a half smile. "I assure you, I'm handling it fine." As fine as she could with an extreme exhibitionist who enjoyed strutting like the cock of the walk, something she'd discovered during the first encounter with Les Massey at his arraignment.

Daniel propped his hand on the back of her chair and leaned closer. "Just another quick question."

He was nothing if not persistent. And darned if he didn't smell good, too. "I said I'm not going to—"

"Are you alone?"

*That* she wasn't expecting—a query posed in a provocative tone that sounded as if he was quite capable, and willing, to end her solitude.

Fortunately Joe picked that moment to return to the table, prompting Alisha to spout out, "I'm with him," followed by a wave of her hand in the clerk's direction. After all, Daniel Fortune didn't have to know that her companion was blissfully married. She certainly didn't want him to think that she was so pathetic she'd been forced to spend New Year's Eve without a date, even if she had been dateless for some time now.

In the blink of an eye, the A.D.A. straightened and restored himself to consummate professional. The iceman returneth. "Good to see you again, Mr. Alvarado."

"Same here." Joe shook Daniel's offered hand with gusto and grinned like a down-and-out miner who'd struck gold. "The way you handled the Richardson case last year was amazing. I still don't know how you managed to get a conviction without the victim's body."

"I owe it to the San Antonio PD's spotless investigation."

Good answer, and good grief. When Alisha noticed Joe's starstruck expression, she expected him to fall prostrate at the A.D.A.'s feet and kiss the large shoes he walked in. "Joe, I'm sure Mr. Fortune would just as soon forget about work tonight."

"You're right, and I'm being rude." Joe gestured toward the chair next to Alisha. "Why don't you join us? My wife should be here in a minute."

So much for Alisha's pretense that Joe was her date. Daniel sent her a quick glance, as if asking her permission to join the party, which she didn't give, and not because she wouldn't like to have him join them. Because she *would* like for him to join them, and that wasn't necessarily advisable. Considering her status as a part-time public defender and his as full-time defender of the public, for all intents and purposes they were enemies. Especially now with the high-profile Massey case hanging over her and his office in charge of convicting him, not to mention her unwelcome attraction to the prosecutor.

For what seemed liked infinity, he simply stared at her and she stared back, until she heard, "Sorry I'm late."

Alisha released her gaze on Daniel to find Julie Alvarado standing at the table, all five feet six inches of head-turning brunette. The kind of woman you wanted to hate—model-beautiful—but was simply too nice to despise. A social worker who devoted her life to protecting children and spoiling her husband. "Hi, Julie. We were starting to worry you might not get here in time."

"I was beginning to wonder, too." Julie tossed her bag on the table and leaned to give Joe a kiss. "Sorry, honey. I had something I had to take care of tonight. An emergency removal of three kids. What a way to end the year."

Joe stood and wrapped an arm around her shoulder, looking very proud, and rightfully so. "Mr. Fortune, this is my wife, Julie. Julie, this is Daniel Fortune."

"We've met," Julie said. "I testified during one of your trials."

"The Henson trial," Daniel said. "That was a tough one."

Julie regarded Joe again. "The one where the boyfriend put his girlfriend's five-year-old daughter into a coma because she spilled her juice on his CD collection."

Alisha inwardly cringed when she recalled the details she'd only read about. Thank God she'd still been working at her former firm defending rich executives involved in white-collar crimes, and that so far when appointed by the court she'd only represented misdemeanor offenses and not heinous felonies.

"Are you sure you don't want to join us?" Joe pointed to the empty chair beside Alisha. "We can count down together."

Alisha counted to ten before Daniel said, "Maybe some other time. Enjoy the rest of the evening."

With another glance at Alisha, he strode away with blatant confidence, his wide shoulders straight, his large hands dangling at his sides, while heads turned as he passed. No doubt about it, he was a natural attention-getter. He'd certainly gotten hers on more than one occasion.

After Julie sat down beside Joe, Alisha pushed the glass of

champagne, compliments of the A.D.A., toward her. "Take this. I still have some left."

Julie exchanged a veiled look with her husband. "I don't care for any champagne, but I guess it will work for a toast." She held the flute aloft. "To the new year. May it not royally suck."

They all touched their glasses together with a shared "Here, here." Joe and Alisha took sips of their drinks while Julie merely pushed the untouched glass aside.

Joe narrowed his eyes and said to Alisha, "That Daniel Fortune is something else. You should do him, Hart."

She nearly gasped. "Why would you even think such a thing?"

He looked at her as if she'd just plummeted several rungs on the intelligence ladder. "Because he wants you."

What a colossal joke. "Oh, sure he does."

"Don't be obtuse, Alisha," Joe said. "I saw the way he was looking at you. In fact, I've seen him look at you that way before at the courthouse. He treats everyone else with indifference, but he treats you like he'd like to get into your drawers—and not the ones in your file cabinet."

She shrugged off the remark. "He razzes me because he doesn't like defense attorneys."

Joe sighed. "Jeez, Hart. Have you been out of the dating loop so long that you don't recognize a few come-ons? The guy's got a hard—"

Julie slapped a hand over Joe's mouth. "My husband is trying to say—and failing miserably—that Daniel Fortune's hot for you."

Alisha found that hard to believe. Yes, she worked at being attractive, both inside and out. Yes, she had worked hard for respect and had enjoyed substantial success in her thirty-two years. But as far as physical attributes were concerned, she had unruly red hair that she futilely flatironed every day only to be sabotaged by humidity—the reason why she'd kept it curly tonight. She was short, not particularly busty and she'd inherited her mother's ample hips. Her skin practically blistered with only a few minutes of sun exposure, and although she didn't have a forest full of freckles, she had more than her fair share. She certainly didn't see herself as the kind of woman that would seriously interest Daniel Fortune. He probably preferred bombshell blondes with more body and less brain.

Julie leaned forward and laid a hand on Alisha's arm. "I can certainly understand why he would be interested in you. You're very pretty and smart."

"And a redhead," Joe added. "Men like redheads. A lot of mystery there. You know, about whether they're natural red-heads or not."

"We're not going to discuss that, Joseph," Julie said.

He gave his wife a whipped-dog look. "Sorry, but it's true. Anyway…" He looked back at Alisha. "You should do him. If I were a woman, I would."

Alisha rolled her eyes. "I'm sure Julie loves hearing that."

Joe aimed his grin on his wife. "She'd do him, too. Wouldn't you, sweetheart?"

Julie batted her eyelashes. "Why would I want to when I have you, honey?"

"Okay, let's say you didn't have me."

Julie shrugged. "Yeah, I'd do him. In a heartbeat."

Joe turned his attention back to Alisha. "See?"

Time to quell the conversation before Alisha seriously considered the suggestion. "I don't do prosecutors, okay?"

Joe looked somewhat frustrated. "You don't do anyone, Hart, and that's your problem. You might be in a better mood if you got laid now and then."

"And you need to lay off her, Joe." Julie smiled, exposing perfect white teeth to match her perfectly lined lips. "When she's ready, she will."

Alisha wasn't ready to do anything other than get out of there. But politeness dictated she hang around, at least for a while longer. Yet she found herself enduring the couple mooning over each other like two besotted teenagers, so obviously in love that only a fool couldn't see it. Even their names sounded perfect—Joe and Julie, lovers extraordinaire. They did include her in general conversation a few times, but only to be nice, Alisha decided. She suspected they'd really like to be home and in bed, carrying on like most happy husbands and wives. That was so far out of the realm of Alisha's comprehension that she found herself growing suddenly melancholy.

Everyone in the world, or at least in the bar, had seemed to pair off. Even Billy Wade, who'd latched on to some big-haired blonde. He was singing "Auld Lang Syne" off-key and the woman didn't even seem to mind. Alisha minded. He was definitely one acquaintance she'd rather forget. In fact, she wanted to forget this whole scene and go back to her apartment. At least there she wouldn't have to tolerate watching everyone engaged in the traditional midnight kiss when a partial glass of warm champagne was the only thing available to wrap her lips around.

She pushed her chair back from the table and stood. "Listen, guys, I'm out of here. I'll see you on Monday, Joe. Bright and early."

"Do you really have to go?" Julie asked.

Alisha slipped her coat on and grabbed her purse from the empty chair beside her. "Yeah, I do. I'm tired."

"I understand." Julie's knowing expression said she did. Only a woman could appreciate another woman's plight of being all alone during a party. "Why don't you have dinner with us tomorrow? It's just going to be the two of us."

"I'll think about it," Alisha said, knowing full well she'd already made her decision. As much as she loved being around the Alvarados, she hated being a third wheel more. "I'll call you tomorrow morning and let you know."

"Be careful, Hart," Joe said. "Lots of crazies on the streets tonight. But God forbid, if you are involved in an accident—"

he hooked a thumb over his shoulder "—I'll be sure to call Billy Wade's number. One-eight-hundred-bad-legal-advice."

"You do that," Alisha said, leaving them with a fake smile before elbowing her way through the milling crowd. Although she shouldn't do it, she couldn't help but scan the area to see if by chance Daniel Fortune was still hanging around. Why, she couldn't say. Even if he was still in the bar, she had no intention of approaching him. By the time she reached the door she confirmed that he had left, and probably not alone.

Right now Alisha had more concerns than Daniel Fortune's sex life. She had plenty to accomplish in regard to the Massey defense, not to mention a few other cases pending. Very few. A couple of divorces involving women who didn't quite qualify for assistance, one contested will, one product-liability case. All basically hinged on settlements before she saw a significant amount of money. But these clients needed her help, and she was more than happy to offer it. Plus, she did get paid when she was selected from the public-defender rolls. The money was decent, although she wasn't sure they would ever be able to pay her enough to make the Massey mess worthwhile.

Yes, she had much to do, and so what if she didn't have anyone to date? No big deal. At least she wouldn't be worrying about contributing to the divorce rate anytime soon. But Daniel Fortune was tempting. He also qualified as a potential mistake.

When she pushed out the door into the cool, misty night, that potential mistake was leaning against the lone lamppost, hands in his pockets, face illuminated by the halogen bulb. Suddenly making that mistake didn't seem like such a bad idea.

*You should do him, Hart....*

Alisha could not imagine that. All right, she could imagine it. And she had. Several times. She certainly wasn't going to make the first move. Or any kind of move, for that matter. But she faced a certain dilemma. She had to walk past him on her way to the pay-by-the-hour parking lot across the street. Of course, she could ignore him—as if that were really possible since he'd already seen her. Or she could sprint to her car with only a muttered good-night.

How silly. She could handle this situation with adult diplomacy.

*This is not that difficult, Alisha.*

Stepping onto the sidewalk, Alisha studied the stars and blurted out the first thing that came to mind. "A really nice night for sex." Oh, crap. She'd been paid a visit by Freud instead of Baby New Year.

Daniel pushed off the pole and narrowed his eyes. "What did you just say?"

Alisha felt the fire rising to her face and more than likely she probably looked as if she'd been slapped. Someone should slap her for the questionable comment. "I said it's a nice night in Texas." *Good save, Alisha.* "Why?"

"Because I could've sworn you said something about sex."

She folded her arms beneath her breasts and prepared to lie. "I'm not surprised you thought that. I hear men think about sex about every six seconds."

"A total exaggeration. More like every ninety seconds." He topped off the comment with the most patently seductive smile she'd ever seen on a man.

"I stand corrected." Although right now standing before him made her want to drop to her knees in brazen worship as if he'd been ordained as a D.A. demigod.

*I'd do him…in a heartbeat….*

A round of *pop, pop, pops* from a series of firecrackers echoing through the streets yanked Alisha back into the real world, where defense attorneys and prosecutors didn't mingle, especially between the sheets. Yes, it happened, that much Alisha knew. But not to her. She'd learned her lesson the hard way, and since that time she'd walked the professional line even though right now she wanted to walk right up and kiss the esteemed

Daniel Fortune. The way she'd fantasized about kissing him for months now. She'd fantasized about a lot more than that.

He broke the silence by asking, "Why didn't you wait inside until midnight?"

She hugged her bag to her chest. "First, it's too crowded. Second, Billy Wade was singing like a wounded banshee. Third, sleep's at a premium these days and I need to get home."

"Yeah. I imagine it is with the Massey case pending."

She attempted to look appropriately incensed—very hard to do in the presence of a man who took charisma to a whole new level. "You're determined to get me to discuss that, aren't you?"

"No. Just making an observation."

And that was the reason for his attention. "You're being too polite to me, Counselor, which leads me to believe you're making nice so I'll give you a clue about my strategy."

"There's a couple of things you need to know about me, Counselor. The Massey case isn't my problem because my job is to prosecute the worst of the worst. Felonies, not misdemeanors. And I don't make nice with a woman to gain information."

"Then what do you hope to gain by making nice?"

"I don't hope to gain anything. At least, not in terms of our professional relationship."

Alisha wasn't sure where this could be leading but she did know it could be down a dangerous path. "We don't have anything other than a professional relationship."

"We could."

That almost shocked Alisha right out of her viselike heels. "I don't think that's a good idea."

"Why not?"

"Because you're a prosecutor and I'm a defense attorney."

"No reason why we can't be friendly outside of the courts."

Alisha could think of one big reason—namely she'd gotten a little too friendly with a colleague and she'd lived to regret it. "Maybe having a personal relationship with associates might work for you, but I've never considered it to be a wise move."

"I don't know if it works for me because I've never done it before."

That was a hard one to swallow. "You're telling me that you've never fraternized with one of the many female attorneys in this town?"

"Never found one I cared to fraternize with." The look he gave her said, *Until now.* Or maybe her imagination was commandeering her brain again.

Turning the topic back to their profession seemed wise. "By the way, I wanted to add my congratulations on your handling of the Richardson case."

"And I should congratulate you on bulldozing the new guy into taking a plea on the Langston case."

"I didn't bulldoze him. I just did some serious negotiating."

"You scared the hell out of him."

She lifted one shoulder in a shrug. "Okay, call me scary. I've been called worse."

"Such as?"

"Stubborn. Single-minded—"

"Sexy as hell?"

Ha! "Can't say that I've heard that in anyone's verbal repertoire when describing me."

"Well, it's in mine, because you are. Especially tonight."

Alisha fought the inclination to look behind her to see what other woman had arrived on the scene. She pointed toward the street. "I'm going to head home now." Before she did something totally stupid.

"Where do you live?" he asked.

"In an apartment north of town, about twenty minutes away."

"I'm a lot closer. Only a few blocks away. The new condo development."

"The one that overlooks the river? That's rather pricey. I didn't know the D.A.'s office paid so well."

"I manage. The view alone is worth it."

"I'm sure it's great."

"You should come over tonight and see for yourself."

Surely this couldn't be happening to her, a tremendously sensual man asking her over. Actually it couldn't be happening, or it shouldn't. "Let me guess. You want me to go over your briefs."

"My briefs are in order, unless you feel the need to do a quality check."

She rolled her eyes for the second time tonight, even though she had a sudden image of doing that very thing. "You're a big boy. I'm sure you're quite capable of tossing out your old underwear when necessary."

"We were talking about underwear?" His grin was teasing and terribly tempting.

She laid a dramatic hand on her chest. "My apologies, Mr. Fortune. I guess I've confused you with all of the other male jurists who just love to throw out those clichéd legal pickup lines."

"You mean things like 'Let's engage in a little discovery'? 'I'll show you mine if you'll show me yours'?"

"Yes, but we can't forget my personal favorite—'Let's go back to my place and study the penal code.'"

He took a step toward her. "How about 'I have no statute of limitations when it comes to making you feel good'?"

From the deep, compelling tone of his voice Alisha inherently knew he was telling the truth. "I've never heard that one before."

"That's because I just made it up. I can be pretty quick on my feet."

She was surprised her feet were still holding her up. "Very creative, Counselor. And to quote another cliché, I don't want to end up as another notch on your bedpost."

He sighed, a rough one. "Why is it that women always think men have ulterior motives?"

"Probably because they do."

"Believe it or not, my reasons for inviting you over don't have anything to do with sex." He rubbed a hand over his nape. "What if I told you that I could just use a friend?"

She could tell him she related to that on a very personal level. "I'm sure you have plenty of friends."

"Sometimes it's hard to know who your friends are in this business."

How true, Alisha thought. "I'm not sure we can really be friends."

"Sure we can." He moved a little closer. "We can have a friendly conversation, like we've been doing since the first time we met."

"Friendly? You call telling me my car was a piece of junk when I asked you about a mechanic the other day friendly?"

"And then you told me in explicit detail where I could drive it."

"True, but you deserved it."

Daniel shrugged. "I think you take everything too seriously."

"And you don't?"

"Yeah, most of the time, but not around you. Beats the hell out of me why you bring out that side of me."

Exactly what Joe had said earlier. "That's because I'm not like most women you know. I don't automatically swoon in your presence." It took great effort on her part not to do that.

"To be honest, I like that about you. That's why I want to spend some time with you. We can watch the fireworks from my living room window. Do you see a problem with that?"

Alisha saw a big problem—namely she'd be sorely tempted to climb all over him if he moved even a millimeter closer. "For all intents and purposes we're opponents."

"We're not opposing each other on any case."

"We could in the future."

"I'm not concerned about the future. I'm only thinking about tonight."

How tempting it would be to take him up on his offer. How very, very tempting. But Daniel Fortune's status as an unflappable attorney was second only to his rep as an in-demand lover.

He took another slow step toward her. "Do you really want to spend the rest of the evening alone, Alisha?"

She didn't want to react so strongly to the way he'd said her name, but she did. "I've been alone before."

"So have I, but it's New Year's Eve. People shouldn't spend the holiday alone if they have other options. Unless you're involved with someone."

"Not currently."

"Then I don't see any real harm in it. Nothing complicated. Just two friends seeing in the new year together."

Alisha hadn't really viewed him as a friend per se, but he wasn't a seedy stranger. After all, he'd made it his life's work putting criminals behind bars. In that regard, he was safe. His magnetism...well, that was another thing altogether.

But she truly didn't want to be alone. Not tonight. She would keep a tight grasp on her control. She would go to Daniel Fortune's apartment and take her chances. "Do you have any wine?"

His gorgeous grin heralded success. "If I do, then you'll come home with me?"

"Yes. To watch the fireworks and have a drink."

"You're welcome to check out my bedpost for notches."

She didn't dare get anywhere near his bed. "No thanks."

"I wouldn't mind showing you my custom-made wet bar. Lots of shelves. And counter space."

"Room enough for two, no doubt."

"Probably so, with a little careful maneuvering."

Alisha felt as if she'd been thrust into some unknown dimension. Maybe he did want to do her. Worse, she wanted to do him. Joe and Julie would be so proud. But caution spoke louder than carnal need. "Be careful, Counselor, or I'm going to rescind my offer."

He looked somewhat contrite. "Sorry, but you walked right into that one."

She only hoped that when she walked into his apartment she'd keep a choke hold on her hormones. "Where's your car?"

"I'm on foot."

She pointed to the lot across the street. "Mine's over there. I'll drive us."

"Save your gas. We can walk it from here."

Maybe walking wasn't such a bad idea. Maybe then they'd be too tired to do anything that might be deemed risky. Maybe they should jog. "Okay, Counselor. Lead the way."

And with only minimal second thoughts, Alisha accompanied Daniel Fortune to his condo, feeling as if tonight she might go anywhere he cared to take her.

## Two

Daniel Fortune liked order, but tonight he'd invited chaos into his world in the form of five feet two inches of prime red-head with an attitude. The reasons he'd asked Alisha Hart into his home had been only partially true. Yeah, he could use a friend, because real friends were rare. But the truth of the matter was he wanted more than her friendship. He wanted her. He had since the first time he'd lain eyes on her. But the timing hadn't been right back then, and timing could be everything. He needed to remember that, otherwise she'd be out of there quicker than he could say "I object."

She wandered around his apartment for a few minutes, picking up various items to study them. Just when he was about to ask her to take off her coat and stay awhile, she pulled the black all-weather jacket from her shoulders and tossed it and her purse onto the club chair in the corner.

"You're very neat," she said as she ran her fingertips over the back of the steel-gray leather sofa.

"I like everything in its place." Daniel liked having her in his place. He liked her sassy mouth. He liked the fact that she gave as good as she got. And he really liked the man-killing dress.

She strolled toward him and pointed behind him. "That is a nice wet bar."

"Thanks. You ready for that wine now?"

"Sure."

Turning his back to her, he took a glass from the marble shelf and pulled the bottle of merlot from the built-in wine rack. He could see her watching him from the mirrored wall behind the bar as he dislodged the cork and he hid a smile as her eyes tracked down his back and lower. She was checking out his ass. He had no problem with that. In fact, he'd be willing to give her a closer, unencumbered look if she asked.

After pouring the wine into the glass, he turned and her gaze zipped up to his face as he offered it to her. "Enjoy."

She took the wine and a sip. "This is good. Aren't you going to have some?"

"I don't drink alcohol. I've seen what it can do to people who can't control their impulses." He'd lived with the sorry results for most of his childhood and faced them daily during adulthood in the context of his job.

She held up the glass. "That's why I'm only having this one. I still have to drive home tonight."

He'd prefer she stay until morning, but that was probably asking too much. "You've only been here a few minutes and already you're talking about leaving."

"I'm just being realistic, Counselor."

"It's Daniel. Tonight we're not attorneys, we're friends." He gestured toward the couch. "Have a seat and make yourself comfortable."

He followed her to the couch, keeping a fair distance just so he could watch the sway of her hips as she walked. Nothing wrong with a little mutual ass-checking.

Alisha settled against the corner of the sofa and he sat on

the opposite end, trying not to crowd her even if he did want to be closer.

"If you don't drink, then why do you keep alcohol around?" she asked.

He stretched his legs out before him and rested his joined hands on his abdomen. "Strictly for socializing."

"I see. Have custom wet bar, will entertain. I'm sure it impresses your friends."

"I don't entertain too often. Hard to find the time. And as I've said before, friends are few and far between these days." A reminder of why she was here, nothing more than simple companionship.

She kicked off her shoes and curled her legs beneath her. "So are the rumors true?"

With her dress now riding high on her thighs, he had one helluva time concentrating on conversation. "What rumors?"

"That you're going to run for D.A.?"

"That depends on party politics. They could decide someone else would make a more appropriate candidate."

"They would be crazy not to consider you."

"I don't have a wife and kids, so that could be a determining factor."

She toyed with the hem of her skirt, drawing Daniel's attention. "Oh, I don't know about that. As a bachelor, I'm sure you would garner the female vote."

"Would I get your vote?"

"That depends. I have yet to see you in action."

"Do you mean in a courtroom?"

She sent him a sly, sexy smile. "Of course that's what I meant."

Damn. "If it's okay with you, I'd like to move off the topic of work."

"Fine by me," she said. "Tell me about your family."

That was one conversation he preferred to avoid, but out of courtesy he offered, "I have a brother and two sisters."

She took another drink of the wine and then set it down on a coaster on the end table. "What about your parents?

He figured she'd ask that next and he planned to keep it simple. "Both dead."

She gave him a sincere, sympathetic look. "I'm sorry, Daniel. I didn't know that. What happened?"

"A car accident about seven years ago." Enough said. He shifted toward her and draped an arm over the back of the sofa. "What about your family?"

"I'm an only child. My mom and dad live in a small town in West Texas."

When he noted the hint of sadness in her voice, he asked, "Why aren't you with them?"

"Well, because the drive takes me nearly a day and I would have had to turn around and come right back home. I did spend Christmas with them, though."

"Sounds like you're a close family." Something Daniel had a hard time fathoming in light of his bitter past.

"Very. They're absolutely the best. We didn't have a lot of money while I was growing up, but it didn't matter. I had everything I needed and a lot of love."

Something he couldn't even begin to relate to. He'd had the material objects because of his banker father, but the man had been bankrupt when it came to love. Daniel opted to keep the conversation focused on her. "I bet you were a cheerleader in high school."

She let go a terse laugh. "Hardly. I didn't have adequate pom-poms."

*Don't do it, Fortune.* But he couldn't prevent his gaze from drifting to her breasts before he went back to her blue eyes. "I don't see anything wrong with your pom-poms."

A slight blush stained her cheeks. "Thanks, but I wasn't the cheerleader type. I was the studious type. I concentrated on making the grade instead of the usual high school stuff like sports and dating, that kind of thing."

"You didn't date?"

"Not really. Not until college, and even then not that much. I was bound and determined to be the best law student ever. I graduated with honors."

"Then you went to work for Gailey and Breedlove."

"Yes. They recruited me."

Daniel prepared to ask something he'd wanted to know for a while now. He'd heard some speculation about her departure, none that he'd been able to verify. "That's a pretty prestigious firm. Why did you leave?"

"It's a long story, but basically I found that the justice scales were tipped toward those who had the money and means to pay for a good defense. That's why I decided to strike out on my own and try to do my part to make things more balanced."

Not the version he'd heard, but he'd settle for her explanation without pressuring her for more. "That's why you signed on to serve as a public defender?"

"Yes, but I want to eventually concentrate on general law instead of criminal law, providing good counsel to those who have the need but not necessarily the money."

"How do you expect to make a living at that?"

"Actually I have a few cases that could prove to be lucrative—provided I win. Just nothing up-front until they're settled. But I'm getting by."

"And I suspect you're working your ass off."

She patted her hip and smiled. "Believe me, it's still there."

"I've noticed. And I'm glad."

She looked somewhat self-conscious as she twitched on the cushions. "By the way, how is Jim Krauss in court?"

For a moment he wondered if she had a thing for his colleague. Nah. The guy was about as boring as they come. And married. "He's fairly good. Why?"

"I'm wondering what I'll be facing during the Massey trial, if it goes to trial."

"I thought we weren't going to discuss that," he reminded her.

"Just curious."

"Krauss better be at his best since you're damn good."

"How would you know?" she asked. "You've never really come up against me."

The images the comment evoked had every muscle in his body coming to attention. "True, I haven't. But I'm sure we'd both enjoy it immensely."

"You're certainly confident, Counselor."

"Remember, it's Daniel tonight, and you're not all that short on confidence either."

"No. I'm just short."

"Your hell-on-wheels attitude makes you seem a lot taller."

She laid a hand above her breast. "Attitude? I don't have an attitude."

"Yeah, you do, Counselor."

"It's Alisha," she said, throwing his words back at him. "And you have to have a little bit of an attitude in this business to be taken seriously, especially if you're a woman."

He gave her a long glance from face to feet, pausing in between. "Believe me, it's more than obvious you're a woman, attitude or no attitude." When he moved closer and pushed a wayward curl from her shoulder, she immediately tensed. "Relax. I'm not going to jump you."

"Do you think I'd be here if I really believed you would?" she said without looking at him.

"Something's making you nervous."

"Okay, I admit it, being here with you makes me nervous." She sent a quick glance his way. "Are you happy now?"

He could think of several things that would make him happy. Having her nervous wasn't one of them. "I'm strung a little tight myself."

That brought her attention back to him. "The iceman nervous? The prosecutor who prides himself on being totally in control?"

God, he hated that whole "iceman" thing. "Believe me, I'm not always in control." Right now his control was in jeopardy. "And under certain circumstances, I'm definitely not the iceman."

"You could've fooled me. I've never seen you look the least bit on edge."

"Maybe you haven't been looking hard enough. Or maybe you just don't want to see it because around you I'm always on edge."

"Around me?"

Time for the truth, regardless of the consequences. "Yeah. Every time I'm near you. Don't pretend you haven't noticed this thing between us."

"What thing?" Her sudden inability to look at him contradicted her denial.

"The one we've been skirting for the past few months."

"I have no idea what you're talking about."

"Okay, have it your way. I'll spell it out for you."

"Please do."

When Daniel inched a little closer, this time Alisha didn't move. In fact, she felt as if her bottom had been bonded to the cushions or perhaps she was simply mesmerized by his aura.

"I noticed you for the first time last year, while you were still working for Gailey and company," he said. "But I also noticed you were with Troy Moreau most of the time and I sensed something was going on between the two of you."

He had that one nailed. "We worked together quite a bit." The truth. "Nothing more to it than that." A lie.

The look he gave her said he didn't exactly believe her. "Back then I didn't approach you for that reason and because I was involved with someone, too."

"Who?" Did she have to sound so absurdly jealous?

"It doesn't matter. That's been over a long time. When I

heard you'd been added to the public-defender rolls, I started looking for you."

Unbelievable. "You started looking for me?"

"Yeah. Do you remember that day you negotiated the plea on the Jones case back in August?"

"That was my first case as a public defender."

"Do you remember me coming in to sign off on the deal because the D.A. was out of the office?"

Boy, did she, right down to every detail, including the red diamond pattern on his navy tie. "Yes."

"I didn't have to be there. Hildebrand talked to me about it beforehand and I'd given my okay. I came in because I wanted to see you."

Alisha felt the creep of a blush climbing up her throat. "Really?"

He smiled. "Really. And after that I kept searching you out just so I could talk to you. Didn't you ever wonder why we kept running into each other?"

"I assumed you just found provoking me so much fun, you couldn't stay away."

"I didn't want to stay away from you. The provocation was just a cover for the fact that I wanted to know you better. A lot better."

She was having a difficult time buying any of this. She was having a harder time remaining upright while he was so close. "I bet you say that to all the girls downtown."

"No. And if you're going to say you haven't noticed the chemistry between us, Alisha, then you're lying to yourself and to me."

Confession time, she thought. "All right, maybe I did notice."

"You've also noticed my ass."

Wonderful. She'd been caught. "Unless you have eyes in the back of your head, I don't see how you could know that."

"When I was standing at the bar a minute ago, getting your

wine, I was watching you in the mirror and saw you giving it a look. But that's okay because I've looked at yours more than once."

Alisha's head started to whirl, but it wasn't the limited amount of alcohol that had her thoughts so jumbled. It was him. "Why did you wait until now to tell me all of this?"

He reached up and brushed another rebellious strand of hair away from her cheek. "You kept giving mixed signals every time I was around you. Stop, go, maybe. I was never sure how you were going to respond to any kind of overture from me. But after I saw you tonight, sitting in that bar alone, looking so damn good, it was all I could do not to grab you up and carry you out."

Aha! His true motive. She was the only one alone and, therefore, available. "I thought this was all about friendship."

"I'm willing to settle for friendship, if that's all you want. But it's going to be tough when I've had some fairly serious fantasies about you for months now."

They couldn't be half as wicked as hers involving him. "What kind of fantasies?"

He ran a slow fingertip up and down her forearm. "Like the other day, when we passed each other in the stairwell. You had on that brown suit—"

"Yes, and if I recall correctly, you told me brown wasn't flattering on me."

"I told you that because what I really wanted to do was take it off you, especially when you leaned your arm on the rail, your jacket parted and I saw just a glimpse of right here." He drew a line down from her collarbone to the side of her breast, causing a shiver to run the length of Alisha's body. "That little bit of bare flesh had me wondering exactly what you had on underneath that jacket. Five more seconds and I might have tried to find out."

Alisha shivered. "I see."

He toyed with the silver-and-green chandelier earring

hanging from her lobe. "I'm not sure you do. But let me tell you about my favorite fantasy, then maybe you will see."

Alisha wasn't sure her heart could take much more. It was already beating like a bongo against her chest. But she had to know. "Since you seem to be on a roll, continue."

He grinned. "You know that sofa in Riley's chambers?"

"The ugly plaid one?"

"Yeah. The last time I was there, I'd just seen you in the hall. You asked me about the holiday schedule—"

"And after you'd harangued me about not owning a calendar, you told me what you knew, end of conversation."

"That wasn't the end of it for me," he said. "Just being around you, even for those few minutes, had me distracted. I was requesting a continuance from Riley and I fumbled around like an idiot because I kept imagining us stretched out on that sofa. Naked."

Wow. "Please tell me Riley wasn't watching in this fantasy."

"No, it was just you and me, after hours."

She swallowed hard. "What were we doing?"

"You sure you want details? It's pretty wild."

For a long moment Daniel simply stared at her with those incredible, intense eyes. She still didn't quite believe this was happening. Still had a difficult time believing he wanted her in *that* way.

She was mildly aware of the colorful flashes of splintered lights outside the window and very aware of how much he affected her. "I believe the fireworks have started."

"Yeah, they have." Daniel pulled her against him with one arm and framed her jaw in his free hand, rubbing his thumb over her cheek in a hypnotic cadence. She reacted with low-down heat and a rush of dampness, as if he were touching her intimately. "Happy new year, Alisha." Before she could return the greeting, he laid his lips on hers.

On one hand, she'd hoped he was a lousy kisser, forcing her common sense to come back around. On the other hand, she knew he wouldn't be, and he wasn't. He drove her into merry madness with his soft lips, tantalized her with his tongue until she lost all sense of reasoning or thoughts of why she shouldn't be doing this.

But doing it she was. And worse, she wanted to do more. She wanted to do him.

Daniel prided himself on knowing women well, including all the things that made them hot, made them want and at times even made them beg. But Alisha Hart had thrown him totally off balance. He sure as hell wasn't complaining, because he'd imagined this for months—having her pressed against him, kissing her senseless until he questioned if he had any sense left either. Still, he needed to take it slow. Needed to make sure he was reading her right before he did something that might make her bolt.

But when she broke the kiss and whispered, "Show me the details," *slow* suddenly lost all its luster. *Slow* couldn't describe what happened next. He pulled her up from the sofa and went after the zipper on her dress while she tore at the buttons on his shirt and pushed it off his shoulders. "We shouldn't be doing this," she muttered as she tackled his fly.

"Probably not," he replied as he slid the dress down in a rush.

And that was the end of all meaningless protests. He considered suggesting the bedroom as he relieved her of her bra and panties in quick order, but it was too far away and he was too far gone. After he shirked off his slacks and briefs, they ended up on the couch, facing each other in a tangle of limbs, hands roving over each other as he kept his mouth firmly fixed with hers. He found her breast with his mouth and slipped his palm between her thighs, finding her, as he'd predicted, hot and wet. She released a soft moan as he touched her, moving in sync with his hand as he drove her to the edge. Luckily she hadn't touched him in the same way yet, otherwise he might go over with her.

"I want you," she whispered. "Now."

Exactly what he needed to hear to continue. With the last scrap of coherent thought he told her, "I want to see your face."

He rolled to his back, settled her on top of him and guided himself inside her. His breath hissed out through his gritted teeth and hers caught in a gasp. She leaned down and teased his lips with her tongue, splayed her hands across his chest to explore but failed to move, as if trying to prove she was in control. In many ways, she was.

Daniel had no problem with that. He'd never been territorial when it came to sex. But then, he'd never been with a woman quite like her. With her ruffled red curls spiraling down her shoulders and her blue eyes glazed, she looked like a mixture of fire and ice. She made him hot, made him sweat, made him mutter a curse that made her smile.

"What do you want me to do, Daniel?" she asked, her voice as sultry as her expression.

He palmed her breasts with both hands. "Whatever you feel like doing. I'm at your mercy." And he was.

She lifted up, then moved back down his shaft with agonizing slowness. "Am I doing your fantasy justice?"

"Oh, yeah." Even those two words took a lot of effort when she began to quicken the pace.

Alisha Hart might look like the wholesome girl next door, but it wasn't long before he discovered she made love like a wild woman. She rode him hard and fast, taking him to the limit of his sanity. She raked her nails down his shoulders as he drove into her, touching her without restraint until he felt the grip of her orgasm.

Too soon, he thought when he moved past the point of no return. Too soon and he couldn't do a damn thing about it. With one more upward thrust, hard and deep, he came with a vicious shudder that ran the length of his entire body.

She collapsed against him, their harsh, broken breathing the only sound echoing in the room, their skin slick and damp where they touched. He slid his hands down her back and over the rise of her butt, then back up again, while he kissed the side of her neck, working his way back to her lips.

Alisha Hart was potent poison, deceptive in that she covered her inherent sexuality with a confident, cool exterior. Any man lucky enough to experience all that enthusiasm was probably a goner, and that included him.

Following a sigh, she lifted her head and looked toward the window. "I think the fireworks have ended."

As far as Daniel Fortune was concerned, they had only begun.

For long, listless moments they remained in the same position, Alisha lying atop Daniel with her cheek resting against his heart. She was too exhausted to move, although she had no desire to do so. However, she also had no idea what had gotten into her. Oh, yes, she did. Daniel Fortune had gotten into her, and she'd willingly let him. More importantly, she'd completely let go—something that was quite out of character for her, at least with a man she barely knew. Oh, wait. She'd never been with a man she *barely* knew, and that was why none of this made much sense. Yet she had no real qualms at all, only the sense that she could get used to more of this, and that wasn't even something she dared to consider. This one instance of absolute bliss would be all she'd expect to experience with him after tonight. Otherwise, she'd be setting herself up for a major fall.

"What are you thinking?" he asked, intruding into her thoughts.

"You could use more color in this room."

He tugged her head up and forced her to look at him. "I'm not buying that, because after what just happened I doubt my decor is on your mind."

"Okay. I was thinking about our carelessness."

"I know. It's not like me to forgo a condom."

It wasn't like her either. "I'm personally disease-free and on the pill."

She felt him immediately relax. "Then you can't get pregnant," he said.

"No. Can you give me a gift that keeps on giving?" A fine time to ask, and something she knew better than to ignore. Something she'd never ignored until now. But timeless wisdom hadn't visited her once this evening.

"I'm clean," he said. "Do you want to see the results of my physical?"

"No. I'm going to trust you on this one." She had no choice.

He pushed her hair aside and pressed a kiss on her forehead. "Good, because you can trust me. I wouldn't do anything to compromise your safety."

Another bout of silence passed before Alisha said, "This is absolutely crazy."

"Call me crazy, but you seemed to enjoy it. I sure as hell did."

She certainly couldn't deny that she'd enjoyed it greatly. "Maybe it was the atmosphere or the fact that I haven't been with anyone in a long time."

"I know what you mean. It's been awhile for me, too."

"I find that hard to believe."

"Why?"

"Well, aside from the obvious things, such as you're an eligible bachelor and highly regarded, you're also a man."

"Being a man doesn't have anything to do with it. My job doesn't always allow for an active social life."

Active sex life would be more accurate. "That's true. Neither does mine. But regardless of our reasons for why this happened, we can't take it back."

He frowned. "Do you want to take it back?"

Did she? "Honestly no, I don't think I do. It was… It was…"

"Hot."

"You could definitely say that."

His frown faded into a smile. "Great?"

She answered his smile with one of her own. "Better than great."

He scooted up and propped his neck on the sofa's arm. Alisha rested her chin on his chest and stared up at him, totally enthralled by his mouth, his five-o'clock shadow and those ever-changing green eyes that he kept locked on her. Reality worked its way into her mind, bringing with it more concerns she couldn't ignore. If anyone found out about this tryst, she could be buried. Maybe that wasn't exactly logical, but sometimes logic was influenced by past experience. "Daniel, you have to promise me something."

He got that guy-about-to-panic look. "This sounds serious."

"Relax. I'm not going to ask for a key to your apartment. I just need to know that you're not going to tell anyone about this."

His expression was a mixture of relief and frustration. "Do you think I'm going to scribble your name and number on the bathroom walls?"

"No, but these things have a way of getting around via the grapevine."

"Alisha, we both deal with confidentiality on a daily basis. I'm not going to mention this to anyone. Except my insurance carrier."

"I beg your pardon."

"My shoulders might need medical attention."

Alisha lifted her head and noted several scratches running from his shoulders to his upper arms. "Did I do that?"

"Yeah, unless I have a cat I don't know about."

Heaven help her, she'd scarred him for life. "I'm so, so sorry."

"I'm not."

Mortified, she pressed her face into his chest. "I have totally lost my mind," she said, her words muffled but still discernible.

Once more he lifted her head up with his palms. "You and I both knew this was going to happen sooner or later."

He probably could use an ego check. "I respectfully disagree. I wasn't planning on this at all. I'm not a casual-sex kind of girl."

"I don't think what we did would qualify as casual, and there's nothing casual about you. But you are full of surprises."

"How so?"

"Let's just say if there were ten women in the room, you're the last one I would've expected to be that uninhibited."

She playfully slapped at his arm, right at the point of his wounds. He gritted his teeth and sucked in a breath. "Obviously I'm making things worse," she said.

But when she tried to roll off him, he tightened his grip. "I don't want you to move an inch because I like you right where you are."

If he kept saying such charming things, she might start believing them. "I have to go home now." When she leaned to retrieve her panties from the coffee table, he yanked them from her grasp and held them up.

"'Happy New Year?'" He laughed, a low, grainy, sexy laugh. "I'll be damned. Special-occasion underwear."

She reached up, snatched them back and played keep-away. "I had no idea anyone was going to see them."

"Do you have a pair for all of the holidays?"

"It's one of my quirks."

"Can't wait until Valentine's Day then."

Again disbelief drilled through Alisha. Surely he wasn't seriously thinking they'd still be together next month. "You know, I really do need to go now."

He tightened his hold on her. "You're not going anywhere tonight."

"Says who?"

"Says me. First, you'll have to walk back and it's crazy on the river tonight. You wouldn't be safe."

"You can drive me back to my car."

"I thought about that, but that would mean we'd have to get

dressed, and I prefer you without clothes." He slid his hands down her bare back and gave her bottom a squeeze. "And even if I did take you back, that means you'd have to drive home with all the drunks. I'm not willing to let you do that."

"Then you're going to hold me here against my will?"

"I'm going to hold you against me all night."

Alisha's heart took a little tumble over the sincerity in his voice, the sudden softness in his expression. He brought her mouth back to his and kissed her again. A surprisingly tender kiss, gentle and thorough and thought-robbing. She now faced two options—forcing the issue and demanding he let her drive home or staying with him until morning.

But he was right—driving could be costly in terms of her safety. And being in his bed could prove costly in terms of her emotional distance. Yet when he nudged her aside and stood, staring down on her with his gorgeous body in full view and his hand extended for her to take, she didn't hesitate.

Daniel Fortune might be dangerous, but he was the kind of danger she could definitely enjoy on a daily basis.

## *Three*

Daniel awoke the next morning to find the space beside him unoccupied. He sat up and rubbed a hand down his chest, hoping the hot redhead hadn't fled without at least telling him goodbye. He also had another pressing issue—the tent he'd pitched beneath the sheet. Making love in the morning was among his favorite pastimes, and frankly having more of Alisha Hart this morning sounded like an excellent idea.

He crawled out of bed and discovered he was stiff in a few places he hadn't expected. Sex on a couch had a disadvantage in terms of comfort, but he wouldn't change a thing. The only thing he'd change is the fact they'd both fallen asleep before they'd utilized his bed. He'd just have to mark that down on his to-do list, provided Alisha agreed. He intended to ask as soon as he found her.

Without bothering to dress he began his search in the bathroom, but he didn't discover her there. No one in the guest room either. He walked into the living room and found it deserted. Next stop, the kitchen, where he came upon a pot of coffee brewing but not the missing defense attorney. He did find a note taped to the refrigerator. After pouring himself a cup of the brew, he pulled the paper down and read the scribbled words.

*I had a great time last night, Counselor. Here's my number. Just keep it off the bathroom wall.*

His laugh was part amusement, part disappointment. He'd planned to spend the day with her since neither would be required to work, even though he had plenty of work to do. But the day wasn't close to being over, and hopefully a phone call would remedy her absence.

Alisha Hart was one hell of a woman, and he didn't intend to let her get away that easily. At least, not until he argued his case.

When Alisha answered the phone, she expected to hear her mom or dad wishing her a happy new year. Instead "Why did you run off without waking me up?" came through the line in a deep, provocative tone.

Daniel Fortune was more intoxicating than ingesting a barrel of moonshine. Just the sound of his voice nearly caused her to drop the receiver. "I tried to wake you, but you were snoring away."

"Did I keep you up with my snoring?"

"Not really." She hadn't minded it at all. But she hadn't slept all that well either, mainly because she'd been in a strange bed with a man who by all rights was practically a stranger. However, she had gotten to know him much better last night, and that made her blush like the devil.

"I should've told you to jab me and I would've turned over," he said. "I usually only snore when I'm on my back."

He had been on his back, giving Alisha the opportunity to study all the little details—from his solid chest, which was covered in a thatch of hair that thinned into a stream running down his belly, and below that… Well, that was the stuff female fantasies were made of. "You weren't that loud. It sounded kind of like a purr."

"A purr? I sure as hell don't purr."

"I'm so sorry. I certainly didn't mean to wound your macho pride."

"I'm definitely wounded. Those scratches look pretty bad this morning."

"You're not going to let me forget that, are you?"

"I will as long as you promise me you'll wake me before you leave the next time."

Next time? "Actually I did try to get you up before I left."

"I said wake me up. Believe me, you did get me *up*."

Her face fired up, right on cue. "That's not what I meant. I shook your shoulder. I swear, I don't think a grenade would have roused you. Anyway, I needed to get home and get some work done."

"It's a holiday, Alisha. You should take the day off."

She slid the reduced-calorie TV dinner into the microwave, stirred the good-luck black-eyed peas simmering on the stove and prepared to tell a little fib. "Actually I'm supposed to have dinner with friends, maybe watch a bowl game or two."

"You like football?" He said it with typical male enthusiasm.

"Love it. My mother's responsible for that. Nothing gets her more excited than the gridiron."

"Now I know how to get you excited—turn on the game of the week."

He had her excited now. So much so, she jumped when the microwave signaled it was time to rotate the container. "What are your plans for today?"

"I was hoping to spend the day with you."

"Sorry, but I can't." And she was sorrier she'd lied. Earlier she'd turned down Julie's dinner invitation because she intended to work. She'd turned Daniel down because she needed time to assess where this whole thing was going.

"I can't change your mind?" he asked.

Oh, he probably could if she let him, which she wouldn't. "Maybe some other time." A big maybe.

"I'm going to see you again, Alisha. And next time we'll do it right."

"I didn't know we did it wrong."

He released a throaty chuckle. "I meant *right* as in having dinner. An actual date. I don't want you to think that last night was only about sex."

"It wasn't?"

"I'd be lying if I said I don't want you back in my bed, but I would like to get to know you better outside of bed."

"Do I need to bring out the arguments again as to why we shouldn't even consider that?" she asked.

"You can, but I'm not going to listen. We have no real conflict of interest at the moment and we can be discreet about it. I think we should just go for it and see where it leads."

Probably places Alisha had never been before. In fact, she'd taken that first step last night when she'd gone to bed with him. Correction: gone to sofa with him. "I'll think about it, but I'm not going to promise anything."

"Go ahead and think about it. I'll pick you up Monday night. We can have some dinner."

"Daniel, I—"

"I'm not going to take no for an answer."

"You're definitely living up to your reputation. No negotiating, no settling."

"No holds barred when it comes to us. And this is about us, not about our jobs. We deal with our careers during the day, and that leaves the night open for whatever we want to do together."

Alisha shivered, even in the warmth of the kitchen. "I guess we could have dinner, as long as it's in an out-of-the-way place."

"You can come here. I'll make dinner."

"You cook?" This man was simply too good to be true.

"Yeah. I can cook. I can do quite a few things that would probably surprise you."

She had no doubts about that. "Then I guess I'll see you Monday night."

"And if I happen to see you Monday during the day, I'll try not to touch you in public, although it's going to be damn hard."

She'd definitely avoid the stairwell and Judge Riley's chambers. "Have a nice day, Daniel. And happy new year."

"You, too, Alisha. And if you start having any reservations, just remember us together last night. It's only going to get better."

Any better and Alisha might lose herself totally to this enigmatic prosecutor.

But what the heck. She'd lived in a celibate shell for over a year. Long past time to make up for lost time. After all, what was the worst thing that could happen?

"You want me to do what?" Daniel glared at Allan Vera, the current D.A., hoping he hadn't heard correctly. Maybe he hadn't. All morning he'd been distracted by thoughts of a defense attorney he couldn't get out of his head.

Vera released a rough, irritated sigh. "You heard me, Daniel. I said you have to take the Massey case."

Of all the asinine directives, this one had to top the list. "Krauss is handling it fine."

"I'm taking Krauss off and putting you on it. The city leaders want this one to go away quickly."

"I've got a full caseload and the Jamison murder trial still pending."

"Jason Jamison is still on the loose."

"Yeah, but that doesn't mean he won't be caught soon. In the meantime I plan to build a solid case against him." As far as Daniel was concerned, any man who would strangle his lover and shoot his own brother with calculated precision deserved to suffer all the punishment the law would allow. First, they had to catch him.

"This Massey thing should be easy enough," Allan said. "Krauss has already handled the details. You don't have to do much of anything but show up in court to argue the case."

And in doing so, face off with a woman he wanted so badly he could taste her. The little taste he'd gotten two nights ago hadn't been nearly enough. Now it might have to be, unless he could somehow get out of this whole thing. "I don't have time to handle some frivolous trial just to satisfy the city leaders."

Allan ran a hand over his balding head and kicked back in the office chair, hands resting on his bulbous belly. "Those city leaders make sure you get paid. And they answer to the citizens, who pay your salary."

"I handle felonies, not misdemeanors."

"Don't forget this one involves an assault of an elderly woman who broke her arm. That's serious business. If we don't stop him, someone else is going to get hurt, maybe worse next time. The city wants this guy off the streets, and in order to ensure this they want the best on the case."

Daniel couldn't disagree that the guy should be stopped. He just didn't want to be the one to do it. "Why don't you take it?"

"No can do. I'm about to go on vacation in a few weeks, so I need to take care of my own business. I'm taking the wife skiing in Purgatory."

And in turn sending Daniel straight to hell. The devil would be joining Vera on the slopes before he agreed to this. "We can put Goeble on it. He's got tenure."

"Goeble's a suck-up, not a decent jurist. He's more interested in parading his ass around, pretending to be a lawyer just to impress his father's cronies. As soon as he's able, he'll be out of here to join some high-dollar firm."

Daniel couldn't argue with Vera's assessment of Goeble either. "I'll find someone else then."

"No. You'll do it. Mayor Davies has been inquiring on the

status of the case on a daily basis. He trusts you to get Massey tried and punished to the fullest extent of the law before he causes more harm."

Easier said than done with Alisha acting in Massey's defense. "Do you realize who's representing him?"

Vera pulled a file in front of him and flipped it open. "Alisha Hart, formerly of Gailey and Breedlove. I hear she's pretty good."

"She's damn good." And Daniel knew that on more than one level.

"And that's why we need you to do this, Daniel. If she's a formidable opponent, then we need to throw the best at her. You're the best."

Daniel had worked hard to earn that reputation and now he wanted to curse it. "I'll cut a deal and be done with it."

"No deals."

He held back a string of foul expletives threatening to explode out of his mouth. "No deals? Hell, Allan, I'm not suggesting we let him walk. I can get him some time on the assault charge without dragging this into court."

"We want him in court. People like this Massey guy need to see that we don't tolerate this kind of thing on our streets. Pettigrew insists we make an example out of him, and you know what kind of power he wields with the party."

Daniel didn't like the wealthy city council member and he liked him even less now. "Why is he so involved?"

"It seems his soon-to-be-ex trophy wife has joined Massey's fan club."

"The guy has a fan club?"

"Yeah. They call themselves Masses for Massey. Best I understand, it's made up of mostly women."

"This case has the potential of getting way out of hand."

"True, and I know you'll handle that aspect, as well."

Damn Les Massey for screwing up his life. "I'm still not comfortable with any of this."

"Get comfortable with it. The party's going to be watching you closely. If you play your cards right and get a solid conviction on this one as well as the Jamison case, you're in as the next candidate. You'll be sitting at this desk this time next year."

Right now Daniel didn't give a damn about the party or the election. "Then you're saying I don't have a choice in this matter."

"That's exactly what I'm saying." Vera stood and walked around the desk, laying a palm on Daniel's shoulder and guiding him to the door. "I trust that you'll have this menace tried and convicted so quickly that you won't have to waste more than a minute of necessary time. You'll handle it well."

For months now Daniel had wanted to handle Alisha Hart and he wished he hadn't waited so long. Hadn't been so cautious. Now he wouldn't be able to handle her at all except during the trial, and that would have to be strictly business. At least for now.

As Daniel strode down the hallway on the heels of his anger, Allan called after him, "One more thing, Daniel."

He turned to face his boss, reluctant to even consider what that one last thing might be. "What?"

"You have a press conference at noon to announce that you'll be in charge of this case."

Great. Just freakin' great. "Is that necessary?"

"Pettigrew thinks it is, and he has the mayor in his corner."

Pettigrew could kiss his ass, Daniel thought as he walked into his office and slammed the door behind him. The last thing he needed was to try some idiot who got his rocks off getting naked in public. Getting naked was much safer when done in the confines of a private residence. An unexpected image of Alisha Hart—naked—vaulted into his brain. He jerked back the chair from behind his desk and collapsed into it, cursing his bad luck and overboard libido.

He needed to get his priorities straight. He couldn't let his major need for Alisha Hart's company derail his goals. Since he'd signed on with the district attorney's office at the beginning of his career he'd had designs on the top position. Since that first time as a kid when he'd witnessed his father knocking around his mother—and couldn't do a damn thing about it—he'd vowed to see justice done. His desire to put criminals behind bars hadn't lessened a bit, and neither would his desire for Alisha. At least, not anytime soon.

Right now he was charged with the unenviable position of telling her the news—and being in the line of fire when all hell broke loose.

Alisha breezed into her office to find Joe sitting on the edge of the reception desk, concentrating on the portable TV set in the corner of the deserted waiting room. "Do we have so little business that you're watching cartoons again?"

Joe sent her only a cursory glance before turning his attention back to the tube. "Not cartoons. A press conference. And I think you should be watching it, too."

Crossing the room, Alisha took her place beside Joe and nearly dropped the bag containing her meager lunch. "That's Daniel Fortune."

"Yep. That's Daniel Fortune answering questions about your client's prosecution and the new prosecutor who'll be handling the case."

Alisha tugged off her jacket and tossed it and the bag onto the desk. "Krauss isn't in charge anymore?"

"No, and you're not going to like who's taking his place."

"Please don't tell me it's that creep, Goeble."

"No, not Goeble."

"Then who?"

"The iceman's going to do it himself."

Alisha's mouth hung open for a few seconds before she said, "You're kidding, right?"

"No, I'm not kidding." He reached behind him and handed

her a piece of paper. "He called earlier while you were out, I assume to let you know."

Alisha took the paper from Joe only to find the number to the D.A.'s office. "I can't believe he didn't tell me New Year's Eve."

"I wouldn't think a bar would be a good place to discuss it."

She wadded up the note and tossed it in the waste bin. "Not in the bar. Outside of the bar, after I left."

Joe had the gall to grin. "Well, did you do—"

"No, I did not. I went home and he went home, end of story." And she was telling one whopper of a story.

She tossed Joe the sack. "Here. It's a sub sandwich. Take half an hour to eat lunch, then get moving on the Massey case. Start working on the motions we've discussed. Now's your chance to play attorney before you have to pass the bar. And call the temp agency. Have them send someone over to field phone calls, preferably one who's worked in a law office before. We're going to need all the help we can get."

When she started for the door, Joe asked, "Where are you going?"

"Out."

"Aren't you going to call Fortune?"

"Nope." She turned with a hand poised on the knob. "I'm going to pay him a personal visit."

"I'd like to buy tickets to that little meeting."

"You need to get to work. I'll handle the A.D.A."

Joe unfolded the paper from around the sandwich and crammed a big bite in his mouth. "Good luck," he said without even swallowing.

As Alisha headed for the courthouse, she realized she was going to need plenty of luck and plenty of strength. Just because Daniel Fortune happened to be the most gorgeous, multitalented, intelligent man she'd ever known didn't mean she couldn't hold her own with him. And she would, no matter what he tried to throw at her.

* * *

Alisha Hart strode into Daniel's office looking as if she'd like to throw something at him. Fortunately she set her briefcase down on the chair instead of hurling it at his head. "I believe you know why I'm here."

She sounded calm, but she looked fighting mad—and sexy as hell in her tailored blue dress that gave Daniel just a glimpse of her knees. Really great knees. "You came by to call off our dinner plans?"

"Very funny," she said without one whit of amusement in her tone.

Daniel noticed the partially open door and pointed behind her. "Close it."

She looked over her shoulder, then back to him, before complying. Instead of sitting, she braced her palms on the edge of his desk and leaned into them. "First of all, do you mind telling me why you didn't inform me the other night you were going to be taking the Massey case?"

Daniel greatly minded that her breasts were eye level and the cut of the dress showed a hint of cleavage. He forced his gaze to her face. "Because I didn't know until this morning. And I don't like it any more than you do. And if I recall, we decided not to discuss it the other night. In fact, I remember we stopped talking altogether after a while."

After snatching up her briefcase, she finally sat, giving Daniel only minimal relief. "We're certainly going to discuss it now."

Daniel leaned back in his chair and laced his hands behind his head. "Go ahead, Counselor. But if you're here to make a deal, you'll be wasting your breath."

"It's my breath to waste, and I don't see why we can't come to some sort of agreement and save the taxpayers money."

"What exactly are you proposing?" he asked.

"One count of disorderly conduct, drop the indecent exposure and the trumped-up assault charge."

"You're not serious."

"Do I look like I'm jesting?"

No, but she looked pretty damn good, Daniel thought. So good he almost couldn't think. But he had to think. "Let's start with the indecent exposure. We have a witness who claims she saw his genitals during his little show on the river taxi and that he in fact was aroused." That much he did know, although he knew nothing about the witness. Truth was, he hadn't had time to thoroughly review the case. He sure as hell hadn't prepared for the impact of seeing Alisha again—and knowing he couldn't touch her now. Or later, for that matter. At least not until this mess was over.

Her expression remained battle-ready. "My client was strategically covered by a wide sash, therefore his genitals were not exposed. As far as his alleged arousal is concerned, the temperature was below forty degrees. In those kinds of elements, I highly doubt Mr. Massey capable of an erection."

The last thing Daniel needed to hear coming out of her pretty coral-painted mouth was the word *erection*. "Our witness says otherwise."

"Your witness is mistaken. Or perhaps she was engaged in some wishful thinking." Alisha looked at him straight on. "You know, if Mr. Massey were a woman, we wouldn't even be having this argument."

"Why's that?"

"Because a woman's arousal wouldn't be noticeable."

"Any man worth his salt can tell if a woman's aroused, obvious or not."

"Not in the dark."

"Oh, yeah. Definitely in the dark. I can always tell. One of these days I'll prove it to you."

"We're not going to talk about that." Her gaze drifted away before coming back to him. "My point is, only one witness claiming my client was exposed and aroused isn't solid evidence."

"You can argue that during the trial."

She stared at him again. "I guarantee I will if we have a trial. I'll have my motions on your desk by tomorrow."

Frustrated with her persistence and his own lack of research, Daniel said, "If you're trying to convince me to go easy on this guy, forget it, Counselor. Mr. Massey assaulted a senior citizen. That's a class A misdemeanor. The state isn't going to budge." That fact had been more than apparent during his earlier conversation with Allan Vera.

She grabbed her briefcase and stood. "Okay. Have it your way. Hopefully the presiding judge will see it my way."

Daniel came to his feet. "Anything else?"

"Not at the moment, but if I think of something else, I'll let you know." She swept her hair away from her face with one hand. Today it fell to her shoulders in soft curls, just as it had the other night. Daniel was assaulted by the sudden fantasy of having those curls raking over his bare chest—and lower. He needed to get a grip, and not on her.

"I hope you're ready for this, Counselor," she said.

Daniel rounded the desk and stood before her. Not too close, but close enough to get the full effect of her vivid blue eyes. "I'll be ready."

"So will I."

"But you're not going to win this one, Alisha."

She lifted her chin and sent him a smug smile. "Wanna bet?"

He streaked a hand over his jaw. "Sure. What should we wager?"

Her smile faded into a frown. "I wasn't serious."

"I am." He shoved his hands in his pockets to keep from reaching out to her. "How confident are you that you'll win?"

"Might I remind you, if anyone found out money exchanged hands between us, we'd both be disbarred."

"I didn't say a thing about money."

Alisha eyed him skeptically. "What exactly do you have in mind?"

Something that would be deemed downright dirty. "I'd have to think on it, but I have a few ideas."

"So do I," she said, continuing to clutch the briefcase to her breasts. "If you lose—which you will—I'd consider something involving a little public humiliation. Maybe I'll make you wear Les's sequined toreador outfit, sans pants, and you can give a speech on the courthouse steps."

"You know, Alisha, if you want to get me naked again, you don't have to win a bet. You only have to ask me."

She wagged a finger at him. "We're not going to go there again, Counselor. Not now."

That "not now" thing gave him some hope. "Later?"

"You're going to continue to give me a hard time, aren't you?"

"I'll give you whatever you want me to give you," he said.

She drew in a shaky breath and her eyes took on a hazy cast. No way could he miss it. "I want you to consider keeping this case out of court."

"I'm not talking about the case and you know it."

"I know, and we can't talk about what's happening between us," she said. "We certainly can't act on it."

At least she'd admitted there was an "us." "True, but this trial isn't going to stop me from thinking about it." He took her hand and pulled her forward. "And you'll be thinking about it, too."

"Daniel, this isn't a good idea at all," she said without much conviction. And even more telling, she didn't yank her hand out of his grasp.

"Yeah, I know. That's why I'm not going to do anything but this." Lifting her hand, he turned it over and brushed a kiss on her palm, followed by a streak of his tongue, before releasing her. "If that's what I have to settle for right now, then I'll live with it."

After a slight catch of her breath, the confidence returned to her face. "A hand kiss. And I thought chivalry was dead."

He brushed her hair from her shoulders and rested his mouth at her ear. "Sometime in the future I'm going to kiss more than your hand, starting with that sexy mouth of yours, then I'm going to move my lips lower until—"

She pulled back and started backing to the door. "We're going to behave ourselves during this trial, Daniel."

"Sure. Whatever you say." But he bit back a laugh when he realized she was trying to convince herself as well as him.

"I'm going now," she said without making a move to leave.

"Fine. I'm not stopping you. Not this time."

"Since when have you ever stopped me?"

He couldn't resist getting in one last comment before she disappeared. "I sure didn't stop you Saturday night. And I'm not going to stop you if you decide you want a repeat performance in the future. But it's going to be your decision. You know where to find me."

"Yes, I do. Opposing me in a courtroom." With that she jerked open the door and rushed away, leaving Daniel assessing his total loss of logic.

For years he'd walked the straight and narrow, never veering off course, never doing anything that could ruin his aspirations, especially not with a woman. But Alisha wasn't just another woman. She was tough. She didn't give a damn about what his status could bring her. And most important, she was nothing at all like his mother—a woman who suffered abuse from her alcoholic husband at the expense of her own children's sense of safety. And still she'd stayed with him, until staying had cost her her life.

But that was all in the past, where Daniel intended to keep it. He also intended to see where this thing with Alisha Hart might lead. Hopefully not down the path of destruction.

## *Four*

As if her little encounter with Daniel Fortune hadn't been bad enough two days ago, now she found herself at the jail for another meeting with Les Massey. She'd had very little sleep and too much to think about—namely the prosecutor. Right now she had to think about her client, who sat across from her giving her a suggestive smile that probably worked on most women but not on her.

She shuffled her notes to keep from looking at him. "Okay, Mr. Massey, we need to go over a few things before I have to go before the judge for the hearing."

"I'm all yours, Ms. Hart. Knock yourself out."

When she finally looked up to discover his orange prison-issue jumpsuit unzipped to his sternum, she wanted to knock him out. "First of all, in reference to the woman you pushed—"

"I told you I didn't push her."

"All right, the woman you allegedly pushed while making

your escape down the walkway following the river-taxi incident—"

"I wasn't escaping."

"You were running."

"I was sprinting. No one was after me except maybe a few girls. They were trying to take my sash." And he looked proud of it.

"You don't remember even accidentally nudging the woman?"

"I don't even remember her. In fact, the last thing I remember was running headlong into the cop. He cuffed me and brought me down here."

Alisha leaned forward and gave him the full extent of her scowl. "One of you is lying."

"She's lying. I didn't push anyone. I'm not that stupid."

Since the guy delighted in putting on a show half-naked in public, leaving himself wide open for arrest, Alisha could definitely debate that. "Next point. You haven't been formally charged with a concealed-weapons violation, but it's a possibility. Did you have a gun?"

Now Les scowled. "I swear I didn't have one. Where would I have stuck it?"

Where Alisha had wanted to stick Billy Wade's toupee on New Year's Eve? She didn't dare ask that for fear he might confirm her suspicions. "I only know that the prosecution has a witness's statement that claims you tossed something into the water and it looked a lot like a gun. I don't want any surprises if they happen to recover it from the river."

Les sat back and rubbed his chin with one tanned hand. "It was probably the maracas."

"Maracas?" This was the first she'd heard about that.

"Yeah. I was shaking them while I was singing 'Jingle Bells' on the riverboat. I was going to throw them to this group of girls standing on the riverbank, but I missed and they fell into the water."

Good thing, otherwise he might have hit one of the girls in the head, resulting in another assault charge. "Okay, this is where we stand. I'm going to argue against the weapons charge, but my guess is we're going to have to go to trial on the other charges."

"There's going to be a trial?"

Wake up and smell the coffee, you jerk, Alisha wanted to say to him. Instead she said, "Yes, and that means you'll need to clean up your act and be on your best behavior."

"Do I have to cut my hair?"

"Wouldn't hurt."

"Oh, man." Les collapsed back into the seat and sighed. "I was hoping it wouldn't come to this. I've got better things to do than get tied up with a trial."

Like she didn't. "Well, you're going to be tied up and locked up until then. If we're lucky, the trial will be scheduled within the month."

"I have to stay here a whole month?"

Weary of Les's whining, Alisha gathered her notes and shoved them into her briefcase. "Most likely yes. And while you're here, try to keep your clothes on, okay?"

"I'll try, but there's this woman jailer and I think she has the hots for me."

Oh, how she wished she could order full-body restraints for the streaker. "The last thing you need is to seduce a jailer. Otherwise you'll be spending a lot longer than a few weeks in here, guaranteed. Any questions?"

Les unfolded from the chair and stuck out his chest like a barnyard rooster heading for the henhouse. "Nope. I'll let you know if I think of anything."

"You do that. I'll be back when we're ready to discuss your testimony." If she decided to put him on the stand, assuming they went to trial, which she honestly hoped they didn't.

Alisha called for the guard, and as she turned to go Les said, "I thought of something."

She faced him again. "Yes?"

He gave her a lecherous once-over. "Since I can't give you any money, I've thought of how I can repay you."

Oh, joy. "That's not necessary. The state pays me."

"But I'd like to show my gratitude in some way. Maybe we could have some dinner?"

"How do you intend to pay for that?"

He hesitated a moment. "Good point. Maybe I'll get a job."

He said it as if that whole concept just now occurred to him. "Good idea, Mr. Massey." She wanted to suggest the cabaret club on the interstate that catered to women but refrained.

Alisha strode out of the conference room as quickly as her feet allowed. Ironic that she'd been asked to dinner twice in recent days by two men—an egotistical exhibitionist and an irresistible testosterone tank. One wasn't at all her type. And the other, well, for all intents and purposes, he was a nemesis. A handsome hunk and expert lover who still plagued her thoughts on an hourly basis.

Funny, sleeping with the enemy again had never looked so good.

"Mr. Fortune, you have a call on line one."

In the process of readying to go home, Daniel took a quick glance at his watch. He needed to get out of there. Otherwise he'd be late to his function, even though he wasn't too thrilled about an evening of schmoozing. "Who is it, Lucy?"

"It's Ryan Fortune, sir. He says it's important."

Daniel had hoped the call might be from Alisha Hart, even if it did pertain to business. He hadn't seen or heard from her in over a week aside from official correspondence, and he'd missed her—a lot. But if his cousin was calling at this time of day, it was bound to be important. He picked up the receiver and said, "Hey, Ryan. What's up?"

"Plenty."

That one word, said with serious concern, worried Daniel. "Anything I can help you with?"

"Yeah. First, are there any leads on Jason Jamison's whereabouts?"

"Nothing substantial yet, but they'll get him."

"I hope they do. Real soon."

Daniel knew the man well enough to know when he was holding back, like right now. "What else is bothering you, Ryan?"

"I've been getting some threats."

"Threats?"

"Yeah. Some messages on my voice mail. Someone saying they're going to hurt someone I love."

Daniel experienced a sick feeling in his gut. "Have you reported this to the police?"

"Yeah. So far the calls have been untraceable. I'm almost a hundred percent sure it's Jason making the threats."

"I'm going to make a few calls to the Red Rock Police Department and the sheriff's department. I'll make sure they send out extra patrols. You also need to up your private security. I could call Vincent and see if he can handle it."

"Don't bother your brother. He's still on his honeymoon."

True, Daniel thought, but Vincent's extended trip with his new wife had a lot to do with protecting her. Natalie would be Daniel's star witness in the case against Jamison since she'd witnessed him murder his presumed wife. Provided Jamison ever turned up again. "I'm sure he has someone handling things at his company in his absence."

"Don't worry about it. I've got another…" Ryan paused as if trying to gather his thoughts. "I've got another security company here locally that can take care of it. I just wanted to let you know what's happening."

"I appreciate it. And, Ryan, we will catch the bastard."

"I hope I live to see that happen."

"I don't think it's going to take forty years."

"Life is short, Danny. You never know when it's all going to come to an end."

Daniel's concern increased. He'd never known his cousin to be anything but positive. "Are you sure you're okay, Ryan?"

"Yeah, I'm okay. And I need to go. Lily's waiting dinner on me. Thanks for talking with me, Danny. I appreciate it more than you know."

"Anytime, Ryan. Feel free to call to check in, and I'll do the same."

After shared goodbyes, Daniel grabbed his coat from the back of his chair and loosened his tie. The conversation left him with a sudden sense of foreboding. Something was definitely wrong with Ryan. He never stumbled over his words. He'd always been sharp and succinct. Maybe it was just stress. God knew the man had had enough of that lately.

Unfortunately Daniel didn't have much time to worry about that now. After he made the necessary phone calls to the authorities, he needed to get home and grab some dinner and a shower in preparation for a social event heralding the upcoming opening of a family-crisis center, a place he'd supported both financially and emotionally. He knew all about families in crises. Despite that fact, if he had his way, he'd stay in tonight and look over the Massey case. Correction: if he had his way, he'd be spending the evening with one Ms. Hart.

Unfortunately that wasn't in the cards. At least not tonight. Not unless she happened to show up at the reception, too. Not out of the question since a good deal of the law community would be in attendance.

He probably wouldn't be so lucky. But if she did show up, the possibilities were limitless, even if wisdom told him to stay away from the lady before it was too late.


"You're late, Hart."

Nudging the office door closed with her bottom, Alisha

crossed the waiting room and tossed her briefcase on the desk behind which Joe was seated. "Late for what?"

"Your appointment. You were supposed to meet with a prospective client forty-five minutes ago."

Alisha slapped her palm to her forehead. "I forgot. Did you reschedule?"

"I tried, but she wanted to wait." Joe hooked a thumb behind him. "I got her some coffee and stuck her in your office."

"Any idea what this is about?"

"She's a referral from…" Joe looked at the sparse schedule on the computer screen. "Someone named Laci Wagner sent her."

"She's a former colleague. I worked with her at Gailey and Breedlove." And a good friend, or at least she had been before the debacle that had caused Alisha to leave her former firm. "Hold all my calls while I talk to her. What's her name?"

"Sheila White. A nice woman."

"Good." She didn't mind talking with a nice woman after counseling her current client, the self-serving stud muffin.

Alisha breezed into the room and encountered a tall, rail-thin lady, her gray hair pulled back into a long braid. The woman's gaze darted around the room as if she wasn't sure where to look.

Alisha rounded her desk and held out a hand. "I'm Alisha Hart, Ms. White. I'm so sorry you've had to wait. I was tied up with a client longer than expected."

The woman sent her a tentative smile to go with a brief handshake. "It's Mrs. White, and I don't mind if you call me Sheila. And I didn't mind waiting because this is important."

Alisha sat and pushed her chair beneath her desk while Sheila reclaimed the chair before her. "Now tell me what I can do for you."

"This is about my son's accident. He was paralyzed from the waist down." The mist of tears in her eyes caused Alisha's heart to clutch. She pulled a tissue from the holder and handed it to the distraught mother.

"I'm sorry," Sheila said as she swiped at her eyes. "It's still so hard to talk about."

"No apology necessary. As soon as you're ready, I'd like to hear how you were referred to me."

She recaptured her composure much quicker than Alisha expected. "I clean Miss Wagner's house, but she says she can't help me because the place where she works is representing the woman who hit my boy." She pushed an envelope forward. "Miss Wagner told me to give this to you."

Alisha took the sealed envelope and opened it to find a handwritten note.

Alisha,
I'm really going out on a limb here, but in good conscience I feel that I must. Mrs. White needs your help in filing a wrongful-death suit. It's rumored that the woman who injured her son had two prior DUI charges we made go away. Her name is Nancy Kenneally, of the electronics dynasty Kenneallys. She's ruined this family's life and she needs to be stopped. Attacking her checkbook couldn't hurt. Just don't let anyone know I've sent her or my ass will be gone before the ink dries on this letter.
Laci.

Alisha wasn't sure what shocked her more—Laci's willingness to take such a risk by revealing confidential information or the fact that if she agreed to represent the Whites she'd in turn be taking on her former firm. Then again, revenge could be very, very sweet.

Setting the documents aside, Alisha folded her hands before her. "Tell me about the accident."

Sheila plucked her purse from the floor, withdrew a photo and handed it to Alisha. "This was my Barry last year when he was a junior in high school."

Alisha studied the picture of the gangly, smiling young man dressed in some kind of track uniform. "He's a very nice-looking boy."

"He was a cross-country runner. Last summer he was out jogging near a park and that Kenneally woman ran him down." Anger had replaced the sorrow in her voice. "They said it was an accident. They said Barry ran out in front of her. He doesn't remember what happened, but I still don't believe it. When the police got there, her car was up on the curb."

"Did anyone see the accident?"

"One lady did and at first she said the woman lost control of the car. Later she told the police she didn't say that. I think she's lying now."

Alisha wondered if the witness had been paid for her silence. "Was Mrs. Kenneally brought up on charges?"

"They had an investigation and nothing came of it. Now she's walking free while my only boy's going to spend his life in a wheelchair. What's left of his life, anyway."

"If you decide to go through with this lawsuit, it could take years to settle."

Sheila lifted her chin. "I want to go through with it and not because of the money. If she doesn't go to jail, then at least we'll get our day in court." Her gaze faltered. "But my husband and me, we don't have any money to speak of. We're just simple, hardworking people. And Barry's insurance coverage isn't going to last much longer."

These were the kind of people Alisha felt compelled to help, not the Kenneallys of the world who bought their own brand of justice. "I tell you what, Mrs. White. I'll conduct some research and if I decide to take this on, I'll do so on contingency."

"What does that mean?"

"You won't pay any money up-front. If we win, then I'll take a percentage. If I lose, you won't be out anything."

Sheila's eyes went wide. "You'd do that for me?"

"Yes, but that's standard in this kind of situation." Alisha stood and extended her hand. "I'll call you in the next couple of days after I review all the facts and determine if we have a good case."

Sheila rose and took Alisha's hand, shaking it vigorously. "Thank you, Miss Hart. I appreciate anything you can do for me and my son."

"Not a problem. I'll see you out."

After escorting Sheila to the door, she turned back to find Joe kicked back in the chair, feet propped on the desk, hands laced behind his neck. "Do you want to ride with me and Julie?"

She strode to the desk and lifted his feet up, placing them on the floor. "Ride where?"

"The reception for the new family-advocacy center. Or did you forget that, too?"

Yes, she had. And she wanted to forget about it now. "I think I'm going to bow out. I've got the hearing tomorrow morning and I need to prepare."

"You're as prepared as you'll ever be. And you need to get out and have some fun."

"I don't consider sucking up to the entire population of San Antonio's legal eagles fun. I can do that any day of the week."

"Yeah, but not with little finger sandwiches and free booze. Besides, Julie's worked hard to help this place get off the ground. She'll be disappointed if you're not there."

He had a point, and Alisha had an obligation to be there if only for that reason. "What time?"

"We'll pick you up around seven."

"I'll drive myself."

"It's not a problem, Alisha. That way, if you and I want to get tanked, Julie's volunteered to drive. She can't drink."

"Why not? She certainly isn't going to be the only one."

Joe grinned. "Because she's pregnant. That's why she didn't have anything on New Year's Eve."

Alisha was caught somewhere between elation and envy. She hated that envy and hated herself for feeling it. "That's wonderful, Joe." She rounded the desk and gave him a quick hug. "You're still going to finish law school, aren't you?"

"You bet. I'm in the home stretch and I can't quit now."

If only she had more to offer him financially. After all, he basically ran the office, serving as a clerk, paralegal and part-time receptionist all at the same time. "If you're willing to stick with me after you go back to school in a couple of weeks, I'll work around your schedule and see what I can do about a raise."

Joe held up his hand. "Don't worry about it. You're going to have to bring in that temp, and that costs money. Julie and I will manage. She'll get paid pregnancy leave and we've saved some, plus her parents are willing to help out. They have the money and the means."

Alisha thought a minute. "Well, if Mrs. White's case pans out, it could mean quite a bit of money."

"Are you going to take it?"

"Yes, I think I am." For that and other reasons aside from the possibility of a large settlement. "Of course, we both know that could take awhile. In the meantime, I'm going to rely on you to help me with the particulars."

"Not a problem." Joe came to his feet. "I'm going to head home, unless you need anything else."

"No. You go ahead. I'm about to leave, too. I have to make myself beautiful for tonight."

Joe laughed. "That shouldn't take too long."

"You are so amusing, Alvarado."

"And you don't even realize how attractive you are. But you can bet Daniel Fortune does."

Daniel had never seen Alisha Hart look quite this beautiful, although the way she'd looked on New Year's Eve ran a close second. Normally she dressed in corporate conservative, a look befitting her position. But tonight...well, she wore a formfitting little black stretchy dress that hugged her tightly, long-sleeved but cut low at the neck and back. And those spiked heels… Man, he could imagine her wearing only those and nothing else. He better quit imagining it or he'd end up spending all evening hiding behind one of the buffet tables.

For the past hour they'd been doing the avoidance dance, maintaining their distance while exchanging glances every now and then. Just watching her move through the crowd had him considering things he had no business considering— namely getting her alone and in his bed.

"Good to see you tonight, Counselor."

Daniel turned his attention from Alisha to the owner of the booming voice, Van McAllister, former state Supreme Court justice and champion of many worthy causes. He'd been instrumental in seeing the center they honored tonight come to be.

Taking Van's outstretched hand, Daniel gave it a hearty shake. "Good to see you, too, Van. You did a great job on this place."

Van scoffed. "I just helped with the fund-raising and did a little conceptual planning. The committee did the rest. And I think they did a fine job."

Daniel took a moment to survey the area. "It's a good design."

"A remarkable design." Van pointed to the upper floor. "We have transitional housing up there." He pointed behind him. "And offices at ground level. Every kind of assistance you can imagine, including counselors and legal help. Just say the word, one of those offices could be yours."

Daniel frowned. "Mine?"

"Yeah. I could use a good legal director. It would only be part-time in the beginning, but it could lead to bigger and better things. Of course, I know you have your sights set on the D.A. position, once Allan gives it up."

Yeah, Daniel did, but that wasn't a guarantee he would be the party's choice, especially if he happened to lose the Massey case. And with his current workload, not to mention

Alisha Hart as opposing counsel, that just might happen. Nah. He'd win, no matter what it took. "I'll keep that in mind."

Van slapped him hard on the back. "Good deal. I can't keep the position open forever, but it's going to take a few months to get this thing going, so you have some time to decide."

"I'll do that." Daniel really didn't have any intention of doing any such thing. Heading up a legal team for a nonprofit organization, albeit a worthwhile one, didn't seem like something he'd try. At least not at the moment.

Right now he really wanted to find Alisha. He couldn't risk seeming too friendly with her, but he could catch her long enough to have a casual conversation—and maybe invite her back to his place.

He needed to get that thought out of his head immediately. Unfortunately he hadn't been able to force her out of his mind. But if he wanted to do the prosecution of Massey justice, as well as focus on the Jamison case, he had to stop thinking about her. Too much to do, too little time—and a whole lot of distraction, he realized when he finally caught sight of her again.

She stood near the double French doors leading outside, a glass of wine clutched in one hand and a sour look on her face as she spoke to some guy who seemed to be standing way too close to her. Her body language alone said she didn't want him near her, yet he kept inching closer.

Daniel saw an opportunity to intervene, although that was pretty damn dangerous when he realized the man's identity. Troy Moreau, a high-dollar attorney and high-handed jackass, the same man rumored to have once been involved with Alisha. The guy had given the prosecutors in his office more than their fair share of trouble on more than one occasion of late.

Daniel weighed his options carefully. If he approached Alisha, Moreau might take the hint and leave. Or he could stand his ground and stick around anyway. Daniel couldn't bodily force the bastard to leave her alone, although the thought was tempting, considering Moreau now had his hand resting casually on the small of Alisha's back. The gesture was too possessive, too intimate. If Alisha had given any indication she welcomed the attention, he'd stay right where he stood. But she hadn't, and Daniel could no longer stand by and let her endure the advances one more minute.

Just as he started forward, Alisha yanked Moreau's hand away and spewed something Daniel couldn't understand, but he knew she wasn't telling Moreau to enjoy his evening. Worse, she looked visibly shaken as she stormed out the doors, leaving Moreau sporting a self-satisfied smile.

Why he felt the need to rescue her, Daniel couldn't say. Chances were, she didn't need rescuing. But he could at least make sure she was okay.

## Five

"Are you okay?"

Alisha recognized his voice all too well and suspected she knew why Daniel Fortune had arrived unexpectedly. Obviously her little scene with Troy had drawn unwanted attention, at least from the prosecutor now standing a few feet from her, arms draped over the veranda's railing. Even his profile was striking. Striking a chord of longing in Alisha.

She stared out at the sloping grounds to the intricate play yard positioned at the end of the hill. "Nice night, isn't it? Not even cool enough for a jacket. I was just trying to remember how long it's been since I've been on a swing."

"You still haven't answered my question," he said.

"I don't understand your question." A lie. She understood it completely.

"I saw Moreau harassing you and I wanted to make sure you're all right."

And to think she'd been so careful to keep her voice lowered when she'd made that verbal jab at Troy's anatomy. She turned and propped an elbow on the railing to find Daniel still staring off into space. "I promise you, Counselor, I'm fine. Troy seems to think that if he gives the word, any woman will gladly join him in bed and thank him for it later."

"But not you."

"Not me." Not anymore.

Daniel finally looked at her, his handsome face washed in the glow of a lone tiki torch set out in the corner of the veranda. "Are you sure that's all it was, a proposition?"

A proposition that entailed taking up where they'd left off, something Alisha didn't care to share—or to even consider, for that matter. "Look, Moreau's a shark, and although it took me awhile to realize that, I washed my hands of him the minute I walked out of my former firm."

"If you say so."

"I say so." Alisha once more surveyed the playground to keep from staring at Daniel. Confronting Troy again served to remind her why she needed to avoid any further involvement with the prosecutor. Fellow attorneys made dicey bedfellows, no matter what side of the law you happened to land on. "Isn't your public awaiting you inside?"

"I've already made my rounds."

"So have I. I better get back inside and find Joe and Julie. If I'm lucky, they'll be ready to leave soon."

"They've already left."

Alisha's gaze snapped back to Daniel. "How do you know?"

Daniel turned and leaned a hip against the rail. "Because he stopped me and told me that if I saw you, I'm to tell you that his wife ate something that didn't agree with her and he needed to take her home. He sends his apologies and hopes you don't have any trouble finding a ride."

Oh, lovely. "Guess it's time to call a cab."

"I'll give you a ride."

She just bet he could. "That's not necessary."

"I know, but I want to do it."

"And how do you propose we manage that, Mr. Fortune? Just waltz out of here together and in doing so start the rumor mill spinning out of control?"

He hinted at a grin. "I think waltzing through the crowd without the benefit of music might be fairly obvious. We don't have to leave together. I'll get my car from the valet and I'll park at the end of the lot. You can pretend to be going to your own car and I'll pick you up."

Apparently he'd planned the whole thing in great detail. "And if someone sees me getting into your car?"

"It's dark outside. And even if someone did see us, I could always say you were having car trouble."

She'd be borrowing trouble if she agreed to this and putting more than her reputation at risk if she couldn't resist him. "I'm still not sure this is a good plan."

"Sure it is. I take you home, we say good night and you go inside alone. Nothing more than that."

He sounded sincere, but could she really trust him? Better still, could she trust herself? Of course, she could avoid cab fare. She could hop out of the car before he even had a chance to park. "Okay, you're on."

He pushed off the railing and smiled. "I'll go back inside first. Give me about ten minutes to get my car and I'll meet you at the end of the drive."

"Exactly what kind of car am I looking for?"

"A black sports coupe," he said as he headed for the entry.

"That's rather vague."

With one hand on the doorknob he said, "The license plate is personalized. You can't miss it."

"What does it say?"

"WIN AGAIN."

That figured. Daniel Fortune was all about winning, and Alisha would do well to remember that. He might be cordial outside the courtroom, but come time for Les Massey's trial, she had no doubt he'd morph into a barracuda.

Yet as he slipped back inside the building with a confident saunter, Alisha couldn't help but remember the way he'd touched her the other night with unexpected gentleness and how he had seemed sincerely interested in her life. How he'd put her at ease in a very short time and brought her to a sensual plane she hadn't visited much until him. If at all.

That was before things had changed. Before they knew they would be facing off in a professional venue. Before their careers had intruded. Like it or not, Daniel Fortune would have to remain off-limits, and Alisha truly didn't like it one bit.

Pulled next to the curb near the last row of parked cars, Daniel watched Alisha stride toward him, fishing through her purse as if searching for keys. She had the role-playing down pat, and he had the strongest urge to find out what other kind of roles she'd be willing to play in his bed.

He rubbed a hand over his face to erase that image, yet he wasn't too successful. He shouldn't have offered to take her home. Correction: *drive* her home. He needed to avoid her, but for some reason he couldn't stay away from her, and that was irrational. He didn't do foolish, and hadn't since he'd shaved his entire body for a swim meet back in college. When it had grown back, it had itched like hell. Now he had a new kind of itch for an attractive defender and he didn't dare try to scratch it. At least not tonight. But after the trial was over he planned to take up where they'd left off. Unless she didn't agree to that plan. He had more than a few ways to encourage her and he would use each and every one if necessary.

Alisha looked to her left, then to her right, before yanking open the car door and practically hurling herself inside.

"Let's go," she said, her voice winded.

"Seat belt first."

She sent him a classic go-to-hell look. "Okay, but you drive while I'm putting it on."

Daniel turned his attention from her to the ignition only to see someone coming toward them. And that someone wasn't anyone he needed to see at the moment, especially with opposing counsel squirreled away in his vehicle. "Get down."

"Why?"

"Because my boss is heading this way."

Instead of crouching in the seat, Alisha draped herself across the narrow console and, of all things, dropped face-down on his lap. He couldn't think of anything more damaging to his dignity, because in about two seconds tops he would give the stick shift some competition.

Daniel turned the ignition, jammed the car into first and sped past Allan without even bothering to wave. He turned up the drive leading to the exit while Alisha remained in the same position. He could feel the warmth of her mouth penetrating his slacks and immediately jumped into third gear while shifting the car into second.

"Is it safe now?" she asked.

He couldn't lay any claim to feeling very safe right now, considering her lips were moving against his groin. Although he was nearing the exit—and close to combusting—he told her, "Wait until we get on the main road."

A patient driver he was not, but he welcomed the stream of passing traffic coming in both directions, allowing him a little more time to keep Alisha's face in his lap, even if it was sheer torture. When the cars had cleared, he laid his hand on her head, intending to nudge her up. Instead he stroked his palm over her hair that tonight was straight and soft. He wasn't sure which way he liked it better—untamed curls or sleek sophistication. Both ways, he decided.

When the traffic cleared, he turned onto the street that would lead them to the interstate. "You can get up now."

She straightened and tugged at her skirt. "That was interesting."

"Tell me about it." He started to make a suggestive comment, but when he took his eyes from the road to look at her, he noticed her troubled expression. That concerned him more than his current predicament. "Are you sure you're okay?"

She propped her elbow where the edge of the door met the window and rested her cheek on her curled hand. "I'm just tired. I haven't been sleeping all that well."

Neither had he, and the major reason was sitting next to him. "I know what you mean. But I've always been somewhat of an insomniac."

"Me, too."

All conversation suspended until he turned onto the interstate. "You're going to have to give me directions," he told her.

"I'll let you know when to exit."

If only she would let him know what she was thinking. And then his own thoughts came spilling out before he had a chance to stop them. "Were you and Moreau involved?"

"Define 'involved'," she said as she continued to stare out the windshield.

He shouldn't push. He should tell her never mind. But he had to know, and that wasn't like him. He wasn't normally possessive with women. He'd seen enough of that behavior in his father where his own mother was concerned. "Were you lovers?"

"You could say that. He definitely screwed me, and not only in the way that you're thinking."

Daniel didn't even want to think about Moreau with his hands on her, but he did think about it, and it pissed him off. "Is he the reason why you left the firm?"

"I told you most of the reasons the other night, so let's just say he was the last straw."

"Then it ended badly." At least it had ended, and that relieved Daniel.

"Yes, but it had nothing to do with a lovers' quarrel, if that's what you're assuming. It had to do with his lack of ethics when we were working together on a criminal-negligence case. You might remember it since your office was involved. Richard Callan was the defendant, a prominent home builder. He was responsible for the faulty wiring that caused the deaths of two kids in a fire."

"I remember it, but I wasn't handling it."

"Maybe if you had been handling it the man would have ended up behind bars, where he belonged."

"You wanted to lose the case?"

"Wouldn't have bothered me in the least. Callan got off because we put the victim on trial."

"How so?"

She sighed. "In the process of investigating the case, I uncovered information that the kids' mother had been dating a few men, and she was on a date the night of the fire. She'd left her boys in the care of a fourteen-year-old sitter. The sitter survived, but the boys perished. And on top of that, the mother wasn't married to her youngest child's father, as if that should really matter in light of the fact her children were killed due to negligence. Troy was sitting first chair and he said he wasn't going to use it, but he did, despite my protests."

"Who was the prosecuting attorney?" Daniel had his suspicions, but he waited for confirmation and got it when she said, "Goeble."

That explained a lot. "He didn't try to keep the testimony out?"

"He tried, sort of, but he wasn't successful. We based our case on the supposition that if she'd been home instead of out with a man, her sons wouldn't have died. Never mind that Callan had a history of using substandard wiring that had resulted in more than one fire, even if it hadn't caused any deaths before that. I sat there and watched the jury return a not-guilty verdict while this poor woman fell apart. It made me sick and sad and totally disgusted."

Daniel knew that feeling well during the few times when he hadn't received a conviction. "And you'd had enough."

"There's actually more," she said. "As it turned out, Troy went to the senior partner and told him about my protests, that I wasn't a *team player.* He received the associate position we were both vying for, and I got the shaft."

The sorry bastard. "They fired you?"

"No. I quit. Now here I am, trying to right my wrongs by representing the common folk, and I end up with the Massey case. Isn't that grand?"

Daniel glanced at her and caught her smile. "No offense, but by taking on criminal defense, you're still representing less-than-respectable people the majority of the time."

"No offense taken, and that's true. But that's also only temporary. I don't plan to spend the rest of my career as a public defender. Crime, even petty crime, isn't exactly my cup of tea. But it pays the bills for the time being."

"You're going to try your hand at being a plaintiff's attorney?"

"Some of the time, yes."

"Not like Billy Wade, I hope."

She laughed. "Definitely not. No slick TV ads or eight-hundred numbers. I'm very selective about what I choose to handle. I have to make sure that my clients have been wronged and that the lawsuits aren't frivolous."

"You're going to take on the evil corporate giants, one client at a time."

"Something like that. At least I can try."

Daniel admired her fervor. Hell, he admired her more every time he came in contact with her. Admired her brain as much as he admired her body. She was one of a kind. One in a million. One woman he found damn hard to ignore. "You know, even when the system fails, it's still a good system for the most part. But we all know it's flawed. My failures drive me to work harder."

She sent him a questioning look. "I didn't think you'd ever failed, Counselor."

He was failing to put her out of his mind. Failing to forget that he wanted to be with her more than he'd wanted anything in a long time. "I don't always win," he said.

"But you do most of the time."

"Yeah." But winning the Massey case didn't seem as important as winning more time with her. That mind-set created a huge hazard in terms of his goals, especially if he lost the trial due to lack of concentration. He needed to stay grounded. He needed to quit wanting her, and that was highly unlikely.

"Right here," Alisha said, pointing to the exit.

The conversation turned to navigating the streets leading to her apartment—a typical three-story, sprawling complex that Daniel guessed would fall into the midrange rent category. At least the neighborhood looked relatively safe, he decided as he pulled into the space Alisha indicated.

He stopped and turned off the car, earning him a questioning look from Alisha. "Thanks for the ride," she said. "I'll see you in court tomorrow morning."

"Tomorrow morning?"

"The Massey hearing. Motions, that sort of thing."

Damn. He was worse off than he'd thought. "Oh, yeah. Guess I need to check my schedule more often."

She unsnapped her seat belt and sent him a smile. "You know, if you're not quite ready, we could postpone it."

"I'll be ready." He was ready right now—to kiss that sassy look off her face.

"I hope you sleep well tonight."

"I would if you were with me." He shouldn't have said it, but he couldn't seem to stop his mouth from spewing what was foremost on his mind.

"We're not heading down that road tonight, Counselor."

She was trying to depersonalize the relationship by going

back to the "Counselor" thing. "I'm only being honest, *Alisha*."

"And I'm going in now."

He unsnapped his seat belt. "I'll walk you to the door."

She pointed straight ahead. "My door is right there. You can watch me to make sure I get inside safely, if that's your concern."

"I'll be sure to do that." He'd watch every little move she made, all the while wishing he could go through that door with her.

"Good night, Daniel."

She had one leg out of the car when he noticed what she was leaving behind. "Aren't you forgetting something?"

She frowned. "If you're going to say a good-night kiss, forget it."

"I wasn't, but that's not a bad idea."

"Yes it is."

He gestured toward the floor of the car. "Your purse."

"Oh."

She scooted back inside and they both reached for the bag simultaneously. In the process, they practically bumped noses, and Daniel inadvertently touched her leg covered in a sheer stocking. He couldn't stop his hand from sliding up her calf, couldn't stop his face from turning to hers. Couldn't prevent his mouth from finding her mouth for the bad-idea kiss that wasn't supposed to happen.

But it did happen—with the force of an explosion. The purse dropped back onto the floor, their arms came around each other and the fight to prevent this very thing was completely lost.

Daniel didn't give a damn. He only cared about how she responded to the kiss—with a challenging play of her tongue against his that left no doubt in his mind she needed the contact as much as he did.

He pulled away and pushed her hair back to kiss the spot

behind her ear, then her throat, before lowering the sleeve of the clinging black dress to kiss her bare shoulder. He slid his tongue along the rise of her breasts, then worked his way back up to nibble on her neck, then back down, taking the material lower and lower with one hand while he slid his other up her thigh, higher and higher.

Before things went any further, he brought his mouth to her ear and whispered, "Let's take this inside."

"We can't, Daniel."

"You want it as badly as I do." He confirmed that when he found the juncture of her thighs with his palm and discovered dampness and heat radiating through sheer silk. "You want me to come inside."

Her breath caught and then released slowly. "Yes, I want it." She tugged his hand from beneath her dress. "Which is why I'm not going to let you in."

Daniel collapsed against the seat and rubbed a hand over his jaw. "No one's going to know, unless the misconduct police are lurking behind the hedge."

"You're probably right. No one would know, but I'd know. And let's face it, if you come into my apartment, you know what will happen. We'll be up all night and we have to be in court early tomorrow."

Daniel would be up all night in every sense of the word. "Okay, I hear you. But I don't like it."

"You don't have to like it. You just have to accept it." This time she picked up the purse on her own and opened the door. "I'll see you in the morning."

Unfortunately he'd see her in a courtroom, not in a bedroom. "Yeah. In the morning."

At least she left him with a smile when she said, "Hope you get some rest."

Sure. That seemed about as impossible as not giving her another thought.

Alisha strode to the apartment without looking back, and

Daniel couldn't help but laugh when she dropped her keys twice before finally unlocking the door. She might pretend she could turn off their attraction, but he knew better. She wanted him as much as he wanted her. And someday soon he'd have her again.

Alisha wanted to scream, loudly, when she had to rush out of the shower to catch the ringing phone. After tucking one towel around her dripping body and wrapping one around her wet hair, she clasped the receiver and delivered an irritable, "Alisha Hart."

"Did you get home okay?"

She'd hoped the caller would be Daniel, pleading his case again. How stupid was that? "Yes, Joe, obviously I'm home. I realize Julie wasn't feeling well, but it might have been nice if you'd told me you were leaving. I would have gone with you."

"I figured Daniel Fortune would take care of you. Did he?"

"I don't have to answer that."

"He took her home," Joe said, obviously relaying the information to his wife.

"Nothing happened, Joe." Unfortunately. "He brought me here and left immediately. I'd appreciate it if you'd keep that to yourself."

"Not a problem. But it's too bad you didn't get to do him before he took on the case."

Oh, but she had. Not that she'd admit that to anyone. "By the way, how is Julie feeling?"

His chuckle sounded a lot like a growl. "Oh, she's feeling real good right now. She made a quick recovery as soon as we got into bed."

Wonderful. That's all she needed to hear—Joe and Julie getting it on between the sheets when her sex life was nil. Of course, that could change with one phone call to Daniel Fortune, if she gave in to the little voice that kept telling her to go for it. "Remember, we've got the Massey hearing in the morning. I need to make sure everything's in order."

"You've done everything you can, Alisha. The rest is up to Judge Slaphappy."

"Slaphappy?"

"That's what they call him at the courthouse. He's got that whole Texas vernacular down even though he grew up in Jersey. He's kind of weird."

"Just as long as he's fair, I can live with weird." Maybe Judge Slagle would be able to relate to the somewhat bizarre Les Massey. "Good night, Joe. Give Julie my best."

Not five seconds after she hung up the phone rang again. "Alisha Hart," she answered, followed by a sigh.

"I forgot something."

She was about to forget her manners. "Make it quick, Joe. I still have some work to do before I go to bed."

"Julie has her first doctor's appointment in the morning, and the hearing's scheduled at the same time. But I can—"

"Go. I can handle it without you."

"I'll be in the office first thing and we can go over the arguments then if you want to, before you and I have to leave."

"Fine."

"And think of it this way. You and the iceman can conference all by yourself afterward, maybe in his office, on the desk…"

"I'm hanging up now, Joe." And she did.

Just as Alisha was about to dress for bed, the damn phone rang again. This time she barked out, "What do you want now?"

"You know what I want."

A full-body shiver coursed through Alisha at the mere sound of Daniel's voice. "A bedtime story before you turn in, Counselor?"

His laugh was low, masculine and oh so sexy. "I'm not ready for bed yet. In fact, I'm not even home yet."

"Where are you?"

"Outside your apartment."

Needing confirmation, Alisha walked to her living room window and parted the curtains. There he was, sitting in his car in the same space he'd been occupying when she'd left him. "What are you still doing here?"

"I was just thinking about something."

"About what?" As if she didn't know. She'd been thinking the same thing, too. Thinking about it in living-color detail, as a matter of fact.

"You look cute with your hair in a towel. And I'm wondering what you have on under that robe."

She snapped the curtain closed and began to pace the room. "Wouldn't you like to know?"

"That's why I'm asking."

And he'd definitely asked for it. "Nothing."

He groaned. "Thanks a lot."

"Sorry," she said, even if she wasn't really. She was getting warmer by the minute, though.

"I need a favor from you." The way he said it, in a late-night husky voice, almost had Alisha saying, "Anything." Instead she chose to admonish him one more time. "We've already been through this, Daniel. I'm not going to let you come inside."

"I want to be inside of you. Real bad."

"Would you please can the suggestive comments?" Before she ran out to the car and tackled him like a noseguard.

"All right. But that wasn't what I was going to request anyway."

"Then what?"

"Tomorrow morning don't wear a dress. I won't be able to concentrate. In fact, make sure you're covered all the way up to that great neck of yours."

"I do believe you think that if you sweet-talk me enough, I'm going to let you into my apartment and into my pants."

"I didn't think you were wearing any."

"Go home, Daniel." *Before I let you in.*

"I will. But there's one more thing." He paused. "It's going to happen again between us, Alisha. Soon. I promise you that."

The line went dead, and Alisha's entire body, from the roots of her wet hair to the ends of her water-logged toes, came completely alive. Damn Daniel Fortune's confidence. Damn his overt sexuality. And damn herself for reacting to him so strongly.

When she heard the sound of his car pulling away, she headed for her bedroom closet and pulled out her favorite outfit. A nice beige tailored jacket, matching above-the-knee skirt and black silk shell. She intended to win this case, and if she had to use questionable tactics to achieve that goal, then so be it. Distracting Daniel Fortune certainly couldn't hurt, because no doubt tomorrow morning he would do the same thing to her.

## Six

Damn if she didn't wear a dress. Not exactly a dress but a skirt that to most would be considered professional. But to Daniel it was distracting because it revealed a good deal of her legs. Everything about her this morning was distracting—from her hair bound by a low ponytail that spiraled down her back to that pair of three-inch spiked black high heels.

She definitely stood out in the courtroom among the matronly court reporter with teased silver hair and Les Massey who'd cut his hair and actually looked somewhat respectable dressed in a cheap black suit. Daniel turned his attention back to Alisha. More accurately Alisha's mouth. She had great lips, and he knew that intimately. All night long he'd been thinking about that mouth. Hell, he'd been thinking about all of her. If he'd gotten more than four hours' sleep, he'd be surprised. And he didn't expect to get much sleep in the near future if he had to face her with any frequency.

They stood as the honorable Judge Grady Slagle entered

the courtroom. Tall and rail-thin was an understatement when it came to the man's frame. His hair had crawled off the top of his head and traveled to his upper lip in the form of a bushy mustache, and his thick, horn-rim glasses made his eyes look comical.

"Y'all be seated, folks," he said as he sat on his judicial throne. After they were all settled in, he turned his attention to Alisha first. "Now if counsel would be kind enough to state their appearances for the record, we can get this over and done with real quick."

"Good morning, Your Honor. Alisha Hart for Mr. Lester Massey."

"All righty then." Slagle leveled his bug eyes on Daniel.

"Daniel Fortune for the people, Your Honor."

Slagle grinned, revealing a yellowed set of crooked teeth. "Well, boy howdy, Mr. Fortune. They've sent in the big dawg. How'd you get saddled with this one?"

"Just answering the request of my superiors," Daniel said, shuffling the papers set out on the table before him.

"Okeydoke, let's dispense with some of this business. First of all, Ms. Hart, I respect you giving it a good shot, but your motion to dismiss all charges is denied. Now let's start with your motion to repress the statement from the witness who talks about a weapon. Wanna comment on that, Mr. Fortune, since I'm not seeing a formal charge yet?"

Daniel expected that, and he also expected the probability he'd get shot down on it. "The witness claims he saw Mr. Massey throw something into the river that appeared to be a gun."

Alisha gripped the arms of her chair. "Your Honor, as far as I'm aware, no gun has been recovered."

"That true, Mr. Fortune?"

Krauss had really screwed up this one, and Daniel was going to take the brunt of it. "Yes, sir, that's true."

"Then if we ain't got a gun, that pretty much voids your

witness's statement and I'm going to grant Ms. Hart's motion to suppress. And since you no longer have a witness's statement, I'm thinking that means you won't be bringing that charge. Unless you expect the investigation to turn up a weapon in the near future." He stared at Daniel expectantly, awaiting an answer.

"As far as I know, the search has been suspended for the time being."

"Because no weapon exists," Alisha interjected. "The only thing my client had on his person was a set of maracas."

"Maracas." Slagle grinned, then cleared his throat exaggeratedly. "Well, as far as I'm concerned, due to lack of evidence, I'm going to assume the prosecution isn't going to try to introduce this again."

Daniel tugged at his tie. "No, sir."

Slagle picked up another document. "Okay, I'll hear arguments on the motion to dismiss the indecent-exposure charge."

"Mr. Massey's genitals were not exposed," Alisha said. "He—"

"Your Honor," Daniel interrupted. "We have a witness who claims she did, in fact, see Mr. Massey's genitals."

"Where is she, Mr. Fortune?" Slagle asked.

"Unfortunately unavailable today. But she will be here during the trial."

Alisha turned her glare on him. "According to the penal code, even if Mr. Massey's penis was inadvertently exposed…" That's when the court reporter's shoulders began to shake and a snort came out of her mouth, drawing everyone's attention and momentarily suspending Alisha's commentary. "As I was saying," she finally continued, "according to the code, a person commits an offense if he is exposed and if he has the intent to arouse."

Daniel leveled his gaze on hers. "According to the statement, Mr. Massey was aroused."

Slagle picked up another document and slid the glasses up

on the bridge of his nose with one bony finger. "That would be from a Miss Ramsey, who states here, 'I saw it when that sash blew up. Like, you couldn't miss it. I mean, like, the thing was *huge* and saluting the flag.'" He regarded Daniel again. "I'm guessing she means 'thing' as in privates?"

Daniel hated this whole thing. "If you'll read on, she does use the clinical terminology later in her statement."

At that point, Alisha leaned over to speak with Les Massey, and Daniel immediately noticed the creep putting his hand on her shoulder. The exchange looked a little too intimate. But then, seeing any guy with his hands on her made Daniel's blood pressure rise.

She straightened and addressed the judge again. "Your Honor, Mr. Massey states that even if the sash had blown up, he would not have been exposed because it was fashioned like a diaper."

Slagle didn't bother to conceal his laugh. "A diaper?"

"Yes, sir. It covered his buttocks and his genitals before being secured at his waist in a bow."

"Was he wearing a diaper at the Alamo?"

"No, sir. He wore a full-length open duster and a pouch."

"A coonskin tail, sir," Massey said, looking very pleased with himself.

"What about at the zoo?" Slagle asked.

"A loincloth," Alisha answered, her gaze drifting to her hands folded before her, the first sign of her discomfort. "And I find it unusual that out of hundreds of witnesses, this Miss Ramsey is the only one who's come forward with the exposure accusation."

Daniel saw his chance to step in and took it. "Regardless, she stands by her assertions."

Alisha finally looked at him. "Considering the incident took place at night, the light was limited, so I don't see how she can be so certain she saw anything from where she was standing on the other side of the river."

Daniel cleared his throat. "Might I remind defense counsel that it was the holiday season and the area was decorated with various lights."

"And might I remind the prosecutor that if these lights provided ample illumination, then one would assume more than one witness would have seen Mr. Massey's 'thing.'"

Good point. "Maybe she was the only one looking."

Alisha released a sarcastic laugh. "Yeah, right. It's bad enough we're wasting time and money trying this case that the state is determined to make my client into a hardened criminal." Her gaze zipped from Daniel to the judge, who appeared to be greatly enjoying the exchange. "No pun intended."

Slagle tented his clasped hands beneath his pointy chin. "I'm inclined to agree that this is a stretch."

Daniel was already getting whipped and the official trial hadn't even begun. "But—"

"Now, Mr. Fortune, you gotta let me finish. I'm going to let the jury decide on Mr. Massey's intent and whether he let the bull out of the barn ready to breed, so the motion to suppress Miss Ramsey's statement is also denied."

Somewhat of a victory for Daniel, but the victory was short-lived when Slagle said, "Ms. Hart, I am going to allow the subpoena of Mrs. O'Reilly's medical records."

He knew exactly where Alisha was going with that one—attack the assault victim's credibility. "I'm inclined to question the necessity of that, Your Honor."

"Save it, Counselor," Slagle said. "You'll both have your day in court because Mr. Massey will be bound over for trial. On that note, this is your lucky day, Mr. Massey. I'm going to make this a real speedy process. I've cleared my docket for a week from next Monday to start the show. Any problem for either of you counselors?"

Daniel did a mental countdown. That gave him all of ten days to get up to speed on the particulars, when he wasn't juggling his normal caseload. "No problem," he said anyway.

"That sounds fine," Alisha added. "But I would respectfully ask the court to consider letting Mr. Massey be released on his own recognizance until the trial since he can't afford any bail."

Now that would thrill Vera, Daniel decided. "Your Honor, we went through this during the arraignment. Mr. Massey has no real job, lives with so-called friends and has no real ties to this community. I don't believe—"

"Neither do I, Mr. Fortune. Mr. Massey will just have to be a guest of the state until he appears in court." Slagle turned his attention to Massey. "And in the meantime, young man, I'm warning you to keep the garden hose in the shed. Is that clear?"

Les tugged at his tie. "Yes, sir. I sure will, sir."

"Good." Slagle regarded Daniel and Alisha. "Anything else you two would like to say?"

Daniel and Alisha muttered "No" simultaneously.

Slagle banged his gavel—a little harder than necessary, in Daniel's opinion. "Then this hearing's officially adjourned. But I have a couple more things to talk about, off the record."

Just when Daniel thought he might actually make a quick escape, he was about to endure a lecture. For a brief moment he worried that somehow Slagle had become privy to the private dealings between opposing counsel. Pure and simple paranoia. No way Slagle could know.

"I'm sure that you, Mr. Fortune, and you, Ms. Hart, saw the coverage on one of those national news shows this morning?" the judge asked.

Daniel exchanged a glance with Alisha and realized she was also in the dark. "I'm afraid I missed that," he said.

"I did, too," Alisha added.

Slagle stroked his mustache like a pet. "Well, it was mighty interesting. And now that this case has gained national attention, we're going to have one hot media fiasco on our hands. I don't think I have to tell you two what that means and I also don't want to see either of you grandstanding for the cameras and trying this case in the press. Is that understood?"

"Yes, Your Honor," Alisha said.

"I understand completely." And Daniel did because he'd been through this situation on more than one occasion. He suspected Alisha had not.

Slagle stood. "See y'all in court."

Daniel collected his notes and shoved them into his briefcase while Alisha spoke with her client before they carted him off. He hated more and more that this case continued to stand in his way of pursuing her. Not that he hadn't done his share of pursuing last night.

He could use a crash course in resistance, he decided as from the corner of his eye he watched her gather her things. He watched every little move she made up until the time she left the courtroom without giving him a second glance.

He needed to ignore her, forget her for the time being, an exercise in futility. Truth was, he didn't want to ignore her. He just plain wanted her.

The minute Alisha left the courtroom, the crush was on. Several reporters stood at the end of the corridor, held back by a line of stoic security guards. The only way out meant walking right through the cameras and chaos.

"Hope you're ready for the first circus act, Ms. Hart."

Alisha caught a whiff of his cologne first before she turned to find Daniel standing behind her, one hand hidden away in his pocket, the other clutching a briefcase. "Appears to be that way," she said with a fast glance at said circus. "Are you going to go first, or should I?"

He nodded to his left. "I'm going to my offices via the staff elevator."

How heroic. "You mean you're going to just throw me to the wolves all by my lonesome?" she asked.

"It's all a part of the game. Might as well get used to it now."

"And you're not going to say anything?"

"You heard Slagle. We don't need to try this in the press. 'No comment' is always your best recourse in this situation."

Like she didn't know that. "Exactly what I intend to say. It's not going to make the hassle any easier, though, because they're not going to give up."

"True, so you're welcome to hang out in my office until they go away."

Seductive images came to her with clarity. Images of clearing Daniel's desk and having a fine time behind closed doors. "Oh, now that's a good way to raise more than a few eyebrows."

"As far as anyone knows, we could be discussing the particulars of the case. Unless you're worried we might give something away."

"Such as?"

"I don't think I have to verbalize that, do I?"

No, he didn't, although she remembered quite clearly his verbal skills on New Year's Eve, among all of his other skills. "I'll just take my chances with the reporters." That seemed much safer than taking a chance by being alone with him. She knew all too well where that might lead. And she might be tempted to be the leader.

"Good luck." He withdrew his hand from his pocket and held it out to her.

A simple handshake, outlining the boundaries, and that should have relieved Alisha. But in reality it disappointed her. However, this was business, and business came before pleasure, particularly in this instance. As a goodwill gesture between opposing parties to satisfy the press, she took his hand into hers. Before he let her go and walked away, he ran his thumb over her palm, sending a sensual message that nearly short-circuited Alisha's faltering composure.

She didn't have time to be excited over Daniel Fortune, even if she was. She didn't have time to play this game, even though she really wanted to play. Right now she had to face the folly.

With head held high Alisha put on her professional face and

walked the corridor, prepared to enter the bowels of publicity hell. She was met with a chorus of "Ms. Harts" while she elbowed her way through the gathering, several microphones barely missing her mouth.

The crowd closed in on her, impeding her forward progress. "Do you believe that Mr. Massey's recent displays are the antics of a pervert or freedom of expression?" said one slick reporter who looked like a TV telemarketer.

"No comment."

"Do you think his causes are worthy?"

"No comment."

She managed to make it through the double doors, but the questions still came on the courthouse steps. "How do you feel about Mr. Massey's overwhelming support from a large part of the female population in San Antonio?"

A large part of that female population had taken up residence on the sidewalk, some holding signs that read, Masses for Massey, while others chanted, "Free Les!" Mass foolishness at its finest, as far as Alisha was concerned. Just two more steps and she could make a dash across the street to her car. Then she would be home free, for now.

But that wasn't to be when a woman with golden-blond hair and a perfectly made-up face blocked her path. "Ms. Hart, as a rank novice public defender, aren't you concerned that you're outmatched now that A.D.A. Fortune has taken over this case?"

Be it stupid pride or simple stupidity, Alisha said, "I'm not a *rank* novice, otherwise I would not have been assigned this case. I will represent Mr. Massey to the best of my ability and he will receive a better than adequate defense, regardless of who the district attorney has chosen to handle it. As far as I'm concerned, Mr. Fortune is just another prosecutor."

As if Alisha needed a reminder, the woman said, "The best prosecutor in the city. Perhaps even the state."

"And I assure you Ms. Hart will handle her duties well."

Alisha glanced back as the crowd turned toward the sound of the deep, authoritative voice. And there he stood, the iceman himself, immaculately dressed in business-blue, his brown hair combed neatly into place, his self-assured stance presenting the portrait of the state's official deity.

It appeared that he'd decided to play the white-knight role, and although she didn't really see the need, Alisha had to admit she was grateful. Now she could make a speedy escape. When the cameras focused on Daniel, she was approached by a security guard. "I'll see you to your car, Ms. Hart."

She gave him a blank look. "It's right across the street. I'll be fine."

"Mr. Fortune insists. He wants to make sure you're safe."

Okay, so maybe he was a little more of a hero than she'd realized. Of course he was. The man shouted integrity. And overt sensuality.

After they made it to the car, the guard offered Alisha a sealed envelope. "Mr. Fortune asked me to give this to you. He said you left it in the courtroom."

Alisha didn't recognize it at all and believed it must be a mistake, until she turned it over and read "For Alisha Hart— Personal and Confidential" printed in the corner. More than curious over its content, she almost opened it right there, then opted to wait until she returned to the office.

She thanked the guard and headed out of the parking lot, but before turning onto the street she glanced Daniel's way again and their gazes met. He subtly lifted his hand and sent her a smile, seemingly without missing a beat with the press inquest. Although the weather was cool, she felt the need to turn on the AC in order to alleviate some serious heat.

On the drive to the office Alisha chastised herself for repeatedly falling under Mr. Fortune's spell. She continued that mental bashing all the way into the office entry.

"Did it go that badly?" Joe asked when Alisha leaned against the door as if she needed it to stay vertical.

"Actually, no. There won't be any weapons charge and we can subpoena the elderly woman's medical records."

"Then why are you the color of hospital bedsheets?"

Alisha pushed away from the door and started to drop her briefcase onto the chair before remembering it contained the mysterious envelope. "I always look pale, Joe. I am pale."

He shook his head. "Not that pale."

"It's stress," she said as she walked into her office. Once there, she set the case on her desk and removed her jacket, leaving her wearing only the sleeveless black shell. At least she wasn't quite as warm as she'd been in the car—or in Daniel's company. "Did you talk to the temp agency?" she called to Joe.

"Yeah. They're screening applicants now. Aren't you even going to ask me how it went at the doctor this morning?"

How inconsiderate of her not to remember. She went back out to the reception area. "I'm sorry. How did it go?"

He grinned. "Great. It's a boy."

"I didn't realize Julie was far enough along to tell."

"She's not. I'm just sure it's a boy."

"I hope it's a girl. You deserve that."

Joe studied her for a long moment and frowned. "You have a hickey, Hart."

Alisha's eyes went wide. "I do not!"

He pointed. "Yeah, you do. Right there at the bend of your neck."

Pivoting around like a demented top, Alisha went back into the office and grabbed a mirror from her drawer. When the reddish spot came into view, she stifled a gasp. Daniel Fortune had left his imprint on her person like an oversexed teenage jock, and she'd let him. And how could she have not seen it until now? Easy. She'd gone to bed in a rush last night and dressed in a rush that morning. The jacket had thankfully concealed it. She hadn't had time to do a hickey search, not that she'd ever dreamed she'd have one. In fact, this was her first hickey. At age thirty-two, how miserable was that?

She mentally rummaged around the treasure trove of excuses she'd heard in her formative years coming from the girls who got all the hickeys in high school, as well as all the guys. "I must've burned myself with the curling iron," she called out.

"You're hair's straight today," Joe called back.

"Oh, I meant the flatiron."

Joe's chuckle had a fingernail-across-the-chalkboard effect on her nerves. "I'm betting that's a big ol' lip-smacking hickey you got from the iceman."

"Shut up, Joe," Alisha said before slamming the door.

Just when she was seated with the case in her lap, ready to reveal the contents of the mysterious envelope, the intercom buzzed. "Drop it, Joe."

"This is business. Mrs. White called and asked if you've reached your decision about taking her case."

Because of her preoccupation with the A.D.A., Alisha had almost forgotten. "Yes, I have. I'm going to represent her. Call her and set up an appointment. We're on the docket for a week from Monday with the Massey trial, so I should be able to work her in the following week."

"Not a problem, considering your schedule is kind of light."

That light schedule made Alisha all the more determined to do well on the Massey case. As much as she hated the process of gaining notoriety, she recognized that the publicity could earn her more clients—and hopefully those who preferred to keep their clothes on.

At the moment her concern centered on the piece of paper she withdrew from the envelope. Slowly she unfolded it and read the message penned in surprisingly meticulous handwriting.

*Meet me next Tuesday night at P.C.'s Bar at 8 p.m. I've enclosed a map. We need to talk.*

Alisha had no clue as to the exact location of said bar or exactly what Daniel needed to discuss. And why on a Tuesday? His request brought about more questions, and the answers would come only if she joined him. But did she really dare to show up?

## Seven

Sequestered in a corner booth at half past eight, Daniel started to believe Alisha wouldn't bother to show up. He hadn't seen her since the hearing the previous Friday, hadn't spoken to her by phone and he couldn't deny he missed talking to her.

None of this made much sense. Not his need to see her. Not his inability to escape thinking about her for more than an hour at a time, if that. Nor did inviting her to meet him with the possibility of getting caught hanging over their heads. But the rural, out-of-the way lounge generally attracted blue-collar locals and retirees, the reason why he'd chosen this setting. Tonight only three men sat at the bar around the corner, watching some sitcom, paying him little mind. The chance they would be seen together was minimal, and it looked as if the chance Alisha might make an appearance was probably slim to none.

Just when Daniel had decided she wasn't coming, he spotted her crossing the smoky room past the pool tables. She wore low-riding jeans and a black turtleneck sweater instead of her standard suits. Basically every inch of her skin was covered, yet Daniel reacted as strongly as if she'd strolled in wearing nothing at all.

He stood beside the booth and signaled her over when she caught his glance. As usual, she looked composed, at least superficially. But when she made it to the table he noticed the wariness in her eyes.

"Have a seat," he told her, indicating the booth. When she complied, instead of sitting across from her, Daniel slid in beside her.

She presented a pretty serious scowl. "Don't you think it might be best if you moved to the other side of the table?"

"No. If you're worried someone's going to see us, then look around. This isn't the kind of place that draws our usual crowd. And this way we have our backs to everyone in here."

She leaned around him and surveyed the area. "I can't argue that. Do you come here often?"

"Once in a while, when I want to hide out." Like tonight.

After setting her purse aside on the table, Alisha turned and leaned her back against the paneled wall. "Okay, I'm here. Now tell me *why* I'm here."

"Because I wanted to see if you're doing okay."

"That's it?"

He shifted toward her and draped an arm over the back of the booth. "Yeah. I've been concerned about all the attention this case is getting. Especially after that fiasco on the courthouse steps."

"I'm fine. Really."

Daniel braced for some serious business. "Alisha, there are a lot of crazies out there. If you start getting any kind of threats, let the police know. Or better still, call me and I'll handle it."

"Threats?"

"Letters. Phone calls. That kind of thing."

"The only phone calls I've been getting are from nosy reporters requesting interviews. I have Joe fielding those. And as far as letters are concerned, I've received a few, but mostly letters supporting Mr. Massey. I haven't received any threats at all."

"Good, but be prepared. More than likely you'll get a few."

She looked altogether skeptical. "I appreciate your concern, but you could've told me this over the phone."

"True, but I have an idea that I want you to consider."

Suspicion crossed her face. "What would that be?"

"I have a small two-bedroom cabin out on Lake Mondo. You're welcome to use it this weekend to get away from all the bedlam."

"That's very nice of you, but I don't think that's necessary."

"You might change your mind the closer it gets to the weekend." And he planned to help her change it.

"Then you're saying that if I want to escape, I can run out to your cabin and be alone?"

"Not alone. I plan to be there. We can leave on Saturday and return on Sunday."

"I should have known there was more to this than a friendly offer."

"That's exactly what it is, a friendly offer. You can stay in the spare bedroom, if that's what you want." He didn't want that at all, but if that's how he got her there, he'd leave the option open.

"And that's two days I could use to get ready for the trial on Monday."

He expected all the arguments and he planned to shoot them down one by one with whatever means necessary. "You can bring your work with you."

"And give you the opportunity to peruse my defense? No way."

"I don't have any plans to peruse your defense." He had other things he'd rather peruse. "Besides, it's an open-and-shut case, Alisha. If you're not prepared by Friday, then you should've asked for a continuance."

That brought about some serious fire in her eyes. "I am ready. In fact, I could take you on tomorrow if I had to."

He really wanted her to take him on tonight. "Great. That means you can go this weekend."

"Daniel, that's insane. I don't know what you expect to accomplish by doing this."

"I want to be able to keep an eye on you."

Her smile came into play. "Is that all you want to keep on me?"

Time to lay it out in the open. "All right. My reasons are twofold. I would feel better knowing you're safe. And I admit it, I wouldn't mind spending some time with you alone. Might help us concentrate better on the trial."

"Oh, I get it. Screw like bunnies until we don't want to screw anymore?"

She still didn't get it, but then neither did he. Not really. "Alisha, when we were together on New Year's Eve, it was hot but it was rushed. I'm not complaining, mind you, but there's something to be said about taking things slowly. And the fact is, this isn't just about lust. I like being with you."

She drummed her fingers on the table. "I'm sure you can pull out your little black book and call some woman to serve as your weekend girl."

"I don't want another woman. I want to be with you. Only you."

"I'm just not sure if we should even consider this."

At least she sounded as if she was considering it. "It's only two days," he said. "Actually a day and a half."

"You know, we keep going over the same territory. Ethically speaking, it's not a good idea. I have much more to lose than you because I have to maintain strict client confidentiality."

He replied, "And I have no intention of holding you down

and torturing you to get you to talk about Massey." Holding her, yes, torturing her, no.

She just sat there, seemingly digesting his words. "I still don't think we can afford to see each other socially right now."

"And I can't not see you socially."

She rolled her eyes to the pitted ceiling tiles. "Come on, Daniel. It's not that difficult."

"Maybe not for you, but it is for me." He moved a little closer and lowered his voice. "When you walked into Slagle's court last Friday, I had one hell of a time concentrating on my business. Didn't help that you had on that damn skirt."

"It was decent enough."

"It nearly killed me, and I figured that's why you wore it, even when I asked you not to. You were using it as a weapon and, lady, it worked. I had trouble forming a coherent sentence."

She lifted her chin a notch. "I don't care for anyone telling me what I can or can't wear."

"You wanted to distract me and you did. But that's okay. It's one of the things I admire about you. You're your own woman. And it doesn't matter what you're wearing, you still do things to me. So if you think that turtleneck's going to discourage me, you're dead wrong."

She rimmed her finger around the tight collar. "I'm wearing this turtleneck because of you, and it has nothing to do with discouraging you."

He frowned. "Care to explain that?"

"It seems, Counselor, you left a calling card the other night. It's just now beginning to fade."

"You mean—"

"A hickey. Isn't that special?"

Daniel couldn't stop his laugh. "I'll be damned."

"I happen to bruise easily."

"You must, because I didn't mean to do it."

"Well, you did. And worse, Joe saw it first."

Oh, hell. "You didn't tell him it was me, did you?"

"No, but he was making some assumptions because you took me home after the reception. I denied everything but I frankly doubt he bought it. I'm sure I looked guilty."

He laid his palm on her knee. "Are you going to deny that you haven't thought about us together even once since that night?"

She picked up a squat fake-crystal saltshaker from the table and studied it. "Maybe once or twice."

He rimmed her knee with a fingertip. "You weren't even the least bit preoccupied when we were in court together?"

She set the shaker down and turned her blue eyes on him. "Okay, maybe a little, but I handled it okay. So did you."

"Not that well. And that's going to continue to be a problem all throughout the trial, unless we find some way to put a stop to it."

"That's easy. We just make a conscious effort not to think about each other."

He opened his palm and laid it on her thigh. "Do you really believe you can do that?"

"Sure." She didn't sound at all confident.

Daniel wasn't at all confident. Turning everything off wasn't realistic. "I don't think I can do it. In fact, I know I can't. But it might help if we spend some time together beforehand."

Regardless of their surroundings and without any hesitation, Daniel braced his palm on her waist, leaned over and brushed his lips across hers.

Her eyes went wide. "What was that for?"

"Just trying to convince you that my plan's a good one."

"You're going to have to do better than that."

She didn't have to tell him twice. This time he kissed her thoroughly. Kissed her until he realized that in a matter of moments he was going to make an offer she would probably refuse, and one he shouldn't make.

She pulled away and smiled. "I have to say that was a good attempt."

"We could go back to my place and I could work on you some more."

"We could, but we should put that on hold until this weekend."

Mission accomplished. "Then you're going to go?"

"I'm warming up to the idea."

He shot her a grin. "You'll go. In fact, I'm willing to bet my car on it."

"Your ego has reached enormous proportions, Mr. Fortune."

"It's not that complicated, Alisha. All you have to do is say yes, and we'll leave all this Massey stuff behind. I won't ask anything of you that you're not willing to give. You'll run the whole show."

"Does this mean you'll cook?"

"Yeah. You won't have to touch a pan."

"Do you leave the seat up?"

"When I'm alone, but I'll try to remember to take care of that."

She narrowed her eyes. "You'll avoid touching or kissing my neck?"

That was a promise he wasn't sure he could keep. "I'll try to refrain from leaving any love bites." At least, obvious ones.

"And you'll promise you won't touch me at all unless I ask you to?"

That one was really tough, he thought, but he said, "I promise."

"We won't talk about the case?"

"Not one word."

She hesitated for a few moments before finally saying, "I'll think about it."

Daniel let out the breath he didn't know he'd been holding. "Good. You can give me your answer tomorrow."

"Fine. I'll let you know."

He pointed at the plastic menu propped up behind the silver napkin holder. "Do you want something to eat?"

"I've already had dinner, but you go ahead."

"I grabbed something before I got here. How about a glass of wine?"

"No thanks. I need to get home."

Daniel didn't want her to leave, unless they were leaving together. But he'd already pushed his luck by proposing the weekend getaway. "I'll walk you to your car."

"I'm parked right outside. I'll manage."

He slid from the booth and held out his hand. "I insist."

She seized her bag, came to her feet and stood before him. "I insist you let me go by myself. Otherwise we both know what could happen."

He grinned. "That's true. All the more reason for me to walk you to your car."

She smoothed his collar, then patted his butt. "You could use a few lessons in patience." Then she walked away, tossing a smile over her shoulder, indicating she knew full well she had him exactly where she wanted him—ready to explode.

He continued to stand there until she disappeared out the door, leaving him behind to analyze where this situation was heading. He didn't care. He cared about her, more than he wanted to acknowledge. And for Daniel Fortune, that was as rare as losing.

"Are you busy?"

Alisha looked up from the stack of mail to find Julie Alvarado standing in her doorway. She pulled off her reading glasses and waved her in. "Please rescue me from these riveting reads."

Julie moved into the room with enviable grace and took the chair across from Alisha's desk. "Just thought we could visit while I'm waiting for Joe to get back from the university. We're going to have lunch together, if that's okay."

"Of course it's okay. He's been working so hard lately, he could use a break."

"I thought I wasn't going to get past all the media vultures hanging around outside."

"I was hoping they would have given up by now."

"Believe me, they haven't." Julie studied the mountainous piles of letters divided into two stacks. "What is all that?"

Alisha pointed to the pile on her left. "Fan mail." At Julie's puzzled look, she explained, "Mostly from women and a few from men who support Mr. Massey's cause."

Julie wrinkled her nose. "The guy is a mental case."

"Unfortunately not mental enough to try an insanity defense by definition of the law. He's a bit of a megalomaniac and extreme in his tactics, but by all rights he's entitled to express himself."

Julie pointed to the smaller stack of letters. "And what are those? Bills?"

"Actually you could call them un-fan mail." She took the one from the top of the stack and began to read. "'Dear Ms. Hart. You harlot! Have you no shame? Leave that Massey man behind and repent!' I didn't even know people used the term 'harlot' anymore."

"Obviously this woman does."

Alisha turned the page around, slid it toward Julie and pointed to the signature. "Unless some cruel parents named their daughter Horace, this came from a man. But this is mild compared to some of the others."

Julie looked considerably concerned. "How bad are they?"

"Nothing too terrible. Just more verbal bashing. Oh, but there is an interesting one, although it's a fan letter. Some inmate in Wisconsin saw me on TV the other day and he wanted me to know that he *accidentally* robbed that bank and would I consider representing him on his appeal. And if I can't, he'd like to date me."

They both laughed until Julie's expression turned serious once more. "These really aren't that funny, Alisha. They could mean a threat to your safety."

"I'm not too worried about it. The police have been kind enough to patrol the area in case the press or any protestors get out of hand." More than likely at the request of the prosecutor.

"But that's only while you're here at the office. You should let someone know about these letters. In fact, you should tell Daniel Fortune."

Alisha grabbed a paper clip and began to unfold it. "Actually I mentioned them last night." But only the nice letters, otherwise he might've camped out at her office door.

"You saw him last night?" Julie sat back and smiled. "Then there is something going on between the two of you. I thought Joe was just imagining things."

Alisha glanced up to find Julie looking at her expectantly, awaiting confirmation or denial. Denial would be best. But then, she didn't have any gal pals with whom to discuss the particulars of the relationship with Daniel, and right now she could use some sound advice. Julie also dealt in confidentiality. She could trust her. "Yes, something has been going on, as stupid as that seems."

"For how long?"

"Try New Year's Eve."

Julie scooted up in the chair, her eyes flashing excitement. "Really? You two got together then?"

"You could say that. I went to his place."

"And?"

How should she put this? We did a little slow dance on the sofa. We got up close and personal on the couch. "We did it."

"Oh, wow. That's great!" Julie's grin faded into a frown. "It was, wasn't it?"

"You could say that." And more.

"Then why do you look so disappointed?" Julie laid a hand over her mouth. "Oh, no. Last night he told you he didn't want to see you anymore, didn't he?"

"Actually, no. He still wants to see me." The paper clip was now one long, unraveled wire.

"Then what's wrong?"

Alisha wrapped the wire around her ring finger. "It's all wrong, Julie. We're opposing each other on a high-profile case."

"I don't know why anyone has to know what's going on with you two behind closed doors, as long as you're careful," Julie said. "People do it all the time. And if you're worried about your behavior with him on New Year's Eve, the same thing happened to me and Joe. We were out on a blind date and I ended up in his bed. We've been together ever since."

Alisha only felt minimally better and all too human. "It's getting complicated. He's asked me to go away with him this weekend."

"Are you going to do it?"

"I don't know. It's risky. If anyone finds out, it could be a huge problem."

"Maybe you should withdraw from the Massey case."

"I've considered that, but it's too late. It wouldn't be fair to my client." And it could mean passing up a golden opportunity to prove she was a top-rate attorney.

"Can you be objective?" Julie said.

"Yes, I believe I can. As long as I don't look at Daniel for any length of time in the courtroom."

Julie laughed. "You have it bad for him, don't you?"

Alisha touched her fingertips to her fiery face. "It's probably just temporary lust." But that didn't ring at all true in her mind—or in her voice.

"Only one way to find out," Julie said. "Go with him this weekend. Spend some time together and see what happens. If you find you don't have anything beyond the sex, then you'll know for sure. You can walk into that courtroom knowing it was fun but it's over."

Alisha raised her gaze from the poor, misshapen clip and centered her eyes on Julie. "What if I find out it's more than just the sex? Or what if I'm so enamored of him by Monday that every time I look at him I break out into a cold sweat?"

"Then you can walk into the courtroom wearing a blindfold."

They shared another laugh that was interrupted at the sound of an opening door and Joe calling, "Julie, are you here?"

"Yes, I'm here." She sent Alisha a knowing look. "Don't worry. I won't tell him a thing until you say it's okay."

"I appreciate that, Julie. Now go have a nice lunch with your husband."

Julie stood and grinned again. "And you have a nice weekend with your *friend*."

After Julie left out the door, Alisha pondered her suggestion. Spending the weekend with Daniel could be perilous. She might discover she actually did like him, and that was silly. She already did like him, more than she should. Liked his body, his mind, his confidence. That didn't erase the fact they were crossing lines that shouldn't be crossed, and not being able to be with him seemed totally unfair. But as they said, sometimes justice was blind. Then again, so was love.

"Mr. Fortune, Ms. Hart's on line two."

Daniel grabbed the phone like some lovesick kid awaiting an answer from a prospective prom date. "About time you called me."

"I'm still thinking about your proposition, but I need more time."

"How much more time?"

"Tomorrow. If I do decide to go, I have one condition. And it's a big one."

Daniel turned his chair around to face the shelves behind his desk in order to hide his satisfied grin from anyone who might happen to come through his door. "Okay, I'm listening."

"If what you say is true—that this is not just about sex—then you'll respect my wishes if I decide we don't sleep together."

"That decision will be all yours. Like I said, I won't touch you unless you ask me to." He might need to borrow some handcuffs to keep from doing that, but a promise was a promise.

"Where is this place exactly?"

Daniel spun around at the sound of the knock and his boss saying, "I need to speak with you ASAP."

"Hang on," he told Alisha, then put his hand over the receiver. "I've got to finish up this call, then I'll meet you in your office."

Easy as you please, Allan dropped into the chair across from Daniel's desk. "I'll wait until you're through."

He gripped the receiver and brought it back to his mouth. "I'll have that information to you by this afternoon. And if you have any more questions, feel free to call me tomorrow. I have a meeting pending at the moment."

"Daniel, is someone in your office?"

"That's correct."

"Oh, God. It's not the D.A., is it?" she asked.

"You're right on that count."

"Okay, I'll talk to you later then. I'm sorry if I bothered you."

"No bother at all. Have a good afternoon."

Daniel hung up and scooted closer to his desk. "What's on your mind, Allan?"

"Just wanted to see how it's going with the Massey case. You're going to be ready by Monday?"

"Not a problem."

"Are you sure?"

Daniel was only sure of one thing—he was pissed off over Allan's untimely interruption and his doubts in his abilities. "Have I ever not been prepared for a case?"

"No, but this is probably one of the most important cases you've ever tried."

Daniel quelled a litany of oaths threatening to tumble out of his mouth. "It's a case involving a public nuisance charged with misdemeanor offenses."

"Don't forget the assault, Daniel."

"I know that. But the victim's testimony might be shaky." *Shaky* pretty much described Mrs. O'Reilly, and Alisha knew that. Why else would she want the eighty-year-old's medical history?

Allan thankfully headed to the door. "I'm counting on you not to let me down. The party's counting on you, too."

"I won't." He hoped.

"And one more thing," Allan said, his hand poised on the doorknob. "I can't recall ever seeing Alisha Hart. Is she as good-looking as I hear she is?"

"I haven't really noticed." Definitely grounds for perjury.

"That's good. A looker in the courtroom can be an unwelcome distraction."

Daniel hadn't been able to concentrate for the past two weeks, thanks to the public defender. And if Alisha did decide to join him this weekend, maybe he could get her out of his system, at least for the time being, and get his brain back on business. Then again, she could nix the idea altogether. Maybe she could use a little more convincing.

## *Eight*

"Just stick it on the break room table and I'll be in to get it in a minute."

"That sounds like an offer I can't refuse."

Alisha's gaze snapped to her open office door when she realized the voice didn't belong to her clerk. On the contrary, it belonged to a man who'd plagued her thoughts all afternoon long.

She came to her feet but decided to stay behind her desk. "I thought you were Joe. He went to get us takeout."

Without even so much as a greeting Daniel closed the door and walked into the room, looking as groomed as if he'd just begun the day instead of ending it. How unfair was that when her hair most likely looked like a frizzy fireball because of the sudden onset of winter rain? Wet and cold, the worst kind of atmosphere for her unruly locks. But with the surprise visit from the A.D.A., *wet and hot* would best describe her current state.

"What are you doing here?" Her voice had taken on a tinny quality, reminiscent of her eighth-grade English teacher, Miss Simons, who'd always sounded as if she were being goosed.

"I'm here on business." He strolled to the desk and handed her an envelope.

Alisha turned it over. "What's this?"

"Directions to my cabin."

She gave him a supersized scowl. "I thought you said this was business."

"I wanted to make sure you were ready for the business of having a good time this weekend."

She couldn't deny she was looking forward to it, holed up for two days with Daniel in the love shack—if she decided to go. "I told you, I'm still thinking about it."

His smile came into play slowly. "Lean forward."

"Excuse me?"

"Just do it."

And she did, like some silly schoolgirl who couldn't resist the town bad boy. Daniel circled his hand around her nape and used his mouth on her like a thief wielding a high-powered weapon. By the time they parted, she was ready to hand over all her worldly goods.

She straightened and tugged her jacket down. "If that's all, I'll be going back to work now."

Instead of leaving, he rounded her desk.

"What are you doing?" she asked, as if she didn't know.

"One more for the road," he told her as he pulled her forward into his arms.

And once more she accepted his slow, deliberate kiss. Accepted that he had too much power over her when he kicked her chair away, turned her around, lifted her up on the edge of her desk and then took his place between her parted legs.

His palms came to rest on her thighs, now exposed because her skirt had shifted up to the point of indecency. She really should protest. She really should hop down and push him away. But what she should do warred with what she wanted to do. Wanted him to do.

As if he'd channeled her thoughts, Daniel slipped his hands completely beneath her hem while she tightened her hold on his shoulders. When he broke the kiss, she managed to say, "We can't do this."

"Trust me, we can with very little effort."

"I meant we *shouldn't* do this."

She gasped when he drew a line with his fingertip where the band on her panties met the crease of her thigh. "Do these say anything special today?"

"No. It's not a holiday."

"Maybe not. But I'm guessing your body's definitely saying something about now."

Loud and clear. "You promised you wouldn't touch me unless I asked."

"You're right," he said, but he didn't remove his hand. He continued to rim the elastic band with his forefinger and thumb. She saw challenge in his eyes, knew he was waiting for her to tell him to stop or to go or maybe even to beg. His movements became more deliberate, a little bolder, as he inched a little farther beneath the silk. Her pulse thrashed in her ears, throbbed in the place so close to his fingertips.

Alisha couldn't begin to understand why she continued to throw caution to the wind where he was concerned. At the moment she didn't want to question it; she only wanted him to soothe the ache, quiet the need.

"Do it," she said in a husky voice that didn't remotely resemble her own.

"Do what?"

"Touch me."

Before he could answer her demand, Alisha heard the buzzer indicating a visitor, followed by the sound of the door opening behind her.

"I'm back, Hart, and I have—"

She jerked Daniel's hand from beneath her skirt and practically jumped off the desk as if she'd been hurled out of a cannon. Daniel faced the window while she turned to the door where Joe now stood holding two white sacks and sporting an I-can't-believe-I-just-saw-that expression.

Joe backed away with a muttered "Excuse me" and closed the door.

Only then did Daniel face her. "Damn."

Alisha tightened her curly ponytail and readjusted her skirt. "Damn is right."

"Sorry." He didn't look at all contrite.

"No, you're not."

"Yeah, I am. I'm sorry we almost got caught before I could finish. But he couldn't have seen what I was doing."

"He saw enough." She moved completely away from Daniel, positioning her back to the shelves on the far side of the room. "I doubt he's at all surprised. He's been on to you since New Year's Eve."

Daniel came around the desk and leaned back against it. "Onto me?"

"After you left the table at the bar, he told me you wanted me."

"Oh, yeah?"

"Uh-huh. And he said I should go for it. Of course, I didn't have any intention of taking him up on his suggestion, even though it turns out I did."

"I didn't realize I was that obvious."

Suddenly chilled, Alisha folded her arms beneath her breasts. "It takes a guy to know how a guy thinks."

"Do you want me to talk to him?"

"No!" She hadn't meant to sound so forceful, but that's the last thing she needed—Daniel and Joe comparing notes. "I'll talk to him. I know he won't say anything to anyone. We can trust him."

"Good," he said. "Because it's fairly obvious I can't trust myself around you."

"And that's probably why we should forget about this weekend."

"No, that's exactly why we should go through with it. If I don't make love to you again soon, I'm going to be ready for involuntary commitment to the psych ward."

He could join her there, Alisha thought. "You're still convinced that spending two days together is going to cure this thing between us?"

"Not cure it but relieve it for the time being. Otherwise we'll never get through the trial. Or at least, *I* won't."

"Then we're going to just tear it up and wear it out so we won't be tempted to jump each other in front of the jury?"

"Something like that."

If she knew what was good for her, Alisha would insist they call the whole thing off. But she only knew one thing— she wanted more of Daniel and less reason. "Okay, I'll go. What time?"

His smile returned and Alisha felt the effects all over her body. "Eight o'clock."

"That early?"

"Yeah, that early."

"If I decide to turn around and head back on Saturday, you're not going to give me any trouble, are you?"

He held up his hands in surrender. "I'm not going to give you any trouble."

"Promise?"

"Promise. But I'm damn sure going to give you plenty of reasons to stay."

He turned and walked out the door without even a goodbye, leaving Alisha alone to plan what she would say to Joe. No planning required. She'd simply pretend it hadn't happened unless he brought it up.

After donning her nonchalant face, she strode into the

small break room to find Joe sitting at the table, several red-and-white cartons set out before him. "Yours is in there," he said, pointing at the sack with his chopsticks.

Alisha rummaged around and withdrew her share of the Chinese food, opting to use the plastic fork instead of chopsticks, otherwise she might end up impaling Joe in the forehead because of her strong case of nerves.

She plopped down in the chair, took a napkin and laid it in her lap. "Did you go over Mrs. O'Reilly's medical records?"

"It's dangerous, Alisha."

"I wouldn't consider it dangerous at all. It's the only chance we have of disproving the assault theory."

"That's not what I'm talking about and you know it."

Alisha dumped a mountain of rice onto a paper plate and began shoveling her kung pao chicken onto the pile. "What *are* you talking about?"

"You and Fortune."

She tossed down the fork and sat back in the rigid chair. "That's rich coming from you. I recall you foisting me off on him on two occasions."

Joe tossed his chopsticks aside and sighed. "Look, I think it's great you two hooked up, but with the publicity this case is getting, you could get caught. In fact, the last two reporters only left about an hour ago. They could've seen him coming here."

"And that wouldn't be questioned considering we're working on the same case. Besides, we're being discreet."

"Yeah, right. Real discreet. That's why I almost caught you getting down on your desk."

Alisha's face heated up, but not from the spicy food since she had yet to take a bite. "We thought you were still gone."

Joe leaned forward, looking way too serious. "If you want to see him, then see him. I'm just saying you need to be careful."

"I am being careful." What a joke.

"And you're going to have to watch what you say to him.

You know how it is when you're sleeping with someone. Things manage to slip out in the heat of the moment."

She stared at him. "Do you really think I'm going to recite case law and reveal my strategy while in the throes of passion? I'm not stupid, Joe." Just smitten.

"I'm not saying you're stupid. I don't want to see you get hurt. I mean, the guy's in his midthirties and he's never been married. What does that tell you?"

"He's a player." Something Alisha already knew.

"Exactly."

"Well, maybe I want to be a player, too."

"Sure. And I want to take up salsa dancing."

Alisha's appetite disappeared along with her patience. She no longer wanted to eat, nor did she want to continue this discussion. She had too much to do before the weekend rolled around, and despite the pesky voice that kept telling her she might be making a mistake, she planned to go to the little cabin by the lake and forget about everything else. And she'd definitely keep her emotions tightly bound in a straitjacket while Daniel Fortune kept her in a constant state of madness.

Punctuality wasn't Alisha's stronger suit, something Daniel realized when she showed up at the cabin at ten o'clock, spewing gravel as she sped up the drive at breakneck speed. He'd been standing on the porch step for over an hour waiting for her, worried she'd changed her mind.

But there she was, getting out of her white sedan that had seen better days, lugging a paisley tote bag over one shoulder. She wore a nylon jacket, sunglasses and a wide-brimmed straw hat fit for a beach, even though the gray skies threatened rain. She also had on a pair of washed-out jeans that fit way too well, chipping away at his determination to keep things light at least for a while.

When she reached the bottom step, Alisha took off the hat

and shook out her curls, then shoved the sunglasses on top of her head. "Sorry I'm late."

"Are you? I didn't notice."

She cracked a smile. "Yes, you did."

He leaned a shoulder against the wooden porch support and stuffed his hands into his pockets so he wouldn't grab her up and haul her into the house. "Did you get lost?"

She set the tote down at her cross-trainer-covered feet. "Actually, yes."

"Why didn't you call me?"

"Because it took me ten minutes tops to get back on track. I spent most of the morning putting out a few fires."

"Problems?"

"Just the usual stuff. I went by the office first to do some work and then I got waylaid by a reporter. He wanted to know if the rumor that Les wears a prosthetic penis is true."

"Is it?" he asked without skipping a beat.

"How would I know?"

"Just checking in case you decide to file that into evidence."

"Oh, wouldn't that be nice, receiving a plastic penis in a box during discovery."

Daniel laughed as he descended the remaining two steps and took her bag. "Well, no reporters here, as far as I know."

She looked alarmed. "As far as you know? Have you seen any around?"

"No, not here. I haven't spoken with any since the day I appeared on the courthouse steps to save you from the hassle."

"You know, I was handling that fine without your help."

"I'm sure you were, but I wanted to make sure you didn't get too overwhelmed by the process."

"Thanks, I guess."

He started up the stairs, held open the screen door and waved her inside. "And this should be the last time we discuss the trial."

"You're right on that count," she said as she moved past

him, the scent of some sort of clean-smelling perfume carrying to him on the breeze.

Once inside the small living area, Daniel set her bag down on the weathered chintz sofa that had once belonged to his mother. The sofa where she used to tell the kids bedtime stories, before bedtime had been disrupted by his father's unwelcome arrival home from work.

Determined to keep those memories at bay, he turned his attention to Alisha, who was giving the room a thorough search. "It's plain, but it's comfortable," he told her.

She turned slowly around before facing him again. "And neat. Don't you have any clutter? Maybe shoes lying around?" She snapped her fingers and pointed. "I bet you have lots of stuff shoved under your bed."

"You're welcome to go look."

The conversation suspended as they stood there, staring at each other as if they weren't sure what to do next. Daniel knew what he wanted to do—toss her over his shoulder and carry her to his bed, and not so she could take a peek beneath it. *Slow down* kept playing over and over in his head. He could do slow for now, and he knew just the thing to help that along.

"Do you know what I want to do right now?" he said.

"I could probably guess."

"I want to take you fishing."

She didn't even try to hide her surprise. "Fishing? It looks like it might rain."

"We'll fish off the dock since my boat's in winter storage. If it rains, we can make a run for it."

"I don't care to fish, but I don't mind watching you do it."

"It's more fun if you participate."

"That depends on the activity."

One potential activity tried to shove caution clean out of his brain. "True. We can stay inside if you'd like."

She picked up her jacket from the sofa and pulled it on. "No. If you want to go fishing, then fishing it is."

\* \* \*

For twenty minutes Alisha sat on a weathered dock and watched Daniel cast his line into the murky green water of Lake Mondo. He wore an open red flannel shirt rolled up at the sleeves over a plain white T-shirt and faded, loose-fitting jeans covering a pair of clunky hiking boots. She liked the image he presented, thoroughly macho male with tousled hair and a spattering of whiskers over his jaw. And those incredible hands…

Just thinking about the interlude in her office threatened to send her up in flames. To distract herself, she pulled a cloth band from her pocket and twisted her hair into a makeshift bun on top of her head. No need to frighten the fish, since her hair had begun to do its usual frizz frenzy in the high humidity.

After a few more minutes she told him, "Maybe you should try a top-water jig instead of the purple worm."

Midcast, he stared down on her. "I thought you said you didn't fish."

"I said I didn't care to fish. I've done more than my share in my lifetime."

"Oh, yeah?"

"Yeah." She hugged her knees to her chest. "Almost every Sunday in the spring and summer, my mom, dad and I would go down to the creek for a picnic. We'd bring bait and my dad's famous fried chicken."

"Your dad made fried chicken?"

"Yes. He's a great cook. After he retired from the steel mill because of a bad back, he took over all the kitchen duty. And that was a good thing because my mother doesn't believe food is done unless it's completely dead and dried out. I didn't know the true color of cooked bacon until I was in junior high. I thought it was black."

He had an odd, almost stoic expression. "Sounds like an unusual arrangement."

"Why? Not manly enough for you?"

"Like I told you, I have no problem cooking. I'm more

of a barbecue kind of guy, though. Steaks and burgers, that sort of thing."

She wasn't surprised. He looked like a grade-A beef kind of guy. A grade-A beefcake. "Is that what we're having for dinner?"

"I haven't decided yet, but probably."

"Did your mother teach you how to cook?"

He shook his head. "I'm self-taught out of necessity. I had to learn to fend for myself."

"So your mother worked outside the home?"

"No. She just wasn't always available."

Alisha found the troubled look on his face disturbing. Obviously there was some kind of a story there, one she might not ever know. Daniel Fortune had secrets, and she'd leave him to them for now.

She crossed her legs before her and leaned forward to watch him bring in the line. "No luck yet?"

"Nope." He lifted his rod and reel and removed the purple worm, tossed it into his tackle box before setting the rod aside and sitting beside her. "I give up. Doesn't look like anything's going to bite."

Alisha had the sudden urge to take his earlobe between her teeth. She studied the darkening skies to distract her. "Probably the weird weather, although when it starts to rain, they may start biting."

"*If* it rains. They're only saying a thirty percent chance."

Alisha looked out over the deserted lake, only a few small houses dotting the panorama. "This is nice. Very peaceful."

"It was until the Christopher Jamison murder."

"That's right. They found his body here."

"Yeah, not too far from here, as a matter of fact."

Alisha shuddered. "You could've gone all day without saying that. It's creepy."

"Sorry, but I think about it a lot these days. I just wish to hell they'd catch his sorry brother."

"Then he's still on the run."

Daniel sighed. "Yeah, but my guess is not for long. I can't wait for the day when I see him put away for good."

Alisha admired the conviction in his tone, but his uneasy expression seemed to put a damper on the outing. "We just can't let go of our jobs for any length of time, can we?"

"Guess it's just the nature of the business." He sent her a sincere look. "But I'll try not to think about work if you won't."

"That's a deal, as soon as I ask you a question."

"As long as it's not about the Massey case."

"No, but it is about another case. Do you remember anything about an accident when a boy was rendered paraplegic after being hit by a car near a park? It happened last year."

He continued to stare out over the lake. "Nancy Kenneally was driving the car. Yeah, I remember." His bitter tone indicated the memory wasn't a good one.

"I was just wondering if you recall any details," she said.

"I remember them too well. Our lone witness decided to get amnesia and recanted her initial statement. Without her the grand jury wouldn't indict. But I know Mrs. Kenneally hit that kid because she'd been drinking."

"Any proof of that?"

"Unfortunately, no. They took her to the hospital due to minor injuries and her lawyer met her there. He managed to stonewall the police, and by the time a blood-alcohol level was ordered, it didn't show anything over the legal limit. But she has a history and a lot of connections. A lethal combination."

"Yes, it is."

He glanced her way. "Why do you want to know?"

"I'm going to represent the family in a wrongful-death suit."

"Good. When you win, then maybe that will give them some peace."

"*If* I win. I'm going up against my former firm. I could be totally outmanned on this one. Unless you want to help me."

He patted her thigh. "Wish I could. I'd like to see that

woman get what's coming to her. Feel free to ask for advice. That much I can do."

"I definitely will."

The rain began to fall, small drops at first, until they came down in a deluge. "Let's get out of here." Daniel stood and held out his hand to her, then grabbed up the tackle box with the other hand. They ran back to the cabin, arriving on the porch drenched and winded from the sprint.

Daniel set his tackle on the glider while Alisha took off her jacket and shook it out. When he removed the flannel shirt, well, she suddenly didn't care if she was soaked and chilled to the bone. The man had a chest that wouldn't quit, very apparent as the wet fabric clung to every inch of solid, supple muscle.

He tossed the shirt on the glider and slicked a hand through his wet hair. "So much for thirty percent."

Alisha swiped the moisture from her face. "You know how forecasts are. Very unpredictable."

"Kind of like you."

Alisha let go a caustic laugh. "I'm not so unpredictable."

"You're here with me, and I wouldn't have predicted that in a million years."

"That's because you're predictably persuasive."

He shifted his weight and hooked his thumbs in the pockets of his jeans. "Can I persuade you to come inside the house before you freeze to death?"

"Sure, but it's not that cold."

"You're cold."

"Why do you think that?"

His gaze traveled to her breasts encased in saturated knit. She didn't have to look down to know what he was seeing. "Okay, my pom-poms are a little perky, so I guess we should go in."

Daniel laughed, a big, boisterous laugh that was as shocking as it was contagious. Alisha followed with a few laughs of her own before she said, "I didn't think it was that funny."

"You're an amazing woman, Alisha Hart."

"And you are a very bad host, Daniel Fortune."

His eyes narrowed. "Why is that?"

"Well, you're blocking the door. And you haven't even offered me a towel so I can dry off and warm up."

He reached out, caught her arms and pulled her against him. Before she could speak, he had his mouth firmly planted on hers, giving her a kiss that would curl her hair if it hadn't already been curly. When they parted, he kept his arms around her and grinned. "Isn't that better than a towel?"

"I'm still wet."

"I can do something about that, too."

And she was tempted to let him.

He opened the front door and said, "After you."

Alisha brushed past him and entered the small living room.

When the door closed behind Daniel, she turned and faced him. "Where's my room?"

She noted the immediate disappointment in his eyes when he pointed to his left. "Right through there. Guest room's on the left, bathroom's in the middle, mine's on the right. You'll find fresh towels if you want to take a shower."

"Thanks." She picked up her lone bag and her briefcase. "I'm going to clean up, then do some studying, if that's okay with you."

"That's what you're here for. Need any help?"

"That's not a good idea."

"I mean help with your bag."

"I can handle it just fine." If only she could handle being so close to him.

"Do you want lunch first?"

She patted her briefcase. "Actually I brought some snacks. That will do until dinner."

He slid his hands in his pockets. "The kitchen's behind me if you want anything to drink."

"I brought some bottled water."

"Guess I'll see you at dinner then."

"Right. At dinner."

She hesitated for a moment, wanting what she shouldn't be wanting. But with Daniel standing there looking so mussed and gorgeous, she couldn't help but want him. Want him or not, she did have work to do, and she'd best get on with it before she discarded her responsibility for a little afternoon delight.

Alisha turned and walked through the small entry, then headed to her left down the hall. She entered the bedroom that was as simple as the rest of the surroundings. A double bed covered in a plain blue chenille spread took up most of the room, leaving little space for anything more than a dresser and a nightstand.

After hoisting her bag on the bed, she unzipped it to retrieve a change of clothes. Her hand immediately went to the black lace nightgown folded neatly on top of her underclothes. She didn't dare show up at dinner wearing that. But after dinner, well, that was a distinct possibility. Might as well admit it—she had every intention of taking up where she'd left off with Daniel, otherwise she wouldn't have bothered to bring lingerie. To deny her overriding desire for him would be futile, and this little work session would only serve to delay the inevitable. She'd already planned her defense for the Massey case, and Daniel Fortune had her feeling totally defenseless.

He'd managed to keep from joining her in the shower earlier. He'd managed to keep from capturing her in the small kitchen during after-dinner cleanup. But he was having a hard time managing his hands at the moment.

As they sat on a braided rug in front of the hearth, Alisha's hair a near match to the fire, Daniel seriously wanted to touch her, beginning with the section of skin revealed right where the oversize shirt parted. He wanted to rake it with his tongue, but the promise to stay away from her neck kept coming back to bite him.

Unaware of his devious thoughts, Alisha swirled the wine

around before taking the last sip and setting the glass on the coffee table.

He gestured toward the open bottle resting beside the now-empty glass. "Do you want some more?"

"No thanks. I don't like to drink alone."

The closest Daniel would get to having some wine would be to taste it on her tongue. The temptation to do just that was overwhelming, but he vowed to remain strong. If she wanted his affections, then she'd have to give him some sort of a sign. So far that wasn't happening, and now that it was nearing midnight, he doubted it would.

Alisha stretched out on her belly and rested her chin on her folded arms. "I'm surprised you haven't said anything."

He'd been talking to her all evening, almost nonstop. "About what?"

"The real me. No makeup, wild hair, ratty clothes."

She had no idea how great she looked at that moment. No idea that she didn't need all the embellishments to keep him totally on sexual high alert. She didn't understand her power, and he found that damn appealing—and unusual. "I didn't say anything because I didn't really notice until you pointed it out."

She smiled a skeptic's smile. "Oh, sure."

"It's true." With the last fragment of his waning self-control, he resisted showing her exactly what he thought about her appearance. "You look great no matter what you're wearing. You don't need any makeup either."

She touched her fingertip to her nose covered by a light shading of freckles. "I'd prefer these not show all the time. Makes me look like I'm twelve, not thirty-two."

"No, they don't. I like them."

"Thanks." She braced her cheek on her palm. "I heard the phone ring earlier. I don't mean to be nosy, but I was worried it might be someone from your office."

"No. No one from the office. That's a private line. I only give it out to a few people. The office calls me on my cell phone."

"Oh, I see." Daniel noted a hint of distrust in her eyes and he figured she assumed some woman had contacted him.

"It was my brother, Vincent," Daniel said, attempting to alleviate her fears. "He's on his honeymoon and he was just checking in."

Her eyes widened. "He was checking in with family on his honeymoon? That's true devotion."

Vincent had been devoted to the family, at least to his siblings. "He's extended the trip and he wanted to see how things are going."

"Are your sisters married?"

"Only to their careers. Susan's a psychologist and Kyra's a VP at an energy company. Vincent was the first one to take the plunge." Something Daniel had never believed would happen.

"Sounds like you've all done well for yourselves. That's a sign of good raising."

They had done well *despite* their raising. "We're all fairly driven, that's for sure."

She rose up onto her bent arms. "Have you ever come close to getting married?"

"No. Have you?"

She shook her head. "Never even considered it."

"Not even with Moreau?"

"Definitely not him. Troy's not the marrying kind. He's only faithful to blind ambition. And if he ever does make that commitment, it would be to further his career."

Daniel could relate to that on one level. "I don't see that as compelling enough reason to marry."

"That's true, but who knows? Maybe you'll find a woman who will give you a reason to settle down, and then you can make everyone happy, including the party."

How could he explain that his own example of marriage had fallen short? He couldn't. Alisha had grown up with parents who had provided security and unconditional love. She'd never understand what it was like to present the face of the perfect family when in reality his family had been anything but perfect. Yet he had the strongest urge to open up and share his experiences with her, but he wouldn't. He needed to keep his pain private, as he'd been taught to do from a very young age. He also needed to head to bed, he decided when he saw her hide a yawn behind her hand.

As much as Daniel wanted to be her lover again, he'd enjoyed her friendship today and he didn't want to compromise that. If she wanted to be in his bed, she'd have to find her way there on her own, without any coercion.

"Time to turn in," he said as he came to his feet.

She looked as if he'd told her to get out of his house. "It's not that late."

"Yeah, it is. And you're tired."

"Not that tired."

He waited for her to hold out her arms to him, to request he lay down beside her, anything that might indicate she wanted to take this further. When that didn't come, he told her, "If you want to get up early, there's an alarm clock on the nightstand. Let me know if you need anything. Otherwise I'll see you in the morning."

He turned away but before he could leave, she said, "Daniel."

He faced her again, hoping she would say that she did need something else, but instead she only offered, "Sleep well."

"I'll try." He'd probably try for several hours at that.

## Nine

Daniel Fortune was a man of his word, Alisha thought as she tossed and turned in a very lonely double bed. He hadn't pursued her, hadn't kissed her again. Hadn't even made any kind of suggestive comment. Maybe the decision to appear before him as the proverbial plain Jane had been a turnoff regardless of what he'd said. But he'd seemed sincere when he'd told her she looked great regardless of her having nixed all the frills. Daniel didn't seem like the kind of man who exchanged honesty for pretty words. He *was* the kind of man she should avoid—habit-forming to the extreme. And that was a habit she couldn't really afford. But she also didn't want to spend this night alone, not with a gorgeous guy right down the hall.

Alisha bolted from the bed and on her way to the light switch knocked her big toe on the corner of the dresser. She quashed a yelp and reminded herself that any injury she might sustain getting to Daniel would be well worth it—if he cooperated. She had a secret weapon made of silk and lace and she intended to use it.

Opening the top drawer in the dresser, Alisha retrieved the negligee and held it up. Hopefully this scrap of a gown would do the trick. She exchanged her normal nonimpressive night-shirt and plain underwear for the naughty nightie and a spe-cial pair of panties—also black silk, with *Surprise!* etched in yellow script across the front. That about said it all without her having to utter a word to Daniel.

After applying a mist of her favorite gardenia body splash, Alisha drew in a long breath, shut off the light and left the room. The short distance down the hall to his bedroom didn't allow her much time to change her mind, not that she wanted to do that. She considered the open door an invitation and walked inside. It took awhile for her vision to adjust to her sur-roundings because the lights were out—and obviously nobody was home. No unmade bed. No signs of life. No Daniel.

That sent a direct blow to her confidence when she con-sidered that maybe he'd used bedtime as an excuse to get away from her. Maybe she'd talked too much and he'd had enough. Maybe he'd decided he didn't like her all that much, if at all. Or maybe he'd decided to return to the dock for a little night-time fishing. Certainly not unheard of but highly unlikely since the rain had yet to cease. Only one way to find out.

Alisha returned to the living room to find the fire had been restoked and now blazed in the hearth. Laid out on the floor on the large braided rug, wearing no shoes, no shirt, ready to ser-vice, was the missing prosecutor. He had his head propped on a throw pillow and his hand resting casually on his bare abdo-men below his navel, where his jeans began. Unbuttoned jeans, but the zipper was still in position. With any luck, not for long.

His eyes were closed, providing Alisha sufficient opportu-nity to give his incredible body a long look-see. His skin ap-peared golden in the firelight and his hair was ruffled as if he'd run his hands thought it numerous times. She wanted to run her hands through it. Run her hands over his entire body, as a matter of fact. First, she had a decision to make. Wake him up or go back to her room like a good girl. But good girls didn't always get the good stuff, so she opted to be a little bit bad.

After taking a few steps forward, she stood by the arm he had resting at his side. And what an arm it was. A thoroughly masculine arm with manly veins and macho muscles. She wanted that arm around her and that hand doing things to her person that she knew him to be quite capable of doing.

Now or never was upon her. Now seemed like a fine idea. "Daniel?"

No answer.

"Mr. Fortune?"

Still no answer. Just when she was about to drop to her knees to try a little physical persuasion, his eyes drifted open and a slow-as-Sunday-afternoon smile curled the corners of his mouth. "Did you really call me Mr. Fortune?"

"That is your name." Talk about stating the obvious.

He surveyed her entire body with a long, painstaking glance. "I thought you were in bed."

"I thought the same thing about you."

"I've been up since you left me. I'm still up." He rubbed his palm down his chest, beginning at his sternum and follow-ing the stream of hair until it disappeared beneath his dis-tended fly.

Without warning, he circled her ankle, slid his hand up to her thigh and toyed with the gown's hem. "Do you wear this kind of thing to bed every night?"

"No. I normally wear worn-out T-shirts."

"I like this better." He rubbed his thumb back and forth over the satin. "I'd like it even better off you."

"Then you take it off me."

He laced his hands behind his neck. "I want to watch you take it off." He had challenge in his tone and heat in his eyes. He also had Alisha completely captive to his raw sensuality.

Feeling marvelously bold, she tugged the hem from his grasp and pulled the negligee over her head, then dropped it on the floor. "Better?"

"Oh, yeah." His gaze drifted down to her panties. "That's a nice surprise."

"I thought so."

He centered his gaze on her eyes. "Come down here. You're too far away."

No sooner said than done, Alisha knelt beside him. He pulled her to him, then flipped her over and pinned her with his body, letting her know exactly who was in charge. She would allow him all the authority he wanted at the moment.

He cupped her face in his palms and said, "Are you sure about this, Alisha?"

Who was he kidding? "I'm half-naked, so I think that's rather obvious."

"No arguments?"

"None whatsoever. The defense rests."

"The prosecution is only getting started." He confirmed that by laying his lips on hers, taunting her with brief kisses before claiming her mouth completely with his talented mouth. He moved his tongue against hers in soft strokes, meticulously exploring, but not to the point of being too invasive. On the contrary, he kept it gentle yet seductive, just the way she liked it.

He broke the kiss to work his soft lips down the column of her throat and kept going. When he reached the rise of her breasts, he sucked a small section of her skin into his mouth, and all too late she realized what he was doing.

"Daniel, you're going to—"

"Leave my mark." He lifted his head and winked at her. "I want you to remember I was here." He lowered his head again. "And here."

Alisha's vocabulary vacated the premises when he drew her nipple between his lips, flicking his tongue back and forth in a steady rhythm that had her squirming beneath him. She slid her fingers through his thick hair, holding on for dear life even though she couldn't hold back the instinctive movement of her hips beneath his groin.

Then he sat up abruptly, leaving Alisha completely confused as well as alone. "Where are you going?" she asked.

He answered her with a seductive smile as he shoved his jeans down, stepped out of them and tossed them onto the sofa. He took his time lowering his briefs, the big tease. To claim she wasn't at all affected by his solid state of arousal would be a complete falsehood. But she didn't have time to look too long before he went to his knees beside her.

He brushed his knuckles across her belly, causing her to tremble almost uncontrollably. She wasn't afraid; she was excited. And even more so when he said, "I want my surprise now."

Hooking his fingers in the lacy band at her hips, he slid the panties down as slowly as he'd removed his own briefs, bringing her to the border of madness. He worked them away and tossed them aside to join her gown resting near the hearth.

"Exactly what I've been wanting," he said. "I'm sure it's a perfect fit."

Daniel's smile was so wildly wicked, and Alisha was so incredibly needy that she couldn't even think of a comeback. She simply couldn't think at all when he parted her legs and moved between them on his knees. His eyes reflected the firelight, his touch created intense warmth when he leaned forward and skimmed his hands up her body. He paused at her breasts and only then did he take his gaze from hers to watch the movements of his fingertips as he caressed her nipples.

After a time, he moved his hands to her sides, splaying his thumbs as he slid his palms down her torso to her pelvis. Alisha's chest rose and fell from labored breaths, from anticipation as he continued on to her hips and down her legs, bending them at the knees and at the same time nudging them farther apart for maximum exposure. She felt only slightly self-conscious when he didn't attempt to hide exactly where his attention had turned. Lowering his head, he ran his tongue along the inside of one thigh before glancing at her again. He did the same thing to her other thigh, as if he intended to send her into complete lunacy. Or make her plead to end the torture. "Please," slipped out of her mouth before she could halt it.

That was exactly what he wanted—for her to beg him to end the sweet agony. And he did, his mouth poised between her thighs as he used his tongue like a feather on her flesh. Alisha couldn't seem to catch her breath when he continued his all-out attack on her senses. He kept his hands in motion, enticing her both inside and out with his skilled fingertips while he coaxed her with his equally talented mouth. She tuned in to the sensations, only vaguely aware that he'd slipped his palms beneath her bottom to lift her closer, driving her further into mindlessness.

Something between a whimper and a scream caught in her throat and came out in a moan when the first strong wave began, followed by a forceful surge when he rose up onto his knees and thrust inside her. Her hips involuntarily bucked with the incredible invasion, and her body clutched when he retreated before he advanced again.

The man had impeccable timing. That was her first random thought. He was bent on propelling her into oblivion, her second thought, when he withdrew from her almost completely before slowly, concisely pushing back inside her, all the while watching her face, his expression showing undeniable male determination.

Alisha thought the abrupt ringing originated from her ears, until she saw Daniel reach over and pick up a cell phone from the coffee table. She wanted to scream, and this time not from pleasure.

Daniel didn't bother to disengage from her body as he answered, "A.D.A. Fortune."

After a long pause he said, "I'm busy." He ran his free hand up and down the inside of her thigh. "Krauss can wake up a judge and get a warrant."

As the conversation continued, Alisha had a difficult time comprehending his steel control, but he *was* in control. Of the discussion and of her. The iceman was totally hot—and melting her with each passing moment.

"I'm going to be in and out all weekend," he said as he moved ever so slightly inside her. "I won't be available. I have something important that needs my attention." His fingertips idled over the place where his mouth had been only moments before, setting the stage for another mind-blowing release, one that Alisha wasn't sure she could endure. But she was more than willing to try.

He hung up, tossed the phone across the room, then turned his fiery gaze on her. "They won't bother us again."

Oddly she hadn't been bothered at all. In fact, the scene had been erotic beyond all bounds, although she did briefly wonder who had been on the other side of the dialogue, unaware of what Daniel had been doing to her. Was still doing to her.

"Put your legs around my waist." His voice was a low, drugging command.

Alisha obeyed and was glad she had when he pushed even deeper. He leaned over and brushed his chest across her breasts as he ground against her, then he lifted his upper body onto straight arms while keeping a steady rhythm with his lower body.

Daniel Fortune was a wonder to behold at that moment, from the perspiration coating his chest in a glittering sheen to the few wayward locks of hair that had fallen across his forehead. His biceps bulged with his effort and so did the prominent veins in his arms and neck. She saw his control begin to slip when she gripped him tighter with her legs and her body. She saw it shatter when she murmured, "Harder."

Daniel thrust again and again and again with almost savage intensity, sending Alisha into the throes of another all-consuming climax. Soon after, his eyes closed and a feral groan filtered through his clenched teeth. He collapsed against her, his heart pounding against her breasts, his body racked with tremors to match her own.

The occasional crackle coming from the fireplace and their ragged respiration were the only sounds in the otherwise silent room. Alisha preferred the contentment and the quiet to after-sex talk. What could she say now that she'd crossed over the line again with Daniel? She could repeat all the reasons they shouldn't be doing this. She could cite all the repercussions of their relationship. None of them really mattered at the moment. Nothing mattered except the wonderful feel of his weight and his warm lips drifting against her neck while he played with her hair as if he found her unruly curls mesmerizing. She found all of him fascinating, from the solid path of his spine to the curve of his taut buttocks to his hair-roughened thighs, territory she investigated painstakingly with her palms. The tone of his golden skin contrasted with her fair complexion, and she found that captivating, as well.

"Man, I think I just visited another dimension," he said without looking at her.

Alisha ran her fingers through his hair, testing the softness at his nape. "I was right there with you."

More silence passed until he finally lifted his head. "Well?"

"Well what?"

"What's going through your mind? And don't say I need more color in this room, because it's got plenty of color."

Alisha suspected her face had plenty of color, too. "That's not it."

His expression grew suddenly somber. "You're regretting this already."

She shook her head. "No, not at all. I was just considering how many rules we've probably broken." And how she'd learned nothing from her experience with Troy. As much as she wanted to trust Daniel, she still worried that this affair could come back to haunt her.

"To hell with the rules, Alisha. I've never broken them with any woman before you, so that should tell you how badly I want you."

She certainly wanted him enough to hurl wisdom out the window. "I know, but I can't help but worry."

"That you won't be able to trust me?"

The man was intuitive as well as an expert lover. "That has crossed my mind."

He rolled off her onto his back and stared at the ceiling. "Whatever happens between us in this house stays in this house. I don't give a damn about your defense of Massey. And I know that when we walk into that courtroom on Monday, none of this is going to enter into it."

If only she could be that sure. "Okay. I believe you." She rested her palm on his chest and slid her fingers through the slight spattering of hair. "We probably should go to bed now. As long as you don't snore."

He turned toward her, propped up on his elbow, his fist supporting his jaw. "You've decided to sleep with me."

She smiled. "I suppose we could sleep."

He stood and pulled her up into his arms, giving her the full benefit of his beautiful body fitted firmly against her. "You are one hell of a sexy woman."

All the responses came back to Alisha then. *Me, sexy? You can't be serious. You're so full of nonsense.* She didn't voice them and instead replied, "I feel the same about you."

"You think I'm a sexy woman?"

She rolled her eyes. "You're so amusing, Daniel Fortune."

"And you make me damn hot, Alisha Hart." He lifted a curl

and rubbed it against his chin. "But you know, you don't really look like an Alisha, especially when we're making love."

Making love. A catchall phrase that had become too easy to toss around. "What do I look like? Maybe Pippi?"

"Lola."

"Okay, I'll be Lola, and you can be…" She tapped a finger on her temple. "Gunther."

"Fine by me." He turned her around and patted her bare bottom. "To my bed, Lola."

"You've got it, Gunther."

Alisha had a seminaked man behind her and her mother on the phone. Not a good combination at all. She would rather hang up and see to that man, but daughterly duty dictated she finish the conversation. However, she was on the verge of burning the omelet and dropping the cell phone if Daniel kept touching her breast.

Wresting out of his grasp, she picked up the pan, dropped it onto a hot pad, turned and leaned back against the counter. Bad move. Now she had a prime view of the premium man standing before her wearing only a towel draped low on his hips. "I'm sorry, Mom. What were you saying?"

"I was saying that your father and I are worried about you representing this lowlife. Do you have some kind of guards around when you have to meet with him?"

"He's in jail, Mother, so of course guards are around. And he's not a rapist, he's an exhibitionist. You don't need to worry. I can handle him."

Her mother's sigh sounded like a deflating tire. "I'm not so sure about that. Leila May came into the post office on Friday and said she heard that his manhood is as big as an elephant's trunk."

That was a new one on Alisha. Just like a child's game of gossip, the legend of Les's "manhood" continued to grow, literally. "I'm sure that rumor got started when he was standing in front of the elephants during his show at the zoo."

"How do you know it's a rumor? Have you seen it?"

"No, I have not seen it, and I don't want to see it." Daniel chose that moment to open the towel and flash her. She sent him a faux frustrated look and centered her attention on the refrigerator behind him.

When he laughed, Alisha immediately reached out and slapped a hand over his mouth, but not before her mother asked, "Is there a man with you?"

"It's the TV." Now she'd resorted to lying to her parents. But a necessary lie if she wanted to avoid more questions. "I've got to go, Mom. Breakfast is getting cold." And Daniel was making her hot.

"Breakfast? It's after noon."

"Okay, brunch. I slept in late." Not that she'd gotten any real sleep since dawn, thanks to the promiscuous prosecutor.

"All right, honey. Daddy says hello. Do you want to speak with him?"

Heavens, no. Not with a practically naked man in her presence. "Just tell him I love him. Love you, too."

She hung up the phone and tossed it aside on the dinette, then gave Daniel a hard stare. "Thanks to you, I was almost busted."

He released another low laugh and rubbed a hand down his chest. "Your mother doesn't approve of you keeping company with a man?"

"She's fairly open-minded about that sort of thing. But she would ask a lot of questions, including your identity. That would mean skirting the truth, and I don't like to lie to my parents." Although she already had.

"You could've told her you met some guy named Gunther."

Alisha went back to the stove and spooned the omelet onto the plate, then yanked open a drawer to retrieve a fork. She turned and held out a bite. "Take a taste."

"I plan to, then I'll try the eggs."

She couldn't move fast enough to avoid his arms coming around her, not that she really wanted to avoid him. He took the plate and set it aside, then hoisted her up on the counter.

"You're bad, Daniel Fortune," she said when he opened her robe, exposing her breasts.

He ran a fingertip over the calling card he'd left last night with his mouth. "It's still there."

"I told you it doesn't take much to mark me. It will probably be there for a few days."

"When it goes away, let me know. I'd be glad to give you another one, anywhere you want me to put it."

Thoughts of last night's interlude came back to her in vivid detail. "I'll keep that in mind, but right now I have to think about going home."

He opened her robe completely, leaving nothing to the imagination and everything at the mercy of his hands. "Are you sure about that?"

No, she wasn't, but if she didn't leave now, she might never go. With the last of her strength Alisha removed those hands and clasped the robe shut. "I had a great time this weekend."

"So did I. It's the first time I've slept all night."

"Almost all night. If I recall, you were quite up before dawn."

He grinned. "Yeah. Sorry about that."

"Can't say that I'm sorry. But now I have to grab a shower and get home."

He laid his palms on her bare thighs below where the robe had conveniently parted. "I'll take one with you."

She frowned. "You've already had one."

"I'll take another one. I have an adequate hot-water heater."

Everything about him was more than adequate. "You're not going to let me go without a fight, are you?"

He brushed a kiss across her lips. "I don't think I am. At least not for another hour or so."

Another hour or so. A reminder that after this little week-end escape Alisha might not see him again, at least until the

trial was over. Maybe not even then. If he lived up to his love-
'em-and-leave-'em reputation, then she could be left a lot
sooner than she would like. But she'd known that when she'd
entered into this forbidden liaison. Still, that didn't make it
any easier.

Without warning, Daniel wrapped her legs around his waist
and pulled her from the counter. When he headed toward the
bathroom, she didn't have the strength to protest. She didn't
have the desire to object. She'd save all her arguments for
court. Right now she wanted to lose herself in Daniel
Fortune—and hope she didn't remain lost to him indefinitely.

An hour later Daniel awoke to find Alisha had left the bed
without his knowledge. If she had already headed home, she
was definitely going to hear about it. He tossed back the covers, grabbed his jeans from the nearby chair and tugged them
on. On his way out of the bedroom he put on the flannel shirt
without bothering to button it. He entered the living room and
saw her bags resting at the door. That gave him some measure
of relief, although he didn't like the thought of her leaving.

In the kitchen Daniel found her wiping down the counters
after clearing away the breakfast they hadn't eaten. "I thought
you'd already gone."

She swiped the dishrag over the stove. "No, but I'm about
to."

"You were going to leave without telling me goodbye?"

After tossing the rag aside, Alisha faced him. "You were
sleeping so soundly, I hated to wake you."

He pulled her into his arms. "First rule—and you already
know it—don't ever leave me again without saying something."

"Okay. What's the second rule?"

He'd never had a set of rules in regard to relationships beyond no rules. No commitment. No exceptions. He'd make
an exception for Alisha. "The next time I see you, wear that
black silk gown again."

She stared at him for a moment, then laughed. "That might seem rather odd during voir dire tomorrow morning."

He could go the rest of the month without having to deal with the damn trial, particularly picking a jury, his least favorite aspect. "I meant the next time I see you alone."

"Which will be after the trial."

Daniel hated that reminder. Hated that the weekend had come to an end and that politics and his profession would keep him from her for at least a few days. "Yeah. After the trial."

"Speaking of the trial," she said. "I have to go so I can get some work done."

She passed by him in a rush, evading his grasp when he reached for her. He'd be damned if he would let her leave without a goodbye kiss. In the living room she picked up her bags and went out the door before he even got the chance to attempt a kiss. But he wasn't going to let the chance pass him by.

Once they reached her car, he took her bags from her, tossed them into the back seat, then pulled her into his arms. "Are you sure you don't want to stay another night? We could drive in together."

"Oh, right. You and me showing up at the courthouse hand in hand, like best buddies."

"Bed buddies," he said with a smile that faded when he noticed she didn't seem to appreciate the humor. "And what I meant was, I could follow you into the city. Make sure you got back okay."

"It's broad daylight, Daniel. I'll be fine. I have my cell phone if I have any problems. Or if you're ready to go now, I can wait."

"Unfortunately I have to pack up and lock up. Plus I thought I might try to fish a little while this afternoon."

"You don't have anything to do to get ready for tomorrow?"

He did, but it wouldn't take that long. "I'm ready." More than ready to drag her back into the house if she didn't get out of there now. He didn't understand why he couldn't seem to get enough of her, but he'd take that thought out and examine it later.

He wrapped his arms around her and kissed her soundly. Kissed her for a long time until he thought they might just go down to the ground and get it on in the driveway.

Alisha pulled away first, then patted his jaw. "It's been great, Gunther."

He patted her butt. "Yeah, Lola. Let's do it again. Real soon."

She gave him a kiss on the cheek, a salute, then opened her door and slid inside. "Do me a favor, Daniel."

"What?"

"Try not to screw me in court tomorrow during jury selection."

"That would probably earn us a contempt charge."

"Ha-ha." She started the ignition, his cue to close the door. He couldn't resist getting one last kiss, even a chaste one, before he let her leave.

She smiled in response. "See you in court."

## *Ten*

"We really got screwed today, Hart."

Joe wasn't saying anything that Alisha didn't already know. Due to a temporary power outage and persistent press, they'd gotten a late start. Even so, the large jury pool should have been to their benefit, but they'd ended up with a less-than-favorable panel for the defense. Seven men, four women, all over the age of fifty-nine except for two, both men in their midthirties. No one near Les Massey's twenty-five.

Joe stood inside her office doorway, one hand braced on the jamb. "Remind me about that whole peer thing again."

"I know, I know." She pinched the bridge of her nose between her forefinger and thumb. "But it could be worse."

"True. We could've gotten the guy who thought the whole way to handle Les Massey was to take him out back and cut off his 'tallywhacker.' Hadn't heard that euphemism since high school."

"Let's hope we don't have others who feel that way and just didn't happen to be as honest about their objectivity."

"Excuse me, Ms. Hart."

Alisha looked up to see the forty-something Penney Smiley, the new temp, standing beside Joe holding a white box tied in a red bow. She had a winning grin that matched her name, a professional demeanor and a pleasant disposition, even if she still had a poufy eighties hairdo complete with wings. "Yes, Penney?"

The woman stepped forward and offered Alisha the mystery gift. "The florist delivered this earlier."

Joe surveyed the package while Alisha untied the ribbon. "Maybe we should call the bomb squad before you open that," he said.

Alisha picked it up and put it to her ear. "I don't hear anything ticking, so I think it's safe." She hoped it was safe. And it was. A dozen long-stem red roses bound by another ribbon with a card attached. She removed the pin, opened the envelope and smiled. *Thanks for the great weekend. Gunther.*

Before she could prepare, Joe grabbed the card from her grasp and read it. "Who's Gunther?"

"Give me that." Penney snatched the card back and handed it to Alisha. "A girl should be entitled to her secrets."

Alisha liked this woman more and more. "Thanks, Penney."

"You still didn't answer my question, Hart," Joe said. "Who's Gunther?"

"None of your business. Any messages, Penney?"

"Only a few from reporters who want an interview with Mr. Massey. I told them absolutely not."

"Good job, Penney. You can go now. And, Joe, you go home to your wife and get a good night's sleep so you're ready to roll in the morning."

Joe straightened his tie and his shoulders. "I'll try, but my wife just can't resist me."

Alisha barely resisted the urge to plant the box in his

mouth. "Julie told me that all she wants to do lately is sleep, so give it a rest."

Joe screwed up his face into a frown. "You women are no fun whatsoever."

Alisha exchanged a knowing look with Penney, then stood. "Fun will be put on the back burner until this trial is over." And that applied to her situation with Daniel, as well. They'd barely looked at each other today, had barely spoken other than to deliver polite hellos. And that was how it would remain for the time being. She did consider calling to thank him for the flowers but thought better of it.

She would take the roses home and remember the weekend while lying awake in her lonely bed. For now that would have to do.

He knew he shouldn't call her, but Daniel found himself picking up the phone and dialing her number. When she answered with her standard, "Alisha Hart," he hesitated for a moment before he said, "You looked good today in court."

"Daniel, you know—"

"I know, but I wanted to hear your voice."

"You heard it several times today."

"Yeah, but it's not the same when you're operating in an official capacity. I like the way you sound now, really sexy."

"Are you trying to make up for stacking the odds against me with that joke of a jury?"

"That's business, Alisha. And I don't want to talk about that. Did you get the flowers?"

"Yes, and they're beautiful. But wasn't that kind of risky?"

"That's the good thing about the Internet. Ordering online provides some anonymity, although I would have preferred to pick them out myself."

"It's the thought that counts, right? And the Gunther thing was very clever. Joe's still trying to figure that one out."

Daniel was trying to figure out why he couldn't keep his

mind off her. Why he'd sent her flowers when he hadn't done that in ages. "I thought that might throw him off track."

"It did."

He stretched out on his back across the bed, wishing she was beside him. Or beneath him. Or on top of him. "Are you wearing that little black gown tonight?"

"No. I haven't even changed out of my clothes yet. I was about to take a shower right before you called."

"Take off your clothes now."

Her breath released slowly. "You're not proposing we have phone sex, are you?"

Not necessarily a bad idea. "No. I'm going to save myself for the next time we're together. I just want to fantasize about you while you're talking to me naked."

"What are you wearing?"

"Not a damn thing." When she didn't immediately respond, he said, "Are you still there?"

"Yes. I just had a momentary lapse of consciousness. Where are you?"

"Lying in my bed on top of the covers. Are you going to do it or am I going to have to come over there and do it for you?"

"That might be really nice."

"Are you serious? Because I could be over there—"

"No," she said quickly. "You need to stay right where you are."

"I will if you'll take off your clothes."

"Okay. Hang on a minute."

He heard her put down the phone, and after a few agonizing moments when Daniel pictured her undressing, she finally spoke again. "I'm done."

"You took it all off?"

"I still have on my panties."

"What do they say?"

"You're crazy."

He chuckled. "No kidding?"

"Yes, I'm kidding. They don't say anything."

"Take them off."

"If you insist."

"I insist."

She paused for another moment. "All done. What now?"

"Run your hand down your stomach."

"I thought we weren't going to have phone sex."

"We're not. I just want you to imagine my hand on you and how it's going to be when we're together again. Are you doing it?"

"Yes." Her voice floated out on a breathy whisper.

"You don't have to stop, Alisha. You can close your eyes and keep right on going. Just pretend it's me touching you."

"I want to wait, too," she said. "I need to wait until you're doing it."

"I want to do it. I'm so hard right now I could forget why I can't see you and be over there in fifteen minutes."

"But you won't come over. You'll wait until the time is right. And, Daniel?"

"Yeah?"

"I'm going to put my hands all over you the next time. And my mouth. Sleep well."

Sleep well? Not in this lifetime.

The line went dead, but that certainly didn't describe his body's current state. He had a painful erection and a long, hard night ahead of him.

Tomorrow he would be forced to focus on the case at hand. He would give no indication that he was battling feelings for the defender that he couldn't begin to comprehend. He would become the prosecutor—committed, reserved, driven—even if it was only a show.

Showtime. And what a show it was, Alisha thought as she scanned the crowded courtroom. Behind the prosecution's table sat a few citizens sporting disapproving stares aimed at the accused. Members of the press lined the walls, including several sketch artists. Immediately behind her, a rowdy, restless group of women of all ages who held up signs that read Masses for Massey and Les is More. She'd expected that, but she hadn't expected to see Anna Marie Pettigrew, the estranged wife of one of the most powerful men in town. Very, very odd indeed and somewhat amusing.

When the bailiff appeared to announce the arrival of the judge, *All rise* took on a whole new meaning. Alisha would swear that the groupies stood and leaned forward, simultaneously centering their gazes on Les. More accurately, below Les's belt.

Judge Slagle braced both hands on his lectern like a preacher about to deliver hellfire and brimstone from his pulpit. A preacher with thick glasses, a shaggy mustache and scraggly thin hair. "Okay, folks, as y'all probably know, we're already two hours late getting started because people have forgotten their manners. Now I don't think I have to remind you that this is a courtroom, not a pep rally. If anyone here sees fit to cause a ruckus, I'll have you removed quicker than a greased-up pig avoiding Sunday dinner. Now y'all take a seat and let's get this show on the road."

After everyone was seated, Slagle addressed Daniel. "You're up, Counselor."

Daniel scooted back his chair, came to his feet and strolled to the jury box. Alisha had avoided really looking at him until that moment, with good reason. But she was enthralled by the way he addressed the jurors, one hand in his pocket and one braced on the railing. He had such fantastic hands with square, blunt fingers and neatly manicured nails. Today he wore a gold ring on his right pinkie and she wondered if perhaps it was a lucky charm. And lucky her, she knew how those hands felt on her body. All over her body. She turned her attention to his wide shoulders encased in a navy-blue jacket that fit him to perfection. That jacket hid one of his finer attributes—his butt—but Alisha knew that terrain well, without clothing of any kind. A first-date shiver ran through her entire body.

"Are you okay, Hart?"

Alisha answered Joe with a befuddled look, proving she wasn't okay. She hadn't been paying attention to the prosecutor's opening remarks because she'd been paying close attention to his finer qualities. And she needed to stop. But before she went back to her notes, she glanced over her shoulder to find that Les's cheerleaders also seemed totally awed by the A.D.A. She wouldn't be a bit surprised if someone held up a new sign that said Females for Fortune. No doubt he would pick up more than a few votes for his future campaign.

Forcing herself back to the situation at hand, she zeroed in on Daniel's voice only to hear him say, "And that is what we will prove."

What exactly was he going to prove? Alisha truly had no idea. She certainly couldn't ask the court reporter to read back the opening statements. That would be grand. *Excuse me, Your Honor, but I was momentarily caught in a carnal frenzy, so if you don't mind...*

"Ms. Hart, your turn."

After clearing her throat, Alisha stood and approached the jurors the same way Daniel had, only she braced both hands on the rail. "Ladies and gentlemen, the prosecution will no doubt try to paint the defendant, Mr. Massey, as a commonplace pervert with violent tendencies. And I will prove that although Mr. Massey's actions might seem unorthodox, he is a man with a cause. Several causes, in fact."

Alisha ignored the sounds of approval coming from across the room, turned her back to the rail and leaned against it. She purposefully leveled her gaze on Daniel. "The prosecution would have you believe that Mr. Massey's behavior was obscene. I would just like to say that many believe the human form is a true work of art. People with names like Bellini, Degas and da Vinci. A work of art that should be appreciated and savored. Enjoyed as a gift." She paused to draw a breath when she noted a definite change in Daniel's eyes. He was remembering their weekend, she could almost bet on it, and maybe that wasn't playing fair at all. But after the jury selection debacle and his inadvertent distraction a few minutes ago, turnabout was definitely fair play. "Mr. Massey has chosen to use his body as an art form—"

"Amen!" resounded from the spectators, followed by a few shouts of "Hallelujah!"

Slagle banged his gavel and sneered. "Hush up now, or you gals are out of here." He looked at Alisha. "Go ahead, Counselor."

Alisha turned back to the jury, fearful that she might stop thinking with Daniel staring at her. He was still staring at her. She could feel it. "As I was saying, Mr. Massey used his body as a means to garner attention for what he believes to be worthwhile endeavors. In this country we are—or should be—able to express ourselves freely. And that is what we will show—that Mr. Massey on three separate occasions engaged in self-expression, not public lewdness or indecency. His conduct was not disorderly, nor did he knowingly knock anyone down. He never intended to cause anyone harm and he does not deserve to be put on trial for exercising freedom. If we can no longer enjoy that freedom, then, ladies, who's to say you might not be charged with some meaningless crimes while at the beach in a bathing suit? Or, gentlemen, mowing your lawn without your shirt? And while you're listening to the prosecution's questionable case, please keep that in mind. Thank you."

After Alisha was seated, Les leaned over and said, "That was great. I like the whole artist thing and that freedom stuff. Makes me sound kind of sophisticated."

That was definitely a stretch. "Don't get too excited. Tomorrow will be the real test when you're on the stand. We'll go over that this evening."

Alisha looked up to see Slagle talking with the court reporter. He straightened and said, "Because of the time, we're going to recess for an early lunch. Court will reconvene at one o'clock."

Everyone rose until the judge retired. Alisha caught a quick glance at Daniel, who was keeping company with a reporter. A gorgeous brunette with big brown eyes and a pink suit that set off her olive complexion. Who wore pink in the dead of winter? Obviously this woman did, and she could get away with it. She could probably get away with anything, maybe even Daniel Fortune.

Alisha didn't have time to worry about that. She needed to concern herself with the case and spend her lunch hour making certain that the jury bought the whole "man-with-a-cause" posture. She had her work cut out for her, both in regard to the defense and the sudden urge to invite Daniel into the stairwell.

Daniel wasn't buying any of that cause crap. Unfortunately the jury looked as if they had bought it hook, line and sinker. *Hook, line and sinker.* That reminded him of fishing, and fishing reminded him of Alisha. Not that he needed any reminders. She'd planted more than a few memories that he couldn't shake, especially during her opening arguments. He wondered if anyone else had noticed how her voice had lowered when she'd talked about bodies. Maybe he'd just imagined she'd been talking to him. Hell, she'd been trying to distract him, and she'd done a damn good job of it. No coincidence that she'd worn that brown outfit or that she'd left her hair down to fall around her shoulders. It swayed every time she moved. *She'd* swayed every time she moved.

Even after making love to her several times, he hadn't even begun to get her out of his system. She was so deeply ingrained in his psyche that not more than five minutes went by when he wasn't thinking about her. Thinking about how she'd felt, how she'd tasted, how she'd kept his undivided attention when they'd talked for hours. She was driving him crazy.

But he wasn't so far gone that he didn't realize something was amiss in his information on the defendant. Tossing aside his half-eaten burger on his desk, he picked up the file and thumbed through it again. No current address of record because he'd supposedly been staying with a friend, and that so-called friend hadn't been located, according to Krauss. Massey's last place of employment was some pizza place. Too many blanks to fill in and not enough time to do it himself. He should have been more involved in the prep for this case instead of following Vera's advice and simply walking into a courtroom virtually unprepared and without the necessary information. But he did have someone who could help.

He picked up the phone and punched the number that rang Sara Utley, a fifty-something paralegal who'd come to his rescue more than once. "I need a favor, Sara."

"Sure. Something to do with the Jamison case?"

"No. The Massey case."

"You mean that naked hunk?"

A huge hunk of trouble, as far as Daniel was concerned. "I need you to see what you can find out about him."

"What am I looking for?"

"Anything we can use against him."

"I'm sure the police have already done a thorough check and come up empty, at least in terms of priors."

"I'm thinking more along the lines of personal relationships. People who might know the real Les Massey. See if you can find something questionable he did in his past."

Sara chuckled. "Like maybe he threw a paper route in the buff?"

That was a possibility. "Yeah. His background info is in the file. I'll leave it on my desk when I go back into court. And I'd appreciate it if you can put a rush on it. Time's running out on this one."

"Sure thing, Mr. Fortune. I'll get back to you when I can. It might be this evening, though."

"I'll be here."

Depending on his witnesses this afternoon—and Alisha Hart's skills—he could very well be there all night.

So far, so good. The first few state's witnesses basically put Les on the scene at the alleged crimes. Alisha kept her cross-examination brief, asking the same questions about Les's dress, his behavior, his effect on the crowd. The man from the zoo offered very little other than Mr. Massey had a pretty good Tarzan yell. And the woman who'd caught Les's Davy Crockett impression had commented she would always remember the Alamo. But now the first of the two most important witnesses for the prosecution was coming up.

"The state calls Misty Ramsey."

"Sounds like the name of a stripper," Joe muttered.

Alisha questioned whether her clerk was right on target. The young woman had tremendously teased platinum hair and large breasts that looked as if they wanted to escape from the tight, low-cut teal sweater. She had on a micromini the color of mud and the most hideous pair of platform shoes the likes of which Alisha hadn't seen since her mother had dragged her to Saturday garage sales years ago. If the fashion police were on the premises, Misty deserved a major citation.

When Daniel approached the stand and smiled, the woman looked as if she might dissolve right into the chair. "Please state your full name and residence for the record," he instructed.

She sat up straight, thrusting her boobs forward. "My name is Misty Rose Ramsey and I live in San Marcos."

"Thank you, Ms. Ramsey," Daniel said. "Now could you tell us your whereabouts on the night of December twenty-third?"

"I was taking a walk on the river. Window-shopping, that sort of thing."

"And on that night did you see the defendant, Lester Massey?"

"Yes, sir, I did."

"What exactly was he doing?"

"He was standing in the middle of a banquet table on a river taxi. It was some sort of dinner cruise, I think."

Daniel stuck his hands in his pockets and slowly paced. "What was he wearing?"

She grinned. "A short jacket with lots of sequins. It was very pretty. And he had this big red sash wrapped around his waist."

"Anything else?"

"A sombrero."

"No pants?"

"No, sir. You could see every inch of his legs. He has nice legs."

A loud whoop echoed through the chamber, causing the judge to bang his gavel, startling Alisha. "If I hear that again, I'm clearin' this courtroom. Go ahead, Counselor."

Daniel walked back to the table, picked up a pointer and returned to the stand. He gestured at an easel holding an enlarged aerial view of the river that he'd introduced into evidence earlier. "Now this is approximately where the taxi was that night. Where were you standing?"

She took the pointer he offered. "Right there," she said, indicating the far side of the narrow canal next to the bridge.

"And Mr. Massey was facing you?"

"Not at first. He had his back to me. But then he was dancing around and he turned. That's when I saw it."

"Saw what?"

"His package."

Was it in decorative paper? Alisha wanted to shout out but quelled the urge.

"Could you be more specific?" Daniel asked.

Misty didn't blush and her gaze didn't falter. "You know, his thing. His genitals."

"Are you absolutely certain that's what you saw?"

She nodded like a bobble-head dog on the dash of a souped-up Chevy. "Oh, yes. It was real big."

More giggles from the peanut factory and grumbles from the puritans.

Daniel glanced at Alisha, challenge in his eyes. "Your witness."

Alisha pushed back from the table and took Daniel's place in front of the stand. "Ms. Ramsey, can you estimate exactly how far away from Mr. Massey you were that night?"

The young woman paused for a moment and pursed her peony-painted lips. "I'm not good at math."

What a shocker. "Think about a football field. Were you that far away?"

"No. Like maybe half of that."

"What time was it?"

"About nine at night."

"Did you have any binoculars?"

Misty rolled her clumpy mascara-laden eyes. "Uh, no."

"Do you have superpowers, like maybe extreme night vision?"

"Objection," Daniel called out, rising from his seat.

Without a pause the judge said, "Sustained."

Alisha forced a smile. "I have one more question, Ms. Ramsey. Since you say that Mr. Massey's genitals were so noticeable, did you happen to see any identifying marks such as a tattoo or birthmark?"

"Actually I do think I saw something like that. Maybe a tattoo, the kind men usually have around their upper arms. Sort of like vines."

She glanced at Daniel to find a look of surprise in his expression over the revelation. If Alisha discovered that was accurate, she would give Les another tattoo he would never forget, using a bobby pin and a permanent marker. Of course, if it wasn't true, that could shoot holes in Misty's testimony and eyewitness account. Having him drop his drawers for verification wouldn't be a banner idea, but she suspected she knew exactly what Misty had seen and she could introduce that during Les's testimony tomorrow. "No further questions."

"Okay, people," Slagle began, "we're going to take a fifteen-minute break before we continue."

Alisha stood and faced Joe. "I'll be back in a few. If Les needs to go to the boys' room, let the guards know. And be sure to escort him, then let me know if you see any tattoos."

Joe groaned. "Isn't that going above and beyond the call of duty?"

She gave him a wink as she backed away. "Just part of the job." When she turned, she almost ran headlong into Daniel. When she moved, he moved, as if they were engaged in some bizarre dance. Finally he stepped to one side and said, "Sorry."

"My fault." She hurried off, the familiar scent of his cologne following her all the way to the rest room. When she found a line of women streaming into the hall, she decided she could hold it, a talent she'd honed during childhood when her dad was inclined to drive nonstop on vacations. She'd been blessed with a boulder-sized bladder, her mother had said, and right now she was grateful. She was also a bit hungry since she'd only had a few peanut butter crackers for lunch.

On that thought Alisha sought out the small break room that housed vending machines and coffee. Although coffee sounded good, she certainly didn't need the caffeine. Just being close to Daniel, even if only momentarily, had her sufficiently wired. She nixed the soda machine, too, and opted for the snacks. Too many choices, she decided as she dug through her jacket pocket for spare change. Whatever she chose, it would have to be something that didn't make her thirsty.

After staring at the machine for several moments, she sensed someone coming up behind her and realized she needed to decide. Gum would work. Fruity gum. Of course, she would have to remember to chuck it before the trial resumed since she had a nasty habit of popping it. Bad molars, her mother had said. What a nice addition to her résumé should she decide to join an Internet singles' site.

*She likes classical music and luxury cars, and she's been blessed with bad molars and a bladder the size of a blimp....*

She was definitely losing it, Alisha decided as she slid the appropriate amount of coins into the slot. Before she could pull the black handle, her hand froze when she heard, "Are you as hungry as I am?"

Oh, God, this was all she needed. A former lover with a fixation on himself and an overblown opinion of his finesse.

She yanked the handle, releasing her frustration and the pack of gum. She didn't want to see Troy Moreau, but she had no choice but to face the sorry music.

"What are you doing here, Troy?"

He forked a hand through his golden hair and favored her with a sleazy smile. "Well, I'm an attorney and this is a court-house, so I thought I'd stay over and watch a little of the afternoon's proceedings. You did a fairly good job this morning."

That was a high compliment coming from him. "You were there?"

"Yeah, standing at the back."

Alisha thanked her lousy stars she hadn't seen him. He'd always delighted in critiquing her, and she wouldn't be surprised if he tried it now. "I have to get back now."

"Let me give you some advice first."

How well she could read him, and she didn't like the subtext one bit. She tore open the package and popped a piece of gum into her mouth. "I don't want or need your advice."

"It's just a small thing. Watch your hands. You tend to wring them. Makes you look nervous."

Alisha wanted to take his tie into her hands and wring it around his neck. "I truly don't care what you think anymore."

She pushed past him, but before she could reach the door he said, "About the White case…"

Reluctantly she faced him again. "What about it?"

"I'm going to be handling it."

A few moments passed before she recovered her voice. "Why are you handling it when it doesn't involve criminal charges against your well-heeled cronies?"

He took a few steps toward her. "I requested the case after I heard you were handling it. Just thought I'd take a shot at something new, like a civil trial. You can never have too much experience."

No, she thought, but he did have way too much arrogance. "How did you know I was representing Mrs. White?"

"We called and made her an offer, and she said she'd hired you."

"Yes, she has."

"It's a good offer. We're willing to go fifty grand."

Alisha couldn't believe his gall. "Fifty grand? That won't even cover medical expenses already incurred."

"That's the best I can do."

"And you can stick that offer—" Alisha stopped, refusing to stoop to his level. "We'll talk about it later. Call and make an appointment."

He dropped down into a chair and assumed his usual insolent posture. "You know, we could have dinner one night. Talk about business. Or pleasure. Whatever you prefer."

She preferred the ground to open up and swallow him whole. "No thanks."

When she started to leave again, he said, "You're way out of your league with this one, Alisha. You can't handle Fortune."

If he only knew she'd already handled him. Straightening her shoulders, Alisha turned and walked to the table, braced her hands on the edge and leaned toward him. "And you're out of your mind if you think for one minute I want to go anywhere near you again." She lifted her gaze to his scalp and frowned. "Troy, I believe you're getting a little thin on top. Maybe you should try one of those new hair-growing products."

Without giving him a second glance she left the room and

turned the corner to see Daniel Fortune standing before her, one shoulder leaning against the wall. She planned to walk past him with only a polite hello, planned not to react to his presence, but she failed when he said, "Are you okay?"

She smoothed a hand down her jacket, praying he didn't see the slight tremble. "I'm fine. Why?"

"I saw Moreau go in after you in the break room."

"Nothing I can't handle."

He pushed off the wall. "I know, but I still worry about you."

She wanted to ask exactly what was worrying him. She wanted to smooth the concern from his face. She wanted to kiss him so badly she was tempted to forget who and where she was. But she couldn't do any of those things, at least not now. She needed to stop by the rest room, throw some water on her face and get back to business. "I'll see you in a few minutes."

When she passed him, he caught her hand and gave it a gentle squeeze, then let her go. She kept right on walking, wondering all the while if he'd meant to provide comfort or throw her mentally off balance.

No. Daniel wasn't like Troy. He'd only meant to remind her that she had his support. She trusted him, something she hadn't thought possible after her involvement with Moreau. Maybe that made her a fool. Or perhaps a woman very close to falling in love.

This afternoon she had a fight ahead of her. She needed to focus on the case and ignore Daniel Fortune, who would be seated only a few feet away—in the role of adversary, not lover.

## *Eleven*

If Alisha was at all shaken, Daniel couldn't tell it from her current demeanor as she prepared to cross-examine the state's most valuable witness. He didn't care about the indecent-exposure charge or the disorderly conduct. The strength of the case hinged on the eighty-year-old assault victim's testimony, and so far, so good. During direct examination Mrs. O'Reilly—who looked like everyone's favorite cookie-baking gray-haired granny—had been a rock. Daniel had all the confidence in the world she would remain that way during cross. If Alisha found some way to discredit her, he'd eat his briefcase.

"First of all, Mrs. O'Reilly," Alisha began, "I want to tell you how sorry I am you've broken your arm."

The lady smiled and rubbed a careworn hand down the blue sling. "Thank you, dear."

"Now I want to ask you a few questions in regard to your health before the accident."

Daniel came to his feet. "Objection. Mrs. O'Reilly's health before the accident isn't relevant."

Without looking at Daniel, Alisha addressed the judge. "There are circumstances in regard to her health that could impact her testimony, Your Honor."

"I'll allow it for now," Slagle said.

Alisha folded her arms across her chest, a sure sign, at least to Daniel, that she wasn't altogether comfortable with the line of questioning. Neither was he. "Do you have any vision problems?"

"Yes, I do. Cataracts. But they're not bad enough to require surgery."

"How close do objects have to be for you to see them?"

"I can see you just fine, dear." She leaned around and looked toward Daniel. "Mr. Fortune looks fuzzy from here."

Alisha turned and nailed him with a quick glance before facing the witness again. "So I assume you can't see clearly more than a few feet away."

"That would be correct."

"Have you fallen before?"

Damn. He knew exactly where she was heading. He rose and called out, "Objection. Irrelevant."

Alisha addressed the judge. "I'll prove the relevance if the court will give me the opportunity."

Slagle tapped his gavel with one bony finger. "Fine and dandy, but let's speed things along. You may answer the question, Mrs. O'Reilly."

Mrs. O'Reilly shifted in her seat. "Yes. I fell a few months ago and had a hip replacement. That's why I use a cane. I tripped after a dizzy spell."

"A dizzy spell?"

"I have bouts of vertigo."

Daniel sat tight even though he wanted to object again, which would only be futile. He would see where this led, at least for now, and hopefully not into a trap from which his star witness couldn't escape.

"Did you have one of those bouts the night of the incident?" Alisha asked.

The woman shook her head. "No, I haven't had a spell in a long time. I was feeling quite fine. I'd been shopping that evening."

This time Daniel wanted to applaud. He relaxed somewhat and tried to hide his smile.

Alisha took a few steps, then came back to the stand. "Okay. When Mr. Massey approached you on the walkway, were there a lot of people around?"

"Oh, yes."

"Were those people watching Mr. Massey?"

"Yes, we all were. Quite a few young girls were screaming and cheering. Of course, I couldn't see him that well. That's why I wanted to catch a better look." She smiled an amiable smile. "At my age, the opportunity to view a handsome young man doesn't come along too often, especially one who is barely dressed. I wanted to see what the fuss was all about."

Several snickers came from Massey's side of the courtroom, prompting Slagle to pound his gavel, and he looked pleased to do it. "Simmer down, people."

Alisha presented her own smile, knocking Daniel for a loop. "Now when Mr. Massey approached you, where exactly were you looking?"

Mrs. O'Reilly's cheeks turned a light shade of pink. "At first his face, but then his red sash caught my attention." More giggles, but this time Slagle didn't bother to pound his gavel. In fact, Daniel could swear he looked pretty amused.

"What happened while you were looking at his sash?" Alisha asked.

"The next thing I knew, I was on the ground."

"Did you see Mr. Massey's hand push you before you fell?"

The woman hesitated. "Not exactly, but he was right there."

"So you're telling everyone in this courtroom that you didn't actually witness him pushing you?"

That sent Daniel out of his chair. "Objection. Counsel is leading the witness."

"I'll rephrase it. Mrs. O'Reilly, did you see Mr. Massey raise his hand and push you?"

The woman who'd been solid as stone looked totally disconcerted. Daniel could relate. "Well, I guess…I felt it," she said.

"Then you didn't actually see him push you?"

Looked like he might have barbecued briefcase for dinner. "Objection. Witness has already answered that question," he said without bothering to stand.

"Sustained," Slagle said. "Get a move on, Ms. Hart."

"I did hear someone say, 'What a jerk,'" Mrs. O'Reilly added.

Daniel didn't doubt Alisha would jump on that, and she did when she asked, "Did this person call Mr. Massey by name or mention him pushing you?"

The woman lowered her eyes. "No, he didn't."

"Is it possible, then, that maybe someone else around Mr. Massey, perhaps one of the young women, could have pushed you down?"

"I suppose that's possible, but he was right there." She tapped her finger on the railing. "Right there when it happened."

Alisha gave her a sympathetic look. "Thank you, Mrs. O'Reilly. No further questions."

Slagle turned his attention to Daniel. "Redirect, Counselor?"

Daniel couldn't think of a damn thing to say. The reasonable doubt had already been planted in the jury's minds, and not one other witness had come forward to confirm Mrs. O'Reilly's claims. He'd have to do damage control during closing arguments. "No, Your Honor."

"Fine," Slagle said. "You may step down, ma'am. Any other witnesses, Mr. Fortune?"

Daniel stood. "The state rests."

Slagle banged his gavel. "Court is adjourned until nine to-morrow morning."

After the jury exited, Alisha addressed Slagle. "Motion to dismiss, Your Honor, on the grounds the state has failed to prove its case."

"Good try, Counselor, but the motion is dee-nied, although it's kind of tempting." Slagle topped off the comment with a condescending look targeted at Daniel.

Daniel remained in place while the courtroom cleared, wondering what the hell had happened. He knew what had happened—he'd been bested by the defense. Considering his own lack of conviction, he should have seen it coming. He should have been better prepared, interviewed the witnesses himself, but he hadn't really cared. His heart hadn't been in this case from the beginning. He'd been totally focused on Alisha Hart. And now he'd have hell to pay for his disregard.

Hell came a few minutes later in his office when he confronted the boss standing by the window and staring out over the city streets. "She kicked your ass, Fortune," Vera said. "Kicked it clean into the next county."

Daniel tossed his briefcase onto his desk and yanked off his jacket. "It's a weak case, Allan. The bulk of it rested on Mrs. O'Reilly's testimony, and she buckled."

Allan turned and gave him a hard stare. "And you let it fall apart. Now what are you going to do to salvage it?"

Daniel collapsed into his chair. "To tell the truth, I'm not sure there's much I can do other than to try to discredit Massey, provided defense counsel decides to put him on the stand."

"She'll have to if she wants to answer to the other charges aside from the assault. I imagine she's going to go for broke."

Daniel suspected his boss was right. "It's going to be tough to make this guy look bad. He's a damn hero to a lot of people. We don't have anything to go on."

"Don't be so sure about that," came a woman's voice from the doorway.

Daniel looked up to see Sara Utley striding into the room. "You found something?"

"I found an ex-girlfriend. It took some time, but I tracked down the guy who's supposedly his roommate. As it turned out, he only let Massey sleep on his couch for a few days. He gave me the number of the former girlfriend, Carol Novak, who lives in New Orleans. I called her but didn't get an answer. I was just about to throw in the towel when her call came in."

Maybe his luck had taken a turn for the better. "What does she have to offer about Massey?"

"Plenty. She saw coverage of the case on the news yesterday. She told me he's never supported a cause in his life. He wants to be in show business and for the two years they were together he was plotting ways to get attention. She's pretty mad at him because he just took off one day without telling her."

"How long ago?"

"About four months." Sara sent him a bright smile. "This is the kicker. It seems the toreador outfit he was wearing on the river is hers. Also—" she fished a notebook from her jacket pocket and flipped it open "—he took several of her favorite CDs and the hibachi grill he gave her on her birthday."

"Did she mention him taking anything of greater monetary value?" Allan asked.

"No. That's it."

Too bad. Daniel would enjoy slapping him with felony theft. "All right. We know for sure what I've suspected all along. Massey's in this for the publicity. But considering she's just now come forward and she lives out of state, that complicates everything."

"She's more than willing to testify," Sara said. "I can book her a flight and get her here in the morning, bright and early."

"At the expense of the taxpayers," Daniel said. "I'm just

not sure it's worth it. We should make a deal on the disorderly conduct charges and cut our losses."

Allan guided the clerk toward the door. "Could you give us a minute, Sara?"

"Sure," she said. "Just let me know if I need to reserve the flight."

"Go ahead and make the arrangements," Allan told her, fueling Daniel's anger almost to the boiling point.

After Sara left the room, Allan closed the door and leveled a hard look on Daniel. "I don't think I have to remind you how important this case could be to your future."

Daniel mustered all his composure to keep his anger in check. "Dammit, Allan, I've told you from the beginning I didn't have time for this. I have the Jamison case pending, not to mention one that landed on my desk this morning involving a parolee who shot a store clerk in the head during a robbery. That clerk happened to have a wife and four kids. That's important, not some guy who's nothing more than a nuisance."

"The party's counting on you with this one."

Same song, second verse, and Daniel was tired of it. "I find it damn hard to believe that my record doesn't speak for itself. That should interest the party, not this nothing case."

"This case is important to the city. This idiot has to be stopped before he wreaks more havoc. Besides, Pettigrew—"

"The hell with P—" Daniel stopped himself and with the last of his waning strength reclaimed his composure. "Look, the best I can do, even with this girlfriend's testimony, is prove that Massey has a different motive for doing what he's done. It doesn't change the fact that the assault and indecent-exposure charges probably aren't going to fly."

"And that proves that the ass is basically a liar," Allan said. "That could go a long way toward erasing reasonable doubt on all the charges."

"But only if the defense counsel decides to call him. And even if she does, she'll have to give me an in during direct examination of Massey, otherwise we can forget about a rebuttal witness."

"Mark my words, Ms. Hart's going to make Massey look like a saint. And my guess is, he's going to play right into your hands."

Probably an accurate guess, but Daniel was sick of the whole thing. He also knew the defendant's counsel well. Very well. "We have no way of knowing what Alisha plans to do, but you can bet she's going to handle whatever we throw at her."

Vera narrowed his eyes. "Alisha? Since when are you on a first-name basis with opposing counsel?"

Dammit to hell. "I'm on a first-name basis with most opposing counsel."

Allan took a seat in the chair across from Daniel's desk. "You know, I haven't mentioned this before, but I'm going to now. I saw her leave with you the night of the reception. I figured, hey, she's a good-looking woman, what could be the harm in it? Besides, I trusted you not to cross any lines. Have you?"

Concerns Daniel had dismissed had come back to bite him—exactly what Alisha had feared all along. "What I did that night has no bearing on this case."

"If word gets out that you've been sleeping with the defense, you could compromise this case. If you lie down and just let this one slide without putting up a fight, it could raise suspicions."

"We haven't discussed this case outside of a professional arena," Daniel said.

Allan came to his feet. "Regardless, you better be prepared to go back into battle tomorrow and win. Otherwise it might be your political future as well as your ass in a sling. And hers, too."

Daniel watched his boss leave without posing any more arguments or defending his relationship with Alisha. In doing so, he would only make matters worse. One thing he did know—he couldn't see her again until this trial was over. Maybe even for a few weeks. He couldn't afford to cast any suspicion on himself, but more importantly on her. His persistence had gotten them into this mess, and it was up to him to get them out of it. Otherwise Alisha might get hurt, and the last thing he wanted to do was hurt her. Professionally or personally. Especially personally.

Alisha would rather be anywhere else, doing anything else, than sitting in a courthouse holding room with the pretty boy from hell.

"Okay, Mr. Massey, we have two options. We can forgo any defense since the state is failing miserably at proving its case, at least where the assault charge is concerned. Or we can put you on the stand and you can tell your side of the story, which may or may not convince the jury to acquit you on all charges."

Les didn't hesitate. "I want to tell my story. I want everyone to know that I didn't mean to hurt anyone."

"As your attorney, I'd advise you to reconsider."

"No way. I want to be on that stand tomorrow."

Exactly what she'd expected. "Then it's time to go over what you need to say. First question, do you have any tattoos on your privates?"

Les folded his hands on the table and grinned. "Nope. Got one on my butt, though. Wanna see it?"

"God, no." Her protest sounded like a gunshot in the empty room. "Any idea where Ms. Ramsey might have come up with the tattoo thing?"

"Yeah. The maracas. I was shaking them between my legs."

"Fine. I'll also ask you about Mrs. O'Reilly."

"Okay, but I don't know why we have to talk about that. You did real good today handling that old lady."

The ageist pig. "Don't get your hopes up, Mr. Massey.

You have to face Mr. Fortune tomorrow. He's not going to go easy on you."

"Piece of cake. I can take it."

Alisha wanted to take her briefcase and cram it where the sun didn't shine. "You need to be direct with your answers. No going off on tangents. Try to stick with yes and no. I don't want any surprise revelations. And for heaven's sake, please do not flirt with the ladies while you're sitting on the stand."

Massey leaned back and rubbed his chin. "When you got it, you got it. They're my public. *My girls.*" He sat forward again. "Which reminds me. A reporter wants to interview me. I told him no, but I can call him back. He says it would be best if he does it now, before the trial is over."

She'd chalk that up to his common sense going on vacation, but he hadn't displayed any common sense to this point. "Not on your life. You keep your mouth closed. What you do after the trial is your business, but you can't say anything until then."

Les slapped a hand on the table. "Not fair. They'll probably forget about me after the trial, unless I go to jail. And I'm pretty sure I won't."

"Again, don't count your chickens before they're hatched."

He looked as if she'd just fed him a mathematical equation. "What?"

Alisha gathered her notes and shoved them into her briefcase. "Never mind. Just remember, no talking to the press."

"But that kind of ruins all my plans."

"What plans?"

He made a sweeping gesture with one hand. "This whole thing. I've waited my whole life for the opportunity. If I didn't think I'd get some good press out of this, then I wouldn't have frozen my jewels off standing around pretending I cared about any cause."

Alisha shook her head, hoping to clear the confusion. "Are

you saying that your whole reason behind these little performances had to do with news coverage?"

Now he looked at her as if she'd taken leave of her senses. "Well, yeah. I want to be an actor and I figure this is the way to get a break. I mean, I've got the looks and the body, but that doesn't matter if no one sees it."

That proved it. He was everything she'd instinctively believed him to be and much more. "Why didn't you tell me this before?"

"I didn't think it mattered. Your job is to defend me, right or wrong."

She was really starting to hate that part of her job. "Just out of curiosity, Mr. Massey, have you ever considered perhaps trying auditions and casting calls instead of going to such extremes?"

"Now you sound like Carol."

"Who's Carol?"

"My ex-girlfriend. She always acted like it was so easy to get a job. Besides, I tried making a few auditions. Never made it past the first call. I even tried to sing on one of those reality shows, but they said I wasn't good enough. What do they know?" He let go a grating laugh. "Those people on the riverboat thought I sang 'Jingle Bells' pretty well."

Alisha really wanted to jingle his bells. "Mr. Massey, if you even hint at your reasons behind your little antics, then you're going to blow this entire case. I'm billing you as a man with a social conscience, not a guy with a desire to make the big time."

"I don't want to start out big. Maybe do some B-movies, a little soft porn."

Alisha had had enough. First Troy, now Mr. Porn Prospect. Could her day get any worse? "It's time for you to go back now. I'll see you in the morning." She stood. "And remember, not a word about this on the stand tomorrow. As far as everyone's concerned, you're an upstanding citizen." She signaled the guard with a look. "He's all yours."

Relieved to get away from Massey, Alisha left the courthouse at a fast clip and elbowed her way through members of the press shouting questions about her impending victory. She sprinted past the crowd of Massey supporters applauding her and chanting her name. They viewed her as Les's champion and had turned the egomaniac into some cult hero, when in reality he'd been playing them all for personal gain, including her.

When she reached the sidewalk across the street, another leading lecher waited for her for the second time that day. She tried to pass by Troy, but he clasped her arm to halt her progress. "Wait a minute, Alisha. I just want to congratulate you."

She yanked out of his grasp. "Fine. Thank you. I have to go."

"I think I deserve a little more from you than that."

"You don't deserve anything from me, Troy, except a swift kick in the butt."

He winked. "Aw, come on now. I taught you everything you know."

Never before had she wanted to slap someone as badly as she wanted to slap him. "You didn't teach me a damn thing. I taught you. If not for me, you'd be working in a dry cleaner's right now."

"And if you hadn't met me, you'd still be a virgin. That should count for something."

She kept a tight grip on her briefcase and her self-control. "It only accounts for my stupidity. At that time I didn't have anything to compare you to, but I do now. Believe me, you've fallen far short." She pushed past him. "Have a nice evening."

Without giving him a chance to respond Alisha rushed to her car. Once there, she sat for a long moment, staring at the courthouse. She could use a long drive to cool off. She could use a stiff drink. She could definitely use some luck tomorrow when she had to question Les. More than that, she could use a solid shoulder to lean on, a warm hand to hold, someone she could trust. And that someone was Daniel Fortune. Good judgment ordered she not even consider that. But when it came to the prosecutor, that hadn't entered into it from the moment she'd landed in his life.

When the buzzer sounded, Daniel checked the clock. He had no idea who would be stopping by his condo this time of night, although he could probably guess at a few possibilities. He didn't want to see any of those possibilities right now.

He depressed the intercom and said, "Yeah?"

"Sorry to disturb you, Mr. Fortune, but a lady named Lola is here to see you."

In a million years he wouldn't have guessed that. He considered sending her away but instead said, "Send her up."

He wanted to pace, but he waited by the door in anticipation of all the possibilities. He had no idea why she would have risked coming to see him, but he assumed it had to be something serious. Whatever it was, he had to admit he was damn glad she'd decided to stop by.

The minute he heard the knock, he opened the door to Alisha, her hair tucked beneath a floppy hat, her clothes covered by a full-length all-weather coat and her eyes concealed by sunglasses even though it was nearing ten o'clock.

She breezed past him, stripped off the hat and shook out her hair. "I know I shouldn't be here, but I went home and changed, then I had a drink at Leal's. I started walking and I ended up here."

He had to agree; she shouldn't be there. But he didn't want her to leave, not until he found out why she looked so strung out. Not before he kissed her good-night, which was all he could settle for in light of their situation. "What's going on, Alisha?"

She pulled off her coat, revealing a pair of faded jeans and a baggy blue sweatshirt. Nothing fancy. Barely any flesh showing. But she might as well have been wearing the black nightgown, considering Daniel's immediate reaction.

Alisha tossed her things onto the chair and walked the room before facing him again. "I'm having an awful day. I thought we could talk awhile."

Now was not the time to invite her to continue the conversation in bed, even though he wanted that. Badly.

He took a few steps toward her, the sofa providing a solid barrier between them, at least for the moment. "I would've thought you might be celebrating your success."

She frowned. "Success as in bullying an octogenarian? Or maybe you mean my lovely encounter with my former jerk of a lover who told me I'm way out of my league."

"I heard him."

She frowned. "What do you mean you heard him?"

"I stood outside the break room door to make sure he didn't hassle you." Only a partial truth. He'd eavesdropped to make sure she didn't take Moreau up on any questionable offers, not that he had any reason to believe she would. But this wasn't about reason. This had to do with plain and simple possessiveness.

"Anyway, he's wrong," Daniel said. "You proved that today in court."

She sighed. "I can handle Troy. He doesn't bother me anymore."

"Then why are you here?"

"I…" She balled her fists at her sides and looked away. "I guess I needed to talk to someone I could trust. Someone who would understand and just let me vent. I thought about calling my mother, but I didn't want to worry her. I considered my friends and realized how short that list is." She turned her gaze on his, her heart in her eyes. "Then I realized you're at the top of that list."

He wanted more than her friendship, but he recognized

she needed a friend more than a lover right now. "Okay. I'm listening."

She strolled to the window, pushed the curtain out of the way and stared into the night. "I'm just sick of it. Everyone plays everyone else. Troy is a prime example. He only cares about what's in it for him. And Les Massey's cut from the same cloth. His only cause is Les Massey. He wants to be an actor." She released a mirthless laugh. "A porn actor. Imagine that. I have to put him on the stand tomorrow and pretend he's an all-around great guy."

She was heading into dangerous territory, and Daniel suspected she didn't even realize it. "Alisha—"

"He doesn't give a damn about animal rights or history. He wants publicity and he's determined to get it—"

"Alisha, listen to me."

Daniel crossed the room, but before he could halt her she said, "And he's orchestrated this whole farce so he can gain media attention. He actually wants to grant an interview from jail. Imagine that. And when I said no, he compared me to his ex-girlfriend who didn't *understand* him—"

He took her shoulders and turned her around. "Alisha, stop."

At first she looked confused, before awareness dawned in her expression and she clamped her hand over her mouth. "Oh, God. I can't believe—"

"Whatever's discussed tonight will remain between us. I promise." But he couldn't promise that she wouldn't misinterpret what he planned to do tomorrow. He also couldn't tell her about it, and that presented one hell of a dilemma.

She shook off his grasp, walked past him and collapsed onto the sofa. "Joe told me this would happen."

"Joe?"

"Yes. He said that when people are intimate, things somehow manage to slip out. Things that should never be discussed. I totally forgot for a minute who you are, which is exactly why this should never have happened between us."

Daniel warred with revealing what he'd discovered earlier that day, verification of what she'd just told him. But he couldn't do it, as much for her protection as it was for his. Especially now. Instead he would blindside her tomorrow. And the resulting destruction could devastate their relationship if she didn't keep it all in perspective.

She was right about one thing—he should never have let this thing between them go so far. Yet he hadn't stopped it because he hadn't wanted to. She meant more to him than any woman ever had. She still did.

Daniel joined her on the sofa and wrapped his arm around her shoulder. "You can trust me. I'm not going to tell anyone."

She laid her head on his shoulder. "I know, but that doesn't excuse my behavior. I'm beginning to think I'm a lost cause."

Daniel was beginning to think he was just plain lost—to her. "It's okay." He turned her face to his and brushed a kiss across her lips. "Let's just forget it."

"I want to forget it," she said. "I want to forget about everything but us right now. Can we do that?"

"You're not going to get any argument from me." And she wouldn't, even if his logical self argued against taking her to his bed. He refused to listen.

Daniel stood and pulled her to her feet, keeping her hand in his as he led her into the bedroom. Once there, he didn't bother to turn out the light, because he wanted to see her. All of her. They didn't say a word as they undressed each other. Didn't speak as he took her down onto his bed. Their only communication came through touches and kisses. Deep kisses, meticulous touches, but not thorough enough before the phone shrilled.

A foul curse spewed out of Daniel's mouth, then another. He considered not answering it, but at this time of night it could be an emergency. Damn his job.

Keeping one arm beneath Alisha, he reached over and grabbed the receiver. "Fortune."

"Hi, Danny."

Another surprise among the many tonight. "Ryan?"

"Yeah. Sorry to bother you. I just wanted to check in."

After giving Alisha an apologetic look, Daniel moved away from her and sat on the edge of the bed. "Sure. I'm glad you called. I've been busy, otherwise I would have called you." But he hadn't, just one more thing to fuel his guilt. "I'm sorry."

"It's okay, Danny. I…" Ryan hesitated, then said, "I need you to promise me something."

"Sure, Ryan. Anything."

"Promise me you'll make sure Jamison gets what he deserves."

Daniel tightened his grip on the receiver. "You've gotten more threats."

"A few."

Damn Jamison straight to hell. "Do you have security in place?"

"Yeah. And there's something else. It's about Emmett Jamison. He's been out of touch with family for a while, so his father, Blake, tracked him down in New Mexico. You know he's former FBI, right?"

That was one of the few things he knew about Jason Jamison's brother. "Yeah. Why?"

"Blake told me Emmett's been out at the firing range every day. Blake's worried he's going to conduct his own search for Jason. He's a good guy and I don't want to see him get into trouble."

That was the last thing the police needed—vigilante justice. "If you can confirm that's his intent, you might want to notify the authorities."

"I'm hoping I don't have to. I'm also hoping they find Jason before the son of a bitch ruins more lives. Or kills someone else."

"They'll find him, Ryan, and when they do, he'll be punished to the fullest extent of the law." Daniel displayed more confidence than he actually felt at the moment.

"I just hope I'm around to see that."

"You will be."

"I won't unless he's caught in the next three months or so."

An eerie sense of foreboding settled over Daniel. "I'm not following you here, Ryan."

"It's almost over for me, Danny. And I can't do anything to stop it."

"You're not making any sense, Ryan."

A long pause followed Ryan's rough sigh. "I've got to go, Danny. Lily's waiting."

"Not until you stop speaking in riddles and tell me what's going on."

"Okay, but what I say can't go any further until I'm ready to tell the family."

"You can trust me, Ryan."

"I'm about to do something. The hardest thing I've ever done."

A sickening feeling settled in Daniel's gut. "What do you have to do?"

"In a few minutes I have to tell the woman I've loved for more years than I can count that I'm dying from a brain tumor and there's nothing anyone can do."

## *Twelve*

"Damn, Ryan. I can't believe this."

The absolute helplessness in Daniel's voice sent Alisha up onto one arm. He kept his head lowered, the phone gripped in one hand as he forked the other through his hair.

"Are you sure nothing can be done?"

Alisha could only make out the muffled sound of a male voice, so she couldn't discern the content of the conversation. But it was bad, she decided. Very, very bad.

After a few agonizing moments Daniel said, "You let me know if you need anything. Anything at all."

He replaced the phone on the charger, then cradled his head in his hands, his elbows on his thighs. With his back to her, Alisha couldn't see his face, but she sensed his distress. She rubbed his back, the only thing she could think to do. "Problems?" she asked softly.

"Yeah."

"Want to talk about it?"

His weary sigh echoed in the room. "I just learned that the man who was more of a father to me than my own father is dying."

Not just bad. Tragic. Alisha said the only thing that came to mind. "I'm so sorry, Daniel."

"So am I. More than I can say."

Alisha wished he would voice his sadness, use her as a sounding board. "I'm willing to listen."

He remained silent for a moment, leading her to believe that he didn't want that at all, then suddenly sat up and turned a bit toward her. He said, "Back when I was a kid, we used to go to see my cousin Ryan on his ranch in the summer."

She recalled what she knew about Ryan Fortune. He was a revered rancher and philanthropist whom Alisha knew only by reputation. A stellar reputation. "Good memories?"

"Yeah. My mom would pack us up and take us, until we'd get the call from *him,* demanding we come home."

"Him?"

"My bastard of a father. He couldn't stand having my mother gone for more than a few days. He hated that she might be happy without him, which she was during those times. I never saw her smile all that much except at Ryan's. But then, she didn't have anything to smile about. None of us did."

Finally the puzzle of Daniel's background was beginning to unfold. "I take it you didn't get along with your dad."

His laugh was caustic. "That's an understatement. Kind of hard to get along with someone who pretends to be the consummate family man during the day, then comes home drunk and knocks his wife around at night."

The truth was much worse than Alisha had thought, but it did explain the sadness and anger she'd seen in his eyes when he'd talked about his parents. "Did he hit you?"

"Yeah, but not to the degree he hit her." He sent a quick glance back at her, then turned away again, but not before she witnessed the fury in his eyes. "Remember when I told you she wasn't always available to cook?"

"Yes."

"That wasn't because she was at a PTA meeting or bible study. She was in bed, nursing her wounds."

A marriage like that was totally beyond Alisha's comprehension. Her father never raised a hand to her mother. Or to her, for that matter. "No one did anything to stop him?"

"We called the police a couple of times, but my mother wouldn't press charges. And my father was a local banker, well respected. No one knew the real Leonard Fortune."

But Daniel had, and he'd suffered for it. "Your mother never left him?"

"No. My brother, Vincent, the oldest, stuck around until my little sister was gone. I left as soon as I could get out of there. And sometimes I regret it. Sometimes I wonder if I could have talked her into leaving."

"Daniel, you can't blame yourself. You can't force someone to do something she doesn't want to do."

"Probably so, but as it turned out, her husband eventually killed her anyway."

It took all of Alisha's strength not to gasp. "I thought you said it was—"

"A wreck. It was. No one knows for certain if he was drunk, because they were both killed instantly in a single-vehicle accident. But I know. He might as well have put a gun to her head and pulled the trigger. Same thing."

He remained silent for a long time before he said, "That's why I appreciate Ryan as much as I do. He provided an escape, even though he never knew it. But it didn't last. One day—I think I was about ten—I begged my mother to let us stay with him for good, but she took us home anyway. We never went back as a family, and that was the last time I cried. I shut down after that out of self-preservation. I stopped feeling altogether, or at least tried. And I swore I would never be like him."

Now it all made sense—Daniel's refusal to drink, his determination to prosecute criminals. His pain. Alisha wanted to reach out to him, but she realized he would have to invite it. "I'm sorry you had to live with that. It's not something anyone could easily forget."

"I forgave my mother, but I've never forgotten, even though I now know the dynamics of domestic violence. And the two times I've had to try a case where a battered woman was involved in the killing of her partner, it's been tough. I might have argued the murder, but I was thinking justification."

"You didn't request to be removed for those cases?"

"I couldn't. No one knows about my sorry situation outside of my immediate family. No one but you."

Alisha wasn't sure which was more shocking—that he'd gone through his life never revealing his horrible past or that he'd chosen to tell her. She scooted up on her knees and wrapped her arms around his neck from behind. "Thank you for trusting me enough to tell me. I only wish I could do something to help."

He took her hand and kissed her palm. "You can. Just be with me."

She could do that without any reservation. She could help him forget, if only for a while.

Daniel took her back onto the bed in his arms and kissed her. A kiss that seemed almost desperate in its intensity. He pulled back to study her face, to touch her mouth, to stroke her cheek, before kissing her again.

She truly wanted to alleviate his pain, to make him forget. Nudging him onto his back, she kissed his face, his shadowed jaw, and then slid her lips down his chest. When she kept going, he tangled his hands in her hair. When she moved beyond the hard plane of his belly, he released a harsh breath. And when she took him into her mouth, he muttered a soft curse followed by her name.

She explored without hesitation, using her lips and hands,

engaging in more intimacy than she had with any man before him. Her ministrations were working, she realized, when she noticed the sound of his ragged breathing and the tautness of his muscles where her palm rested on his thigh.

Suddenly he sat up and bent forward, taking her by the arms and pulling her up. "Not this way," he murmured as he laid her back onto the bed again. "I want to be inside you."

With his solid thigh he parted her legs and fulfilled his desire, as well as hers. He moved hard, moved deep, holding her tightly as he whispered her name. She didn't complain when he cuffed her wrists in one hand and held her arms above her head while he kept his other hand in motion over her body. She didn't worry when the tempo turned wilder, more frantic, because she intuitively knew this was what he needed. She wanted to be the woman he needed. The woman he loved.

Alisha didn't have time to analyze that thought because her own needs took over as Daniel continued to touch her and kiss her. She climaxed with a moan against his mouth. He wasn't far behind her, his body racked with a fierce shudder as he continued to look into her eyes before he buckled against her.

They stayed that way, holding each other, their breathing returning to normal in slow increments. He rested his cheek against her breasts while she smoothed her hand over his hair. She cherished the absolute contentment she experienced in that moment, until she felt the warmth and dampness against her skin.

Alisha moved her hand down to Daniel's face and confirmed what she already knew. She stroked his hair and whispered, "It's okay. I'm here. It's okay…."

She felt his sorrow as keenly as if it was hers, and she cried for him, as well. She let the tears fall silently as she mourned for the little boy whose life had been shattered by violence, and fell totally in love with the man who had taken that tattered past and built something solid from the ruins with his undying pursuit of justice.

The world was lucky to have Daniel Fortune, and she was so very lucky to know him. No matter what happened from this point forward, she would never regret having him in her life.

While one man let go of his past in the arms of a woman, another prepared to face his tenuous future in the arms of his beloved wife.

Ryan Fortune couldn't imagine his life without Lily. Couldn't imagine walking into the room where they had spent so many nights holding each other, loving each other, to tell her what he should have told her months ago. But he couldn't put off the inevitable any longer, especially now that Daniel knew the truth. He owed her that much. He owed her everything.

On leaden legs Ryan walked into the bedroom and paused at the open door. Lily sat up against the pillows, concentrating on whatever book she was reading, her routine for all the years they'd been together. He took a moment to study her, to record all the details of her face, before the tumor took total control, robbing him of the ability to remember at all.

At fifty-nine Lily was still incredibly beautiful, her hair still long and sleek and black, tinged with only a few strands of barely noticeable gray. He questioned what he had done right to deserve such a remarkable woman. He wondered how he would ever be able to tell her goodbye or if he would even be able to say the words when the time came. But the loss of his dignity could never compare to losing her.

When he stepped inside the bedroom, Lily set her reading glasses and the book on the nightstand, tossed back the sheets and patted the space beside her.

"Climb in, my love. You look exhausted."

He was both tired and weary, burdened by his illness and the duty he must now undertake. "We need to talk."

"Of course." He saw the concern in her expression, heard it in her voice. She knew something was going on, had known for a while. He just hadn't been able to find the strength to tell her. He prayed for strength now as he slid into the bed and pulled her against his side.

"We've had a good life, haven't we, Lily?"

She snuggled against his chest. "The best."

"Have I made you happy?"

She raised her head and stared at him. "How could you ask me that? I love you more than I've ever loved anyone. I love you more every day."

"I feel the same." *Get on with it, Fortune.* "And that's why what I'm about to tell you is so damn hard."

"Ryan, you're scaring me." Her fear was reflected in her face.

Truth be known, he was scared, too. Not scared to die, but scared to leave her behind. Scared that she might get it in her fool head to stop living. "I'm sorry, honey. I don't want you to be scared. But I do need you to promise me something before I continue."

He saw the first mist of tears in her eyes. "What?"

"That no matter what happens in the future, make sure the Fortune reunion happens in May. And never forget that you've been the best thing that's ever happened to me."

"Ryan, please—"

"I'm sick, Lily. I have something growing in my head. It's going to keep growing until it sucks the life out of me."

She straightened and touched her fingertips to her lips. "God, Ryan, no—"

He pulled her back into his arms. "I'm sorry. I should've told you a few months ago. I just didn't know how."

The tortured sob she released cut Ryan straight to the heart. He held her close while she cried, fighting his own tears. He damned this disease. Damned his helplessness and the injustice of it all.

Without warning she sat up and returned to the Lily he knew and loved. "We're going to fight this, Ryan. I'm not ready to lose you. We'll call Peter and Violet in the morning and ask them—"

"I've already talked to them." He sat up with his back to the headboard. "Lily, I've seen plenty of doctors, and they've all said the same thing. Nothing can be done about it."

"What about chemotherapy, radiation?"

"They only buy a little bit of time. I don't want to spend the last of my days being sicker than I have to be. I've accepted my fate, and you have to accept it, too. I swear to God, Lily, I can't have any peace unless I know you're going to be okay. I have to know that you'll go on without me and be happy."

She threw her pillow across the room. "Happy? How can I be happy when I know you've given up?"

"I'm not giving up, honey. I've just decided to acknowledge the illness and go on from there."

She stared at him blankly for a long moment. "I can't do this, Ryan. I can't even think about living without you."

He took her hands into his. "You're going to have to think about it, but you also need to think about the good times. You need to think about all the years we've spent together and how lucky we've been. Some people spend a lifetime together and never have what we have."

She collapsed against him, her tears bleeding through his pajama shirt. "I love you, Ryan. I love you so, so much. I won't be able to stand it if you're gone."

He rocked her gently, held on to her tightly and finally let his own tears come. He wanted to freeze this moment in time. He wanted to wake up and realize his cancer had all been a nightmare. He wanted a miracle, knowing that a miracle wouldn't come. Besides, he'd already been blessed with one miracle, and she was in his arms.

Daniel couldn't seem to get close enough to Alisha, even now as they made love in the moments before dawn. She roved her hands over his back, soothed him with her touch as they moved together. He held her face in his palms to watch her, filing the moments to memory—the pleasure in her eyes, the way her lips trembled when she neared a climax—until his own body's demand for release forced his eyes closed. The impact jolted him from the inside out, and he continued to shake long after it was over, his face buried in the softness of her neck.

If he had his way, they wouldn't leave his bed the rest of the day. Maybe not even then. If he had his way, they'd forget about the damn trial and make love well into the night. And tomorrow. And the next day...

"I have to go home and change," she said, forcing Daniel back into unwanted reality.

He raised his head and kissed her softly. "I know. Maybe we could ask for a continuance so we can continue this for the next few hours."

She drew a line down his jaw with a fingertip. "And what excuse should we use to avoid a contempt charge?"

"Contempt for the case."

"You can say that again." She patted his bottom and said, "Scoot."

He rolled onto his back and watched her rise from the bed, giving him a great view of her incredible body. He knew the territory by heart because he'd explored every inch last night with his hands and his mouth. He could get used to seeing her this way every morning, waking up with her every morning. Going to bed with her every night. He was beginning to think he wanted that more than the D.A. position, and that wasn't anything he'd considered before. Ever.

She grabbed her sweatshirt from the floor and slipped it on. "I'm going to use your guest room to take a shower before I leave."

He laced his hands behind his neck. "You can use my shower. I need to take one, too. We could conserve water."

She pointed a finger at him as she backed to the door.

"We'll never get out of the shower if we take one together. Then I'd have to appear in court looking like a prune."

"You'd make a beautiful prune."

"And you are so full of it, Daniel Fortune," she said as she left the room.

Daniel had to admit he was filled with her. He'd never felt this way about any woman before, had never been so consumed that he didn't give a damn about his job. He sure hadn't been so open with any woman, neither had he let down his guard enough to reveal any serious emotions. Not until last night. Not until her. He'd expected the moments to follow to be awkward, but instead they had been incredible. With her help, he'd lessened the burdens he'd carried from his past. And even though he now bore the burden of Ryan's illness, she had eased that, as well. He'd never needed anyone as much as he needed her.

All night he'd been considering how to handle the myriad feelings crowding in on him. He'd come to the conclusion that life was short and he'd waited too long to find someone like Alisha Hart. He'd also formulated a plan, even though he questioned if she would even consider it—especially after what he had to do to her in court today.

Unable to prolong the inevitable, Daniel bolted out of the bed and made fast work of his shower. While he was shaving, Alisha walked into the bathroom dressed in a knotted towel. Even with hair dripping and her face free of makeup, he could take her down on the floor mat and get inside of her right then without a second thought or concern for his responsibility to the courts.

She took the space beside him at the black marble vanity and gave him a long once-over. "Boxers. Very sexy." She traced a fingertip down his butt. "I'm going to be thinking about these all day long."

He lifted the razor before he cut a swath across his jaw. "If you do that again, I won't be responsible for anything I might do to delay your departure."

She grinned at his reflection in the mirror. "Do you happen to have a spare toothbrush?"

He gestured toward the drawer to her right. "In there, a couple of freebies, compliments of my last dentist appointment."

"Very nice." She withdrew one, ripped open the package and grazed his arm when she reached for the toothpaste. Just that minimal contact had him ready to crawl all over her again.

Daniel attempted to concentrate on shaving, glancing at Alisha now and then, smiling when she inspected her teeth. Without asking, she took his hairbrush and ran it through her damp hair, but he didn't mind that at all. He liked her touching anything that belonged to him. He enjoyed watching her routine and he knew for certain what he wanted from her—the opportunity to see her standing beside him every morning.

He set the razor down, rubbed a towel over his jaw and tossed it aside, then circled his arms around her from behind. "You know what we need to do?"

She stopped the brush midstroke and regarded him over her shoulder. "I don't have time."

"I didn't mean that."

She went back to brushing her hair. "Then what did you mean?"

He drew in a quick breath. "We need to move in together."

She stared at him over one shoulder. "Are you serious?"

"Yeah, I am. Very serious."

She turned into his arms. "What made you even consider such a thing?"

"You. I want to see where this goes with us. Living together will let us know if we can get along for more than a weekend or a few nights."

"I've never lived with anyone before."

"Neither have I."

"It's a huge step, Daniel. I'm not sure we're ready for that."

"I am." And he was.

She slicked both hands though her hair. "We need to think about this."

"I have. All night. But you go ahead and think about it." He pressed a kiss on her lips, then nuzzled his face in the cleft of her breasts. "Remember, I have ways to convince you."

"How well I know." She tugged his head up. "But at the moment you're going to have to put that on hold."

He pushed against her. "This?"

"Yes, that."

"Okay." He took a reluctant step back. "For now."

Alisha followed him into the bedroom and dressed while he gathered his clothes. Although he knew he should drop it for the time being, he wanted to convince her that his idea had merit. "Let's talk about the pros and cons about living together," he said as he pulled his slacks on.

She leaned a hip against the dresser and folded her arms across her middle. "Okay. Pros first."

He took his shirt from the hanger and shrugged it on. "You'll be closer to work."

"Then you'd want to live here?"

"Yeah." He tucked in the shirttails and fastened his fly before sitting on the edge of the bed to put on his socks and shoes. "Do you have a problem with that?"

"No. Who wouldn't want to live here? It beats the heck out of my place in regard to convenience. It's a lot nicer, too. The wet bar is a real perk."

Daniel rose and draped his tie around his neck. "Glad you see it my way." He took his jacket from the closet and turned to find her staring at nothing in particular. "We can talk about it more at lunch."

She sent him a warning look. "We're not going to see each other at lunch. We can talk about it tonight. Hopefully the chaos will be over by this afternoon."

And hopefully after the case was over she would still be speaking to him. "Are you ready for today?"

She frowned. "Of course. Why?"

"Just wanted to make sure." That was all he could say without revealing his plan.

"You sound worried, Counselor. Are you afraid you're going to lose?"

"Not at all." He would do everything in his power to get a conviction because that was his job. He hated that job at the moment. Hated that she would suffer because he'd learned to do it well.

After putting on his jacket, Daniel held out his hand to her. "Walk me to the elevator. I'll go down first, then you can leave. Unless you want me to drive you to your car."

She pushed away from the dresser and took his hand. "I can make it by myself, the same way I got here. I'm a big girl. But it's not even six yet. Do you have to be in that early?"

"I've got a few last-minute details to attend to." Namely prepare to interview his surprise witness.

He couldn't resist one more kiss. Or one more compliment that he hoped she would carry with her during the day. "You look beautiful this morning."

"And you are a beautiful man." She sniffed his neck. "You smell great, too. Now get your gorgeous butt in gear and get out of here."

Once at the elevator, Daniel took her back into his arms. "Just remember, whatever happens today, it's not about us."

"I know that."

He kissed her briefly. "Good." But as he stepped into the elevator, the one thing he needed to say, the one thing he should have said last night, spilled out of his mouth as the doors began to close. "And also remember I love you."

## Thirteen

Daniel Fortune loved her? How incredible was that?

Alisha felt as if she floated from her chair when she stood. Felt as if she might not be able to get through direct examination without turning around and shouting out that the most eligible prosecutor was crazy about her.

The world looked completely different this morning. The jury looked less daunting. Judge Slagle looked spiffy, even if his wiry hair flipped up on the ends. And Daniel...well, the way he looked right now in his gray silk suit, his gorgeous hair neatly combed, his face clean shaven, defied adequate description. What she wouldn't give to be able to walk up to the table where he now sat and smack a wet kiss on that devastating mouth. That would be a poor idea, although she wondered if her admiration was obvious. Hiding her feelings for him amounted to trying to conceal a bonfire at midnight. But she had to hide them. She'd allow herself a momentary lapse into giddiness before getting down to business. And business included words from the "naked guy" himself.

Alisha straightened her frame and forced herself back into professional mode. "The defense calls Lester Massey."

Massey seemed to be right up there with the second coming of Elvis, judging by the oohs and aahs and squeals that rose from the fan section when Les made his way to the stage. Alisha wouldn't be surprised if someone tossed a pair of panties at him while he took the oath to tell the truth. His white teeth gleamed against his tanned face. His normally shaggy hair had been combed back to reveal the two gold earrings in one lobe that reflected the light. He cleaned up nicely, but Alisha considered him a charming chameleon. And after today, good riddance. First, she had to sell him to the jury.

Alisha readied to paint Les as supercitizen. "Mr. Massey, is it fair to say that you've always been a champion of causes?"

"Yes."

"Could you explain?"

Les did a good job of feigning humility. "Well, it's kind of embarrassing to talk about myself."

Oh, sure. "Could you try please?"

"Okay. I did a lot of charitable work in college. Building houses and cleaning up parks, that sort of thing. I think it's important to give back to the community. To make people aware of the importance of social issues. That sort of thing."

He was doing much better than Alisha had expected. He seemed almost civil. "Now let's talk about the activities that brought you here today. What was your intent when you posed at the zoo?"

"I wanted to call attention to animal rights, how I think it's unfair to keep the helpless creatures locked up."

"And at the Alamo?"

"I was trying to get people to pay attention to the importance of our past."

"You didn't think posing partially clothed was a bit extreme?"

He presented a little-boy shrug. "Sometimes you have to be a little extreme to get people's attention."

"And lastly the river-taxi incident. What were you trying to prove with that?"

He took on a serious expression. "People forget what the holidays are supposed to be about. Everyone gets caught up in the shopping stuff, so I figured I'd try to convince everyone to slow down and just have fun."

Oh, brother. Alisha resisted rolling her eyes. "That particular night, did you expose yourself?"

"Only my legs and chest." He puffed out said chest. "I never whipped it out for anyone to see."

Alisha would swear she heard a collective sigh. "*It* as in your genitals?"

"Yeah. Those."

"Do you have any tattoos there?"

He looked totally pained by the prospect. "No, ma'am. I did have a pair of maracas." A chorus of laughter rang out. "I mean, I was holding a pair of maracas that night. I accidentally dropped them in the river."

"Could you describe these maracas and explain where you were holding them?"

"They were blue, with flowers and vines painted on the bulb part. I was holding them upside down, kind of between my legs, shaking them."

When the chuckles died down, Alisha turned and spoke directly to the jurors. "Mr. Massey, the night you were on the river, do you recall seeing Mrs. O'Reilly when you exited the taxi and entered the walkway?"

He shook his head. "No, ma'am. I didn't see her and I didn't push her. My grandmother passed away a few years ago, and I still miss her a lot. I'd never hurt an old lady."

Not too bad, Alisha decided, except for the "old lady"

part. "One more question, Mr. Massey. When you decided to conduct this performance, did you intend to offend or harm anyone?"

"No, ma'am," he said adamantly. "If I'd known anyone was going to get hurt, I would've never done it."

Alisha felt more than satisfied by Les's testimony, and she didn't want to push her luck. "No further questions."

When she started back to the table, Daniel passed by her on the way to the stand. She caught a good whiff of his scent and thought she might possibly swoon. Instead she took her seat next to Joe and braced for Daniel's cross-examination. She seriously doubted he could do much to salvage his case, but she knew he would try.

He approached the stand slowly, keeping his distance. "I want to clarify one thing, Mr. Massey. Your only intent in regard to these escapades came from a deep-seated sense of social awareness?"

"Yes, sir. That's right."

"And you have no other reason for it whatsoever?"

"No, sir. I just want people to be more aware."

More aware of Les Massey, Alisha thought wryly.

"A couple of final questions, Mr. Massey," Daniel said. "Did you go to college and get a degree?"

"I couldn't finish. I didn't have enough money."

"What was your major?"

"Uh, I didn't really decide before I had to leave."

"Are you currently employed?"

He looked appropriately dejected. "No. I've worked some odd jobs to get by. But times are tough for everyone."

Poor, poor Les. If he were any more pitiful, Alisha would have to pass out the tissues to the girls.

Daniel walked back behind the table. "No more questions."

Slagle gave his attention to Alisha, and she assumed she probably looked as shocked as he did. That wasn't much of a cross, but she realized Daniel probably couldn't add anything more. Grilling Mr. Charmer could possibly alienate the jury, and maybe that's why the prosecutor hadn't gone for the jugular. Or maybe he sensed defeat. At least he hadn't used anything she'd given him to any real degree, although she suspected he'd been heading in that direction. But Les had held him off with the whole poor-pitiful-me act. Massey had definitely proven he could act up a storm.

"Any other witnesses, Ms. Hart?" Slagle asked.

"The defense rests, Your Honor."

Slagle waved a wiry hand at Les. "You can step down, Mr. Massey."

Daniel remained standing beside the table. "I'd like to request a fifteen-minute recess before we continue, Your Honor."

Slagle checked his watch. "Okeydoke. Fifteen minutes, then we can start to wrap this up."

"You've done it, Hart," Joe said to Alisha as they stood. "No way is the jury going to convict."

Alisha was cautiously optimistic. Experience had taught her anything could happen. "Let's not make any assumptions yet. The prosecutor still has closing arguments. Which reminds me, I need to polish mine a bit. I'm going to find a quiet place and do that very thing. You know the routine. If Les wants to take a trip to the boys' room, accompany him and the guard. Make sure he doesn't pose for the press."

Joe grinned. "Is that with or without his pants down?"

Alisha smirked. "Both."

Although unwise, Alisha couldn't resist searching out Daniel, if only to catch a quick glimpse. But he'd disappeared without her noticing. Oh, well. She planned to get more than a good look at him tonight. And if luck prevailed, closing arguments would go quickly, and then the jury could begin deliberations. Hopefully the verdict would be returned by day's end, then she could put Les Massey behind her, figuratively speaking. Win or lose, it really didn't matter. The only thing that mattered was Daniel and being with him without this case intruding on their relationship. And more important, she realized now that she could trust him. And she did, with all her heart.

Alisha pushed her way through the loitering press outside the courtroom, skirting their questions while a bailiff stepped up and held them back, allowing her to disappear into a back hallway.

When she found an empty conference room, she collapsed into an unforgiving wooden chair and took out her notes. For the most part, she usually winged it during closing, but she liked to make sure she had all her points in order. Fortunately she'd been blessed with a good memory to counteract the bladder and molar problems. She laughed at that thought. Laughed from the sheer joy of knowing that Daniel loved her. Unless he'd been lying. Of course not. He wouldn't just spout out something that important for the heck of it. He had no reason to lie.

Alisha's time was limited, therefore she could not keep recalling those moments. Work took precedence over very pretty words. But before she could review her notes, the door opened on her dream man. At the moment he looked every bit the iceman.

"Sorry," he muttered. "Obviously this isn't where I'm supposed to be having my meeting."

"Obviously not. Unless someone's hiding under the table." She bent down and took a quick look before straightening again. "I don't see anyone, so that means we're alone." And maybe he might take the hint and give her a quick kiss.

It seemed that hadn't even occurred to Daniel when he said, "They're probably in the next room down. I need to find them."

"Daniel," Alisha called before he could leave. "About this morning…"

He looked totally impassive as he stepped inside the room and closed the door behind him. "We can't discuss that now."

Alisha tapped her pencil on the pad, concerned that he

seemed so aloof. "I know, but I just wanted to say I feel the same."

He still looked detached and not at all affected by her declaration. He also didn't respond, leaving her to question whether she'd misunderstood him that morning. Or perhaps he'd changed his mind.

As Daniel turned to go, he stopped short of opening the door but kept his back to her. "Remember, whatever happens this afternoon, I have a job to do."

Alisha gathered he had one heck of a closing statement planned. But then, so did she. Still, a queasy feeling settled in her tummy, and she chalked it up to hunger pangs. After all, she hadn't had any breakfast. Yes, that was it. It had to be it. The trial was basically over, and she believed she'd scored more points than Daniel. Maybe that was the problem. He didn't like losing, even if he'd never been all that enthused with this case from the beginning.

Well, if he did lose, she'd come up with a few wicked ways that would ensure his forgiveness.

Daniel hoped Alisha would forgive him for what he was about to do. Regardless, he had to do it and he could only hope she understood that.

After Slagle seated himself on the throne, Daniel remained standing and said, "The state calls Carol Novak to the stand."

A moment of silence passed, then Alisha said, "Approach, Your Honor," with more poise than he'd expected.

"Come on up, Counselors," the judge said.

Daniel didn't dare look at her as he walked to the bench. He'd let her have her say before he went on the attack.

"Your Honor," Alisha began, "I have no record of this Carol Novak on the witness list presented to me during discovery."

"We were unaware of her role in impacting the state's case until she came forward," Daniel said.

"But—"

Slagle put up a hand to silence Alisha. "Ms. Hart, the state is within its rights to refute evidence through rebuttal. You'll get your turn in cross. Besides, we could use a little something to liven up this case before lunch. Otherwise I might be tempted to take a nap."

Only then did Daniel risk a glance at Alisha. She didn't look as though she appreciated Slagle's attempts at humor. In fact, she looked royally pissed. And after this was over, he imagined she'd be out for blood. His blood.

Slagle shooed them away. "Now step back and let's get going. Bring in the witness, bailiff."

Daniel walked back to the table and picked up his notes. He'd had little time to interview Ms. Novak, although she seemed like a solid witness. But then, so had Mrs. O'Reilly. She could end up doing more harm than good. Not if he could help it. Not if he could ignore Alisha's current glare and keep his mind centered on his duty.

Following Slagle's instructions to the jury regarding the rebuttal process, Carol Novak strode to the stand and took the oath. Dressed in a tailored black suit, with her hair pulled back into a low ponytail, she looked the part of corporate executive, which she was. Wearing an expression that could wither a professional wrestler, she looked the part of a jilted lover, which she had been.

Daniel decided to remain in place to avoid Alisha's glare. Less diversion that way, and he needed all the concentration he could get. "Ms. Novak, could you please state your occupation and city of residence for the record?"

"I'm vice president of finance for a computer corporation based in New Orleans."

Les definitely had something going for him that didn't meet the eye in order to land an intelligent and attractive woman like Carol Novak, and Daniel doubted it involved his IQ. "Do you know the defendant, Lester Massey?"

She fidgeted with the hem of her blazer, the only sign of

nervousness. "Yes, I know him quite well. We were lovers for two years."

"Did you live together?"

"Yes, we did. Unfortunately."

Daniel expected Alisha to object to the barb, but when she didn't, he continued. "During your time together, did Mr. Massey engage in activities similar to those for which he is now charged?"

"No, but he talked about doing it all the time. He considers himself an aspiring actor and he was always planning ways to get noticed. He told me he used to streak during college and he enjoyed the attention. He's very proud of his body."

Slagle's gavel pounding followed a loud whistle from the crowd.

"Did he support any kind of social causes during the time you knew him?"

"No. He didn't support much of anything, including himself. I did that."

Still no objection from Alisha, and Daniel found that strange. She didn't even level one "hearsay" objection. He felt reasonably sure he'd established Massey's penchant for being a publicity hog and a bum. Now he could follow up with that during closing arguments. "Thank you, Ms. Novak. No further questions."

"Any questions for this witness, Ms. Hart?" Slagle asked.

"Definitely, Your Honor."

Daniel turned and headed back to his seat while Alisha headed to the stand. She didn't even offer a cursory glance in his direction. She looked damned determined, though, and about as angry as the witness.

"Ms. Novak, when you were with Mr. Massey, was he ever violent?"

"No."

"Did he ever deny having any desire to support any causes?"

"No, he didn't deny it, but—"

"When you parted ways, did you leave him or did he leave you?"

"He walked out without even saying goodbye. And the jerk took my collection of classical CDs and my toreador outfit that my father gave me."

"Your Honor," Alisha said. "Could you instruct the witness to keep commentary at a minimum?"

"Just stick to the yes and no answers, Ms. Novak," Slagle said.

Alisha studied the ground before bringing her attention back to the witness. "Ms. Novak, how long ago did Mr. Massey leave you?"

"Four months ago."

"Then would it be accurate to assume you're still angry with him?"

"Objection," Daniel said.

Alisha shot him an acid glare. "I have to question Ms. Novak's motivation for coming forward at this late date."

"I'll allow it."

"Yes, I'm angry," Carol said. "Wouldn't you be?"

"My state of mind is not in question here," Alisha said calmly.

Maybe not, but Daniel could imagine what she was thinking—that her revelations last night had something to do with this and that he'd betrayed her.

"One more question, Ms. Novak," she said. "Do you see your presence here today as doing your civic duty or is this a good way to get revenge?"

Daniel shot out of his chair. "Your Honor—"

"Sustained," Slagle said.

"Nothing further," Alisha said as she pinned Daniel with an angry look. "And as they say, hell hath no fury like a woman scorned." Before he could offer another objection, she added, "Withdrawn."

She strode back to the table and met his gaze. This time

Daniel didn't see anger, he saw unmistakable hurt before she reclaimed her seat. He planned to explain as soon as he had the opportunity. He prayed it wasn't too late.

## *Fourteen*

"How do you think we did?"

Alisha noted insecurity in Les Massey's voice for the first time since she'd had the misfortune of meeting him. "I don't know, but we'll find out when the jury comes back with the verdict."

And she predicted that would be soon. Other than that, she didn't dare make any predictions. She'd done her best during closing arguments to undo any damage imposed by the state's surprise witness. She'd stressed that regardless of Mr. Massey's motivation, the prosecution had failed to prove without a doubt that he'd assaulted an elderly woman or that he'd exposed himself to a degree that warranted a conviction. As far as the disorderly conduct was concerned, that still remained up in the air. But if they did find him guilty on those counts, that was little more than a fine and limited jail time, if any.

Daniel, on the other hand, had proved he was a master at his job. He'd painted Les to be a liar supreme and sufficiently attacked his character, all he'd been able to do. If the jury had taken that bait, then Les might be in jail longer than he'd anticipated. And Alisha honestly didn't care. Didn't care if her client was sentenced to a long confinement. She only cared about the biting betrayal brought about by a man she'd thought she could trust. A man she loved. A man who was all about winning, regardless of the consequences.

The conference room door opened and Joe stepped inside. "The jury's back already."

Alisha checked her watch. Only two hours' worth of deliberations. That could be good. Or bad. "All right. Let's go."

She walked down the hall between Joe and Les, all the while hating that she had to see Daniel again. Hating that after this fiasco ended, she wouldn't see him except in this setting, if then.

After they reentered the courtroom and took their places, Alisha concentrated on the jury as they filed in to keep from looking at Daniel. She was afraid she might not be able to hide her heartache. Maybe even afraid she might cry, because that's what she wanted to do at the moment—have a nice, irrational, emotional outburst. Later she just might do that. Right now she had to remain composed when the judge instructed Les to stand.

"Has the jury reached a verdict?" Slagle said.

"We have, Your Honor," the foreman replied and handed off the paper that held Les Massey's fate.

Slagle looked it over, then handed it back to be returned to the foreman. "On the count of indecent exposure, how do you find?"

"Not guilty."

Several excited murmurs came from behind Alisha. Even after the jilted girlfriend's appearance, support among Massey's girls still hadn't diminished. Smitten fools, every one of them. But who was she to talk? She should get up right now and take her place among them—behind the prosecutor.

"On the count of assault, how do you find?"

"Not guilty."

This time Les said, "Oh, yeah," prompting Alisha to give him a quelling look.

"On three counts of disorderly conduct, how do you find?"

"Guilty."

Not exactly a clean sweep, Alisha decided, but it could have been so much worse. She risked a glance at Daniel and saw no satisfaction in his expression, witnessed no high fives exchanged between him and his assistants. But come to think of it, he hadn't really won. Neither of them had, both in terms of the case and their relationship.

"Order," Slagle shouted to silence the unruly crowd. Alisha's temples pounded in time with every bang of his gavel. "I'm ready to dispose of this case, so I'm going to go ahead and sentence Mr. Massey."

Alisha was more than ready to get the hell out of there. More than ready to return to her office and lock herself in. More than ready to get as far away from Daniel Fortune as she possibly could, at least in a physical sense.

"Mr. Massey," Slagle said. "You are hereby sentenced to pay fifteen hundred dollars, and any jail time will be counted for time already served."

The Masses for Massey sent up a resounding cheer until Slagle's nasty scowl silenced them. "However," he continued, "I'm thinking you should do a little community service, so I'm sentencing you to thirty hours at the zoo, cleaning up poop."

Les leaned over and said to Alisha, "Can he do that?"

She replied, "He's doing it, isn't he?"

"Uh, Judge," Les said. "Can I ask a question?"

Alisha didn't have the strength to intervene. The judge could handle him.

"Yes, young man?" Slagle said.

"After I get through with my community service, will it be okay if I leave the state or will I be on parole or something?"

Slagle chuckled. "No parole, and I'm thinking a few of San Antonio's good citizens will be glad to chip in for your bus fare."

Les looked totally perplexed. "No kidding?"

"Yes, he's kidding," Alisha said, almost adding *you moron* to the comment.

"Court's adjourned," Slagle said. "Everyone's free to go, and that includes you, Mr. Massey."

Alisha gathered her things, but before she could get away from her client he said, "You know, I guess that's not too bad, but I was kind of counting on not guilty on everything."

She shoved her notes into her briefcase. "Consider yourself lucky that the jury had enough sense to weigh the facts in light of your lies."

"Maybe I should appeal it."

Oh, good grief. "Maybe you should just forget about the whole thing and go on with your life." Exactly what Alisha intended to do—forget about Daniel and what could have been. Get on with her life without him.

"Okay, I can do that." Les gave her a suggestive grin. "I can probably scrounge up enough money to buy you dinner. I can get a discount at the pizza place where I used to work."

Lovely. Alisha gripped her case and presented a fake smile. "Mr. Massey, from this point forward I am no longer your attorney, nor am I a prospective girlfriend. As far as I'm concerned, I never want to see you again. And if by chance the day should come when you decide to pull one of your half-naked stunts again, you better hope I'm not wielding anything heavier than a loaf of bread."

Alisha strode out of the courtroom to find the press gathered round the vestibule, awaiting comments. She only wanted to slip out before anyone discovered her presence. With that in mind, she took a right and headed down a back hallway toward the side exit in order to escape without detection.

She cursed the fact that she'd had to park so far away, at the back of the lot, thanks to the trial's notoriety. After she heard a noisy commotion coming from behind her, she turned and walked backward a few steps, expecting to catch a glimpse of the A.D.A. Instead she saw a throng of females converging on Les Massey as he displayed the victory sign like a practiced politician. He'd come out of the ordeal relatively unscathed, with basically a slap on the wrist. She wished she could say the same for herself.

On the heels of her need to hurry away, Alisha turned and practically sprinted through the lot. Her steps slowed as she caught sight of a tall figure leaning back against her sedan, shoulders straight, arms folded across his chest. Even before she could register all the details—the immaculate brown hair, the intense green eyes—she knew it was Daniel by his confident stance alone. Her heart took a dive, then took to beating in a crazy cadence. She reminded herself she was still angry with him, that she still hurt like the devil every time she considered how far she had fallen for him—and how far he had gone to win.

Since he was blocking the driver's door, Alisha had no choice but to speak to him, if only to request that he get out of her way.

"We need to talk."

She barked out a laugh. "Why? So you can gloat over your victory?"

"So I can explain."

"There's nothing to explain. You did what you had to do." She fumbled with her briefcase and withdrew her keys, immediately dropping them on the pavement. With lightning speed Daniel retrieved them and depressed the remote, unlocking the car.

"Get in," he said, hanging on to her keys as he rounded the hood and opened the passenger door.

Alisha slid into the driver's seat, resigned to the fact that he would persist until she heard him out. She would give him a few minutes before she told him goodbye for good.

The car filled with the scent of his cologne, and she gripped the steering wheel to keep from reaching for him. She craved him like a love addict craved a fix, knowing that if she fell off the wagon, she would keep coming back for more.

"What happened back there in court had to happen," he said. "I had no choice."

She continued to stare straight ahead. "I know. You used my stupid mistake to make Fortune's Last Stand. Silly me to think that you wouldn't use me."

"Is that really what you believe? That I used you?"

"Yes. I told you about the ex-girlfriend and you tracked her down. If I'd kept my mouth shut, Massey probably would have been cleared on all counts."

"You honestly distrust me that much?"

"Why should I trust you? This is a recurring nightmare with me. First Troy, now you. I've been played the fool twice—three times if you count Les—but never again." And this time it hurt worse than it ever had with Troy. But she hadn't been in love with him.

"Alisha, look at me."

She didn't want to do that, didn't want to see the face she had taken to memory, the face she'd wanted to see every day for the rest of her life. But his touch on her arm acted like a magnet, drawing her gaze to his somber expression.

"I want you to listen to me, and listen carefully," he said. "First of all, I'm not Moreau, and deep down you know that. Second, we both knew the rules and the risks going into this thing."

Damn him. "Don't patronize me, Counselor. Of course I knew the rules. And I broke them. But so did you. You don't have to remind me."

"But obviously I have to remind you of something even more important. I've never told one living soul what I told you last night. This morning I told you something I've never told any woman I've been involved with. I meant every word I said. Right now you're too damn angry to handle anything else I have to say, so I'm going to give you some time to think about it before we talk again."

She fought with everything in her to hold back the threatening tears. "I don't see any reason to talk again. I just can't keep repeating the same mistakes, Daniel. Trust is everything to me, and I'm not sure I can trust anything you've said to this point."

"We're not a mistake, Alisha." He tugged her hand from the wheel and rested it in his, then pressed the keys into her palm. "If you let this sham of a case ruin what we have together, then we both lose."

Long after Daniel left the car, Alisha sat with her forehead resting against the wheel, unwelcome tears rolling down her face and dropping onto her best black skirt. She couldn't stand the thought of facing Joe. Or facing anyone, for that matter. Her emotions were too out of whack to put on a happy face and pretend that everything was rosy and right. In light of that, she took out her cell phone and dialed the office.

"Hey, Joe," she said, biting back a rogue sob. "Cancel my afternoon, okay?"

"Come on, Hart. You have to come in. Julie's here and she wants to congratulate you."

"Congratulate me?"

"Well, yeah. You basically won."

*If you let this sham of a case ruin what we have together, then we both lose....*

"Tell Julie thanks, Joe, but I'm completely worn out. I want to soak in a hot bath and watch some pointless reality show." And have a good cry while she faced the reality of having Daniel gone from her life. "I'll see you in the morning."

Alisha hung up and started the car, wishing home was a little closer. More than that, she wished she'd never handed over her heart to Daniel Fortune.

* * *

When Alisha failed to answer the phone or his messages for the past twenty-four hours, Daniel decided to pay her a visit. He grabbed up his cell phone and dialed her number, reached the damn answering machine again. "Alisha, it's me. I know you're in there because I can see you, and I have to—"

She picked up the phone and barked, "What do you mean you can see me?"

Finally. "Because the curtain's partially parted. I'm parked outside your apartment. I want to come in."

"It's late and I'm tired."

"So am I. Tired of not being with you."

Her sigh filtered into his ear, calling up memories of other sighs that weren't weary. "You're not going to leave, are you?"

"Nope. Not until you let me in. No negotiating, no settling. I'll sit here all night if I have to. You don't want me wearing the same clothes into work tomorrow morning, do you?" His attempt at levity fell flat. He didn't find any humor in this situation either.

After a slight pause she said, "Okay. I'll give you a few minutes, but that's it. I need to go to bed."

He halted the offer to join her. He needed her to know this wasn't about sex, although he still wanted her as badly as he had from the beginning. "I'm on my way."

Daniel tossed the cell phone aside, opting to leave it behind because he wanted no interruptions. He only wanted her back, and that might be expecting too much.

After slipping his keys into the pocket that also contained the possible key to their future, he left the car in a rush. Before he could even knock, the door flew open to Alisha standing there wearing a peach-colored silk wraparound robe and a stern expression. "You have five minutes," she said, moving aside to allow him entry.

He stepped into the small living room, immediately noticing it was clean but not without clutter. The place suited her spirited personality, from the abstract paintings on the wall to the eclectic collection of DVDs.

When Alisha took the small beige tufted chair across from the couch, Daniel remained standing, his palms braced on the back of the sofa. She planted her feet firmly on the floor and folded her hands in her lap. "Okay, Daniel. Say what you have to say and get it over with."

He decided to do what he did best—argue his case—because this was a case he couldn't afford to lose. "You've ruined me."

A hint of confusion followed by a flicker of fear passed over her face. "What?"

"You've ruined me. I can't even consider being without you."

She laid a hand on her chest. "Oh, God, you scared me to death. I thought you meant—"

"My job? No. That's still intact, at least at the moment. But this isn't about my job. It's about us, our relationship."

She no longer looked fearful. She looked resolute. "The way things stand now I'm not sure there can be an *us*."

"Maybe not, unless you own up to a few things first." He sidestepped the sofa, walked to the chair and stared down on her. "Do you compare me to Moreau every time we're together?"

"I don't know what you mean."

"When we make love? When I'm touching you, inside of you, are you thinking about him?"

She bit her bottom lip. "No. Not once did he ever make me feel the way you do."

"Then why are you comparing me to him now? Why do you think that I'd intentionally do what he did to you?"

"Because you want to win."

"Believe me, if I'd really wanted to win, I would've, and nothing could have stopped me. But the truth of the matter is, I didn't give a damn about it. I only cared about you."

Now she looked angry. "Oh, great. You're saying that you *let* me win?"

If not careful, he was severely going to screw this up. "No. You won because you're tough and you gave it all you had. I didn't."

"But you did use the information I handed to you."

Back to that again, and time to clear the air. "What if I told you I knew about the girlfriend before you told me about her?"

"For how long?"

"About an hour before you came to see me the other night."

"And you didn't tell me."

"I couldn't, and you know it." He rubbed a hand over his jaw. "If I'd told you about her, you would've kept Massey off the stand and avoided a rebuttal. Since Allan Vera knew about this witness—and since he suspects we're involved—that would have caused trouble for both of us."

Her eyes went wide. "The D.A. knew about us?"

"He saw us after the reception and he formulated an opinion from that. I didn't confirm or deny it, but I knew I had to fight to prevent any more speculation. I did it to protect you from the possibility of being disbarred."

She didn't speak for a time as she might be finally viewing the situation with logic. "I guess you're right."

"I know I'm right. And I'm right about us, too. We need to be together. Live together."

She hugged her legs to her chest and refused to look at him. "I need some time, Daniel. You're not even allowing me to digest everything you've told me about today."

He took a chance and moved closer to her. "In my experience as a prosecutor I've learned that only a small window of opportunity exists during an investigation, otherwise you might lose a suspect. I also recognize I waited too long to tell my mother I forgave her, and then it was too late. I'm afraid if I wait too long to act on my feelings for you, that opportunity will pass me by, too."

Now for the most important question of all. "Do you love me, Alisha?"

She covered her face with her palms. "Why are you doing this to me?"

He planted his palms on the arms of the chair and leaned into them. "Do you love me?" he repeated more firmly this time.

When she dropped her hands from her face, he saw the first sign of tears, and he hated that. "Yes."

"Then say it, dammit!"

"I love you."

He knelt before her and took her hands into his. "Good, because I love you, too. So much, it physically hurts me to think that we won't be together. Nothing matters except for us staying together."

She didn't look quite so angry, but she didn't look completely convinced either. "Daniel, loving you only complicates things more. We can't afford to find ourselves in this situation again, and I can't afford to remove myself from the public-defender rolls until I get my practice established—provided the court hasn't already removed me."

"No way. You're a good attorney, Alisha. You proved that this week. I would be surprised if you don't move up in the ranks and get handed some felony cases."

"And if that's true, then therein lies the problem. We could very well be facing each other in a courtroom again. We know what happened this last time, and next time it could be worse, especially if we're living together."

"That won't be a problem. I'm resigning from the D.A.'s office." He'd made the decision that morning after being reprimanded by Vera and Pettigrew.

She looked totally shocked. "Would you repeat that?"

"I'm leaving the D.A.'s office."

"When?"

"I'll stick around for a couple of months until I get the Jamison case where it needs to be and handle anything else that might be pending."

"What about your aspirations for being the next D.A.?"

"If the Massey case did nothing else, it taught me that I don't want to play the political game." It also taught him that some things were much more important, namely her.

"What are you going to do now?" she asked.

"I've accepted a job as lead counsel for the new advocacy center. I've decided that for the past few years I've been trying to put my father in jail. Now I'm going to honor my mother by helping women like her and helping families stay together."

Her expression softened, giving him hope. "That's wonderful, Daniel."

"It's what I want to do. But there is another problem. It's only part-time. However, I think I've come upon a solution that would benefit us both."

She hinted at a smile. "What would that be?"

"Come here." He pulled her up, led her to the sofa and positioned her beside him, keeping her hands in his grasp. "If you could use a part-time partner, I'm available. We can start with the White case. Now I'll be free to help you win that one." He rubbed his thumb over her wrists. "And when you move in with me, we can share expenses. I also have some money put aside in trust. The funds were left over from my inheritance. I gave some of it away, but I still have quite a bit left for our kids' college funds."

Her mouth opened, then dropped shut before she said, "Our kids?"

"Yeah, unless you don't want any."

"Aren't we kind of jumping the gun here?"

He grinned. "You're right. But I'll fix that right now." He dipped his hand in his pocket, withdrew the pair of plain white panties and offered them to her for inspection. "For you."

Alisha held them up and read the script splashed across the front in bold black letters. "'Will you marry me?'"

"You bet I will," he replied.

Her smile came into full bloom. "Where did you get these?"

"I bought them. Actually I ended up buying two pair. The lady at the embroidery shop said the silk pair wouldn't work. They thought I'd lost my mind, but I wasn't worried about that because you're worth it."

Alisha studied them awhile longer before draping them on the ring finger of her left hand. "They're too big, but I can have them sized."

Daniel rubbed a hand across his nape. "I thought about a ring, but I decided you might want to pick it out. And we can't really tell anyone for a few weeks, at least until the publicity dies down. I don't want to do anything to hurt you."

"I know that now. I trust you."

Three simple words that meant everything to Daniel. "That's the one thing I needed to hear you say more than anything, other than you'll marry me. We don't have to do it tomorrow or even next month. Just as long as we do it."

She touched his face with reverence, alleviated the ache that had plagued him since yesterday, since the day that he'd realized no other woman would ever move him the way she had. The way she still did, and always would.

"I don't know what I'm going to do with you," she said.

"And I don't know what I'm going to do without you if you tell me no."

She smiled at him. "You won't have to find out."

"Is that a yes?"

"Yes, that's a yes."

They shared a kiss that started out tender and, as usual, turned passionate in a matter of minutes. Alisha pulled away first, but her smile eased any of Daniel's cause for concern. "Are you sure I'm awake? I mean, this isn't some weird dream, is it?"

He pushed her hair away from her shoulders and circled her breast with a fingertip. "Yeah, you're awake, at least for the moment. You look tired. I probably should let you go to bed."

She hid a yawn behind her hand. "I'm not that tired—and I'm more than ready for bed."

He slid his hand beneath the T-shirt and cupped her breast. "You want to try on those panties now?"

She tossed them onto the chair. "Maybe later. You'd just have them off me in a matter of minutes."

He outlined her lips with his tongue. "True. Are you ready for bed now?"

She responded by standing and pulling him to his feet. "Yes, as soon as we dispose of one more thing."

"Our clothes?"

"The wager, or have you forgotten that?"

"I don't see any reason to worry about that since I think we've both won. And besides, I got you in the bargain, and that's all that I want."

She looked at him a long moment before saying, "I really do love you, Gunther."

"I love you, too, Lola. And if you give me five minutes, I'll show you how much."

She began releasing the buttons on his shirt with one hand while undoing his belt with the other. "Oh, I'll give you more than five minutes. In fact, I plan to give you more than you can handle."

"Hey, I'm up for it."

Boy was he, Alisha thought when she lowered his fly.

On the way to the bedroom they tossed clothes aside like debris caught in a whirlwind. They didn't bother to remove the papers strewn across the bed, although said papers soon ended up on the floor. They didn't even bother to turn down the spread or turn off the light.

Their lovemaking started out playful before quickly turning passionate. Alisha experienced joy in the purest sense of the word in the company of the iceman. *Her* iceman, whom she managed to melt with very little effort. But then, she did more than her share of melting, too. They came together with strong desire, with reckless abandon, with shared declarations of love. And in the quiet aftermath she realized she'd been wrong not to trust him or herself. He was everything Troy had never been, never would be.

Alisha settled against Daniel's chest, content and confident that their future together would be as solid as their commitment to see justice done. And before she drifted off in his arms, she acknowledged that sleeping—and making love—with her former enemy and future husband had never felt so right.

*Everything you love about romance...*
***and more!***

*Please turn the page for Signature Select™*
*Bonus Features.*

# Bonus Features:

### Author Interview 4
A Conversation with
Kristi Gold

### Author's Journal 8
Simply Stated: San Antonio's
Allure by Kristi Gold

### Sneak Peek 16
ONCE A REBEL
by Sheri WhiteFeather

# BONUS FEATURES

# The Law of Attraction

## Author Interview:
## A conversation with
# KRISTI GOLD

*A bestselling author, national Reader's Choice winner and romance Writers of America RITA® Award finalist, Kristi Gold has written more than twenty books since her first book debuted in 2000. Recently she chatted with us as she took a break from writing her latest Silhouette Desire novel.*

**What's the most rewarding aspect of writing? The most challenging?**

Writing at times can be very cathartic, especially when you consider that authors possess the power to manipulate fictional worlds and produce a happy ending, even when those endings sometimes seem few and far between. But the most significant rewards, at least for me, have come through correspondence with readers and knowing they appreciate what I do. The most challenging aspect is staying fresh, staying motivated and sometimes staying awake since I tend to write very, very late at night.

**If you couldn't be a writer, what would you be?**
My pat answer to this question has always been: miserable. But if I had to choose another occupation, I'd like to be a nurse. I have a great deal of respect for the women and men who work in the healthcare trenches. They possess a lot of guts, and usually receive very little glory. But what they do on a daily basis is very, very important, if not always appreciated.

**Besides writing, what other talent would you most like to have?**
I've always wanted to be a singer. Trust me, this will never happen. Just ask anyone who's heard me wail.

**What do you consider your greatest achievement?**
You know, that would have to be my three kids. I wasn't equipped with any kind of how-to manual, and they've actually turned out pretty well—so far.

**What is your most treasured possession?**
I have my mother-in-law's love letters sent to her by her future husband as he journeyed by train from Texas to Wisconsin, mailing one at every stop until he found his way to her. They have both since passed away, but what an incredible love story they've left behind.

**Who are your heroes in real life?**
Anyone who makes an extreme sacrifice for the good of all—aide workers, police officers, firefighters, service men and women, shelter volunteers. Those who lead by good example, and not by hollow rhetoric.

**Who is your favorite hero of fiction?**
Wow! This is a really tough one, and as always, a toss-up (Hey, I'm a Pisces, a fish, and we're known to flounder on occasion). I will focus on the male persuasion, and narrow it down to two: Danny Sinclair, from Leigh Riker's *Danny Boy*—an emotionally and physically wounded rodeo cowboy, and Joe Burgett from Kathleen Korbel's *A Rose for Maggie*—a reclusive children's book author. As you can see, they are polar opposites in terms of their chosen careers, but they both possess what I feel is the most heroic quality you can find in a man: honor.

**What is your favorite quote or motto?**
This particular quote by Calvin Coolidge, sent to me years ago by a fellow author while we were still struggling to publish our books, has served to see me through many tough times:

"Nothing in the world can take the place of Persistence. Talent will not; nothing is more common than unsuccessful men with talent. Genius will not; unrewarded genius is almost a proverb. Education will not; the world is full of educated derelicts. Persistence and determination alone are omnipotent. The slogan 'Press On' has solved and always will solve the problems of the human race."

**What is your idea of perfect happiness?**
To wake every morning knowing I can begin my day surrounded by family and friends, many more opportunities to share my stories and a continuous supply of Starbucks® cappuccinos on hand.

**What actress would you want to play you in a movie?**
This one is relatively easy—Stockard Channing. I idolize her. Heck, I want to *be* her!

# Author's Journal

## Simply Stated: San Antonio's Allure
### by Kristi Gold

When I learned San Antonio would provide the setting for *The Law of Attraction*, I was extremely pleased. Where else can you find a magical place that merges Old Mexico, the Wild West and Germany, as well as African-American and Native American culture? An exciting locale that is immersed in history, mystery and romance? A popular location for impressive museums and notable movies such as *The Getaway, The Newton Boys* and *Miss Congeniality*? It's also the eighth largest city in the United States, but don't let the size fool you, or the fact that the metropolitan area is also home to high-tech corporations and sprawling suburbs. It still retains its quaint charm in so many ways, and at times feels almost intimate.

Because I'm a native Texan, and San Antonio is one of my all-time-favorite vacationing spots, I felt that I could convey the atmosphere accurately in *The Law of Attraction* without having to do extensive research, even though any excuse to visit would be a pleasure, not an inconvenience. As good luck would have it, shortly after I acquired the preliminary outline of the story, I attended a weekend writing conference in San Antonio where two of my friends—one New York State resident, who had never visited the city, and one fellow Texan and author—were also present. After the conference ended, we decided to relocate to a downtown hotel and spend Sunday afternoon exploring the sights. Since I was the designated tour guide (even though I had trouble finding our new hotel), I decided to begin with one of the most notable attractions—the Alamo.

Standing on the grounds of the Plaza that spring day prompted memories of my first Alamo encounter, when I was but a mere child armed with some basic knowledge garnered from my Texas history lessons, including the fact that my birthday (the *day*, not the *year*) coincides with the day the mission fell to the Mexican army. Already feeling an immediate connection to the site, I remember being awed by all the people speaking in hushed tones and the palpable respect for the surroundings. You truly could have heard the proverbial pin drop—or camera, as it was in my case. This embarrassing faux pas earned me a few hard looks from visitors, and for several years I was reluctant to return for fear I might be recognized as the notorious ten-year-old camera-dropper.

However, I put aside my irrational concerns and led my two friends into the inner sanctum, only to find that tourists no longer spoke in whispers. I don't know if that's a sign of the times, but I do find that very sad, perhaps because I now understand why that reverence existed in the first place—the Alamo is not only a mission; it's the final resting place of those who paid the ultimate price in Texas's fight for independence, Jim Bowie, Davy Crockett and William Travis, to name just a few. Despite the tourists' absence of awe, and my initial shaky introduction years before, the Alamo's historical significance was not lost on me then, or now, and never will be.

<sup>10</sup> After my friends and I studied the exhibits, we ventured outside to witness the dismantling of huge tents, booms and platforms that had been erected the previous night for a star-studded party celebrating the premiere of the recent remake of *The Alamo* (the movie was actually shot outside of Austin on what is purportedly the largest outdoor film set in history). I am proud to say that although tempted, I did not scour the grounds in search of a paper cup heralding "Property of Dennis Quaid" or a Billy Bob Thornton commemorative pen to claim as souvenirs.

After walking past the gazebo where Sandra Bullock took her infamous dive into the crowd in *Miss Congeniality*, we traveled a couple of blocks to a stone stairway that led to the Paseo del Rio—better known as the River Walk—which is located twenty feet below street level along the banks of the San Antonio River. Now the term *river* generally lends itself to the image of a wide expanse of water. In reality, this river has been channeled into a canal webwork that weaves throughout several downtown blocks. You can actually stand on one side, throw a stone and hit the other side with little effort (I strongly advise against this as you could injure someone, not to mention suffer immediate arrest, neither of which is conducive to a good experience). Both sides of the canal are connected by periodic arched stone bridges, and the *only* boats you will see are flat-bed, open-air river taxis and police patrol watercraft. If you envision taking a trip to San Antonio and climbing aboard a yacht to enjoy the scenery, think again. Private vessels are not permitted, nor is there room to allow them passage.

Back to the afternoon venture. After we descended the stairs, I escorted my companions down the flagstone walkway past the myriad shops, restaurants and clubs to one of my preferred eating establishments—Dick's Last Resort—where the waiters receive their gratuities based on the skill with which they hurl insults. If you are easily offended, this might not be the place for you. But if you don't mind a loud announcement when you inquire about the location of the rest room, great food and an irreverent yet fun atmosphere, I highly recommend it.

During our lunch, the three of us chose a table on the patio to watch the river taxis go by, which led to a discussion about *Attraction's* fictional character, Les Massey—also known as "The Naked Guy" and "The San Antonio Streaker." In the book, you will notice some of the results of our conversation, i.e. Les's performance on the dinner cruise, and some you will not. Fortunately. After we spent several hours plotting Les's strange course, my New York friend left us to join her husband while my other friend and I strolled along the river before settling in for dinner.

A word of warning should you decide to visit: Picking a place to dine in San Antonio can be an exercise in indecisiveness in light of the many quality choices—from Tex-Mex to seafood and everything in between. After some debate, we selected an Italian bistro where we again took a table outside to watch several couples strolling hand in hand, both young and not so young, while listening to varied strains of music— including jazz ensembles, hard rock bands and mariachis—filtering through the doors of an assortment of nearby establishments. The River Walk after dark takes on an electric life of its own; it is a truly unforgettable experience and not to be missed.

Unfortunately our trip ended with dinner,

proving that four or five hours on a Sunday afternoon is just not enough time to take it all in. Four or five days would be satisfactory in order to hit the high points, and there are more than a few. A visit to La Villita, a one-time Mexican settlement that now houses several shops, should be a planned stop, and so should El Mercado, the largest Mexican marketplace outside of Mexico and home to the popular twenty-four-hour restaurant and bakery, Mi Tierra, another of my personal favorites.

As if the downtown area doesn't have enough to do to keep one as busy as a bull in a herd of a hundred heifers during mating season (that's Texan for *real* busy), the outskirts hold just as many must-see attractions. Several other missions are situated in the San Antonio Missions National Historical Park. The King William District (named in honor of King Wilhelm I, King of Prussia in the 1870s) has lovely manicured streets lined with historic homes, and if one has a fondness for foliage and/or wildlife, San Antonio has a beautiful arboretum and a wonderful zoo. If you're up for some theme-park excitement, you can plan a trip to SeaWorld or Six Flags Fiesta Texas. And if you're brave enough to venture into the realm of the paranormal, you could discover that San Antonio is a *spirited* city in a very literal sense.

Now I've personally never seen anything more frightening than a few rowdy revelers who looked as though they might actually topple into the river headfirst, and some seriously scary traffic on the freeways leading into downtown during rush hour. Yet many "ghost" sightings throughout the city, from parks to the police station, have been reported and repeated. For example, the Alamo's grounds contain a thirty-foot-tall national monument to the entity that presumably rose from the rooftop with a ball of flame in each hand, successfully thwarting the mission's destruction (that would certainly deter me). Legend also has it that the founder of the famous South Texas King Ranch, Captain Richard King, frequents the suite bearing his name, which is located at the elegant historic Menger Hotel—

where he passed away in 1885. Teddy Roosevelt allegedly still hangs out in the Menger's tavern where he once recruited cowboys to join his Rough Riders' detachment before the Spanish-American war. And that's just two of the supposedly *thirty-two* apparitions that grace the hotel's halls. Gives a whole new meaning to guests who've overstayed their welcome, huh? If you are sincerely interested in investigating the "otherworldly," I suggest looking into one of the "ghost" tours. Or you could travel to the Alamo Street Restaurant and Theater for a visit with the genteel "Miss Margaret," aka former actress Margaret Gething, who sometimes keeps company with her seamstress, Henrietta, and pal Eddie. I understand that she can often be seen in the balcony during rehearsals and performances, wearing a flowing dress and sporting a "hauntingly" kind smile. In fact, I hear Miss Margaret is very friendly and "spirited."

An overview of San Antonio would not be complete without mentioning festivals, and the city has many. But the best-known is Fiesta San Antonio, an annual ten-day April affair featuring many activities, including athletic events, art displays and colorful parades. Although Fiesta has always served as a memorial event dedicated to those who battled at the Alamo and San Jacinto, it has grown into a celebration of the city's cultural diversity. If you do want to attend, some advice—book early.

So there you have it. Whether you wish to attempt to convene with spirits or to shop, or if you prefer to engage in a little romance or only relax, you'll find no better place to do just that. If you want to walk till you drop, or dance the night away, pack comfortable shoes. If you're prepared to have a good time, I doubt you'll be disappointed.

Although I can talk about the city with great enthusiasm, in order to appreciate this vacation Mecca, you have to be there to experience its appeal. Quite simply stated, there is no denying San Antonio's allure.

Here's a sneak peek...

# *ONCE A REBEL*

## by
## Sheri WhiteFeather

*Enjoy this excerpt of Sheri WhiteFeather's*
ONCE A REBEL, *the ninth book in* THE FORTUNES
OF TEXAS: REUNION *series—available February*
*2006.*

## CHAPTER 1

Susan Fortune approached the barn, the weathered wood calling to her like an old friend, stirring scattered memories, making them swirl in her mind.

In the past seventeen years she hadn't been home much. She'd returned now and then, but always in a rush, a day or two at Thanksgiving, Christmas or Easter.

But being back in Red Rock, Texas, back on the Double Crown Ranch, felt different this time. Because this wasn't a harried holiday weekend, a fast-paced trip she'd crammed into her busy schedule. This was the real thing. A homecoming that turned her heart inside out.

Her cousin Ryan, the Fortune family patriarch, was dying.

Susan moved closer to the barn, the slightly chilled, early-February air stinging her skin. She'd spent the most important time of her life, her senior year in high school, on the Double Crown. Ryan had taken her in after her alcohol-enraged father had kicked her out. He'd offered her a place to stay, a place to feel loved, a home away from home, from the turbulence that had nearly destroyed her.

And now here she was, wishing she could save Ryan, but knowing she couldn't.

Reflective, she looked around, watching the ranch hands do their jobs. And then a tall, tanned man in rugged denims, with a straw cowboy hat dipped low on his forehead, exited the barn. He strode toward a white dually, and suddenly she couldn't breathe, every ounce of oxygen in her lungs refusing to co-operate.

Was that Ethan Eldridge?

Yes, she told herself. It had to be. He'd grown bigger, broader, more masculine, but she recognized him just the same. Even the way he wore his clothes bred familiarity. A hand-tooled belt that he'd proba-bly made himself was threaded through his jeans, and the hem of each pant leg frayed around a pair of weather-beaten boots. When he adjusted his hat in a memorable manner, her girlhood dreams went up in a cloud of pheromone-scented smoke.

She hadn't seen him since they were teenagers, since she'd pined for him like the emotionally torn, desperate-for-affection female she'd been.

Should she call his name? Get his attention before he climbed into his truck and drove away?

Or would that make her look foolish? Susan

Fortune, the reformed bad girl, flaunting herself in front of Ethan Eldridge all over again.

Unsure of what to do, she simply stood where she was, the wind whipping her hair across her cheek. But before she could come to a decision, Ethan reacted to her presence. Like a solitary animal, a cougar sensing an intruder, he slowed his pace and turned around.

Leaving Susan exposed to his gaze.

Chiding herself, she smoothed her hair, batting it away from her face. She wasn't reverting to promiscuity. If anything, she was able to diagnose her teenage self, the rebellious girl who'd paraded other boys in front of Ethan. Susan understood the wild child that had festered inside her. She'd graduated from Stanford and earned a Ph.D. in psychology.

She decided to greet him with a friendly yet noncommittal hello, so she started off in his direction, cutting across the dirt path that separated them. But as she analyzed his catlike posture, she realized that he hadn't identified her.

He had no idea who she was.

Beneath the brim of his hat, his eyebrows furrowed. A frown of curiosity, she thought. A country boy wondering why a citified blonde, dressed in designer jeans and a form-fitting blazer, was determined to talk to him.

Finally when they were face-to-face, with sights,

sounds and smells of the ranch spinning around them, recognition dawned in his eyes.

Those stunning blue eyes.

"Susan?" He beat her to the punch, saying her name first.

"Ethan." She extended her hand, preparing to touch him. "It's good to see you."

"You, too." He accepted her hand, enveloping it with callused fingers.

They gazed at each other, silence sizzling between them. She could feel the soundless energy zapping the air, conjuring invisible fireflies.

So much for her Ph.D.

Suddenly she was a smitten seventeen-year-old, reliving the day they'd met. He had been a ranch hand's hardworking, properly reared son, and she had been as untamed as the Texas terrain, a lost girl aching for attention. So much so, she'd parked her butt on a fence rail, as close to him as possible. Then she'd unbuttoned the top of her blouse, complaining about the heat, trying to get him to look at her.

He did, but only for a second. Just long enough to stop working and offer her a bottle of water. His water. A plastic container he'd yet to open, to drink from.

An elusive boy. A gallant gesture.

In her young, needy soul, Susan had fallen like a ton of shattered bricks, wanting Ethan even more. But she'd never gotten him. Nothing. Not even a kiss.

"I'm sorry about what's happening to Ryan," he said, bringing her back to the present. "You know how much I care about him."

She nodded. Ethan had practically grown up on the Double Crown. He knew Ryan well. "He's such a good man. Everyone loves him."

"I'm sure he's glad to have you home."

*Home.* The word never failed to strike her heart. She'd lived with her parents in Katy, Texas, a suburb of Houston, until Ryan took her in. Sixteen years in Katy and one year in Red Rock. Yet Red Rock would always seem like home, even though she'd moved away from Texas altogether.

Ethan shifted his stance, drawing her attention to his tall, muscular form. He'd been lean and wiry as a teenager, a boy who'd spent all of his free time with the animals on the ranch.

"Ryan told me you became a large-animal vet," she said.

"And he told me you became a child psychologist." A smile ghosted across his lips. "I guess we both grew up, didn't we?"

"Yes, we did." As a girl she used to dream about that uneven smile. Slow and sexy, she thought. One corner of his mouth tilting in a lazy sort of way.

Caught up in the moment, she stole a glance at his left hand. The last she'd heard, he was single, but that was a few years ago. She hadn't made a habit of grilling Ryan about him.

When she noticed the absence of a ring, she sighed. Ethan was thirty-five, the same age as she was, and she'd never married, either. But her work was her priority, the heartbeat of her existence.

Did Ethan feel that way, too? Or was she jumping to conclusions? Just because he didn't wear a ring didn't mean he wasn't involved in a committed relationship. Or that he wasn't looking for a partner, someone to share the ups and downs in his life.

"Did you just get here today?" he asked.

"Yes." She told herself to quit psychoanalyzing him, to leave her textbook curiosity at the curb. "I arrived this morning." She flipped her wrist and checked her watch. "A few hours ago. Ryan is taking a nap, so I decided to go for a walk."

"How's Lily holding up?"

"She's doing the best she can. When I left the house, she was fussing in the kitchen, giving herself something to do." Lily was Ryan's third wife, a woman he'd loved since his youth but hadn't married until many years later.

The wind rustled Ethan's shirt. "How long are you going to stay?"

"I'm not sure. But I'm hoping to help everyone get through this." She noticed the expressive lines around his mouth, the aging process that had altered his features, cutting masculine grooves into his skin.

He reminded her of a model in a cowboy ad. The stereotypical Texan, with his hard-angled cheekbones, slightly crooked nose and lightly peppered jaw. But she knew he was real.

Tangible. Touchable. Flesh and blood.

Even after all these years she still wondered what it would feel like to kiss him.

When she lifted her gaze to his, he dipped his hat even lower, shielding his eyes.

Just like old times, she thought. She'd never been able to break through Ethan's defenses. Even though he'd been attracted to her, he'd kept his distance, making her long for him even more.

Not that she would let herself long for him now. Kissing him, or even fantasizing about it, would be a mistake.

"You must be working today," she said, trying to resume a casual conversation.

"Yes, I am. But I live here, too."

She started. "On the Double Crown?"

"It's only temporary. I'm in between homes right now, so I'm renting the hunting cabin from Ryan." He gestured to the barn. "Of course I'm boarding my horses here, too."

From what she recalled, Ethan had been living on the rough-and-tumble property his father owned. Although she wondered why he was moving, she decided not to ask, not to delve too deeply into his affairs, even if she wanted to, even if everything about him still intrigued her. "I've never been inside the hunting cabin."

"Really?" He shifted his feet, scattering dirt beneath his heels. "There isn't much to see, but you can come by later if you want to."

Surprised by the invitation, Susan didn't know what to say. He'd never asked her to visit him before. He'd never encouraged her advances. Of course, this time she wasn't falling all over him. At least not outwardly. Inside, her heart was skipping girlish beats.

"Thanks," she finally managed.

"Sure."

While silence stretched between them, the wind kicked up, the scent of hay and horses triggering her senses. In the distance cattle grazed, like colored dots on the horizon.

24

"I'd better go," he said. "I have an appointment on another ranch."

She told herself to relax, to not make a big deal out of his offer. "It was nice talking to you, Ethan."

"You, too," he told her.

He climbed behind the wheel of his white dually, and she watched him start the engine. Within no time, he was gone.

The boy with the slow, sexy smile.

She returned to the house and headed for the kitchen, where she found Lily, bustling around the stove.

Struck by the woman's beauty, Susan stood in the doorway, admiring the woman Ryan had married. Even at fifty-nine, Lily had the power to turn heads.

Long-limbed and voluptuous, she wore a mint-colored sweater and a loose skirt, attire that was as unpretentious as her style. Her midnight hair was fastened into a simple twist, leaving the angles of her face unframed.

"That smells good," Susan said, indicating the pot of broth simmering on the stove.

Lily looked up, her large, exotic-shaped eyes radiating warmth. "It's corn soup. An old Apache recipe."

Which made sense, considering Lily was part Apache and part Spanish.

Susan moved farther into the kitchen and watched as Lily mixed several pounds of boiled, shredded beef with a homemade batch of acorn meal. She suspected that Lily had taken her time, peeling the acorns and grinding them, a task that was meant to keep her mind off Ryan's illness, especially on this gloomy morning.

A second later Lily took a shaky breath, then glanced out the window as though someone were stalking her. And why not? Susan knew that a man named Jason Jamison, a cold-blooded killer, had been threatening the family. Of course Ryan had hired a security team to protect them. He wouldn't leave something like that to chance.

"Are you okay?" she asked Lily.

"I'm fine. Just jittery, that's all. There's so much to deal with right now." She turned away from the window. "Will you check on Ryan? And if he's awake, will you tell him that I'll bring him some soup later?"

"Sure. But if you need someone to talk to, I'm here."

"I know." Lily gave her a brave smile. "I'm glad you're staying with us. I like having you around."

Her heart bumped her chest, filling her with a sense of longing, of family, of home and hearth. Lily hadn't been Ryan's wife when Susan had lived on the Double Crown, but she'd gotten to know her later. Mostly from trips Ryan and Lily had taken to San Francisco, where they'd traveled to visit her.

26

"Thank you," Susan told her. "That means a lot to me."

Lily nodded, and they simply gazed at each other, caught in a soundless moment.

After the older woman resumed her task, adding the beef and acorn meal to the broth, Susan left the kitchen, her emotions tugging at her sleeve.

She walked through the great room, her boots echoing on tiled floors, as restless as the Fortune Empire ghosts.

Over the years, the house, a traditional adobe structure, had undergone quite a few renovations. At one point it had been divided into two separate wings, where Ryan and his older brother, Cameron, lived with their families. But Susan knew that Cameron had died over ten years ago, leaving Ryan to pick up the pieces of his brother's lazy yet tremulous life.

She headed to Ryan and Lily's room, a master suite with a private bathroom, hot tub and sauna. The door leading to the sitting area was open, a sign that her cousin was awake. She knocked anyway, a light tap to announce her presence.

"Come in," he called out.

She entered the room and saw him sitting on a small sofa near the fireplace. To Susan, Ryan had always seemed larger than life, an invincible force with his solid frame and darkly handsome features. But an inoperable brain tumor had challenged his strength, creating symptoms he could no longer hide.

"How are you feeling?" she asked.

"Better now that you're here."

He patted the cushion next to him, and she moved forward. He didn't look particularly refreshed from his nap, but she was grateful that he was coherent. Earlier, he'd been too dizzy to converse with her.

She sat down and took his hand, holding it gently in hers. "I love you."

A smile wobbled his mouth. "I love you, too, little girl."

"I'm not little anymore."

He gave her hand a light squeeze. "You're still my baby."

She wanted to ask him about Jason Jamison, to discuss the details, but she didn't want to alert him

that his beloved wife was fretting in the kitchen, looking over her shoulder every chance she got. Sooner
or later Susan would learn everything there was to
know about Jason. Both of her brothers had warned
her about this man, suggesting that she talk to Ryan
about him. Which she intended to do, just not now.

"Lily's making soup," she said, trying to sound
more cheerful than she felt.

"What kind?"

"Apache corn. She's going to bring you some
when it's done."

"That sounds good." He released her hand. "What
did you do today?"

"I went for a walk. Down by the barn." She studied the fireplace, the rugged structure, the natural
beauty of each carefully placed stone. "I ran into
Ethan."

"Really?" Ryan perked up. "How'd it go?"

"Fine. We only talked for a few minutes." She
glanced at her cousin and saw him scrutinizing her
beneath his dark brows. Anxious, she fidgeted, then
caught herself, folding her hands on her lap. "I used
to have a crush on him."

"I know you did, pumpkin. I think everyone
knew."

Embarrassed, she laughed a little, picturing herself as she was, a teenager in tight clothes and too
much mascara. "I wasn't very subtle about it."

"It's hard to hide those kinds of feelings." He was

28

still watching her, looking at her with a knowing expression. "Old crushes run deep." He paused, then said, "Lily was the love of my life when I was in high school. And look what happened to us."

She shook her head. "It's not like that between Ethan and me. I hardly know him."

"The heart doesn't forget."

She leaned forward, tempted to touch Ryan's cheek. She knew he'd loved his first wife. She'd been his childhood friend, the woman who bore his children. But Lily was the fire in his soul. "You're just an old romantic."

"And you're a young woman who needs a good man."

"I have my career."

"And a big, empty condo in California. That's not enough, Susan."

"I'm not ready to fall in love." And especially not with Ethan, she decided. She didn't need the complication. Not now. Not while she was in Texas. "I spent enough time mooning over him."

"Like I used to do over Lily?"

She leaned back against the sofa, doing her damnedest not to lose the fight. Apparently Ryan was determined to drive his point home, to compare his life to hers. "I never pegged you for a matchmaker."

"Are you kidding? Me? The old romantic?" He chuckled under his breath. "It's right up my alley."

She forced a smile, humoring him. And humoring herself, as well.

Because deep down, she wanted to see Ethan again, to summon the courage to stop by the hunting cabin. But she knew she wouldn't.

Susan wasn't about to chase him.

Not ever again.

...NOT THE END...

*Look for* ONCE A REBEL *by Sheri WhiteFeather in stores February 2006.*

**A breathtaking novel of
reunion and romance...**

THE
F RTUNES
OF TEXAS:
*Reunion*

Once a Rebel

by Sheri WhiteFeather

Returning home to Red Rock after many
years, psychologist Susan Fortune is reunited
with Ethan Eldridge, a man she hasn't gotten
over in seventeen years. When tragedy and grief
overtake the family, Susan leans on Ethan to
overcome her feelings—and soon realizes that
her life can't be complete without him.

**Coming in February**

Silhouette®
*Where love comes alive*™

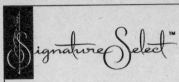

# What happens when new friends get together and dig into the past?

# Ex's and Oh's
## Sandra Steffen

A story about secrets, surprises and relationships.

HARLEQUIN®

Next™

Available February 2006
TheNextNovel.com

HN29

## Silhouette®

# SPECIAL EDITION™

# HUSBANDS AND OTHER STRANGERS

### by

# Marie Ferrarella

A boating accident left Gayle Elliott Conway with amnesia and no recollection of the handsome man who came to her rescue…her husband. Convinced there was more to the story, Taylor Conway set out for answers and a way back into the heart of the woman he loved.

**Available February 2006**

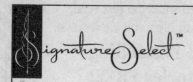

**Firefly Glen...**
**there's nowhere else quite like it.**

**National bestselling author**

**Featuring the first two novels in**
**her acclaimed miniseries**
**FOUR SEASONS IN FIREFLY GLEN**

Two couples, each trying to avoid romance,
find exactly that in this small peaceful
town in the Adirondacks.

**Available in February.**

**Watch for a new FIREFLY GLEN novel,**
*Quiet as the Grave*—**coming in March 2006!**

If you enjoyed what you just read,
then we've got an offer you can't resist!

## Take 2 bestselling
## love stories FREE!

## Plus get a FREE surprise gift!